Heather,

If you enjoy vampires, witches, werewolfs and faries then you may enjoy my own supernatural creation... the CARVERS.

Love Always B. L. Brooklyn

The Carver's Magic

B. L. Brooklyn

This is a work of fiction. Names, characters, places, and incidents either are the product of the author's imagination or are used fictitiously. Any resemblance to persons, living or dead, business establishments, events, or locales is entirely coincidental.

Edited by B.L. Brooklyn and Randi Gause

eBook ISBN-13: 9780996704106
ISBN: 0996704116
ISBN-13: 9780996704113

DEDICATION

For everyone who has ever felt the fire in their blood.

CONTENTS

ACKNOWLEDGMENTS

I would like to thank my family for their patience while I wrote this book. I would also like to express my gratitude to the many friends who saw me through this book; to all those who provided support, talked things over, gave perspective, and assisted in beta reading. I would like to thank Randi Gause, my editor, for her encouragement and insights. A special thanks to Melissa Newell – for that lollipop moment.

CHAPTER ONE
SHANE

"Hey, bartender!" Some guy calls behind me, while I am tendering my last order.

As I turn, I catch my favorite blonde sitting by herself, waiting patiently for her order. Her martini is next on my list of orders to make.

"Bartender!" The same guy calls out again, trying to get my attention. Wiping off my hands on a fresh white rag, I take a good look at the Average Joe wearing a yellow button-up with an orange Manchester United shirt underneath.

Who dresses like that?

I toss the towel on the bar and let out a breath, ignoring the Average Joe. In my book, an Average Joe is a guy who lets his girlfriend dress him.

I nod to him, letting him know I will be right there, but at the moment I am shaking a mixture of vodka, vermouth, and olive juice for the exquisite young blonde in front of me. She's been here every Friday for a month and tips well, so it's worth it. Plus she never gets drunk. She will drink two of these, slowly with her defined, luscious lips, and that will be it. Usually she comes in with a brunette, but right now she's alone and I am more than happy to keep her company as long as I can.

This shy number is twirling a strand of hair, peering up at me every few moments. Inwardly, I am smiling at her. If I were right in the head, I'd buy her a drink, ask her some mundane questions including her number, then find a way to get her back to my house, in my bed, so I can be the one biting on those tasty looking lips of hers.

But I can't.

The thought of only getting one night with her rubs me the wrong way. I would need more than one night to fill my curiosity. To be honest, she's not the type I usually go for.

This precious looking thing has razor-green eyes, that stands out from her hair pulled back in a sideways braid that flows all the way down the opposite side of her neck, hiding a necklace down the front of her turquoise shirt. She is enchanting, for a human.

I place the martini in front of her. "Here you go," my voice sounds more rigid than intended. Sometimes I wish I were a regular human, not having to worry about their race finding out about me and my kind, but as it is, I'm not and I can't, and I may despise them a little because of it. Especially right now.

"Thanks," she practically whispers her reply while pulling a loose strand of hair behind her ear.

"Hey, bartender!" The Average Joe guy calls rudely once more. Ignoring him, I rub my hands tightly against my white rag. I know he's frustrated, and I don't have to look back to know that his girlfriend has walked up next to him and is complaining about my slow service. Most girls don't get on my nerves, but this one is at the top of my list tonight. I want to stuff her mouth with my dirty gym sock kept in place with some duct tape, but I'll just have to settle with putting a rotten taste in her mouth she won't be able to get out for a week.

The blonde is sliding the olive off her toothpick with her teeth very slowly. Yeah, she knows I'm watching, even though she won't look at me. I inwardly groan as I force myself to tend my next customer.

I head toward the Average Joe and his spandex clad girlfriend. She's wearing a fedora over her mangy, dirty blonde hair. Her makeup is screaming Clockwork Orange fan and I am holding in the chastising words that she needs to hear: We like them classy not trashy.

The Average Joe orders Slippery Nipples for his girlfriend and her friends. Then his girlfriend yells into his ear, loud enough for me to hear the entire order: one Chardonnay, Sex On the Beach, Cape Cod, and two Long Island Ice Teas. He gives me their order and adds on two beers for himself.

After I mix their orders, Joe pays me in cash and leaving a dollar for a tip.

"Shane!" A gruff voice calls out.

I cocked my head, looking for the person calling out my name instead of using my title. It's the Douche.

Tonight he's wearing a dark gray V-neck shirt with a stupid oversized cross around his neck, and his black bushy chest hair tufting out. He got chatty with me one night about a year or so back, and now he thinks we're brothers, or friends, or whatever he labels me.

My label for him is Douche.

"Yeah?" I say, not really asking what he wants. His pack of friends are flanking him with matching shaved arms, big watches and shirts that don't fit.

I don't like them.

Grabbing the rag from my black apron, I wipe off my hands. The Douche is looking way too high and mighty. I lift my chin at him. My non-verbal attempt to hear the order I have disdainfully memorized.

The Douche grabs the back of a bar chair in front of him and says a few formal words, as if we are old pals. We're not. I hate small talk. I hate it. Finally he asks for "four Buds and a whiskey." I grab a cup for the whiskey, as the Douche rubbed his hands together as he begins to scan the room. I fill the glass and walk two steps to my left and open the small cooler with the bottles of beer. I pull out four bottles and feel my stomach tighten as I watch the Douche settle his gaze on the blonde bombshell with the dirty martini. He looks her over twice, before rubbing his chin and grins. He moves slowly and steadily toward her, never taking his eyes off his prey. It was only two steps for him but it was like I was watching everything in slow motion.

He stopped millimeters from her shoulder. Too close for my liking and, I know it's not my place to say that, but in all reality, I won't let someone hurt someone weaker than them. This Douche may get a chance to introduce himself but Hell will freeze over before I let her walk out of here with him.

I grew up with four brothers that were like the scum of the earth. All my nightmares are categorized into two groups: things they did to me, and things they tried to do tried to do to me. I would probably be dead ten times over if it weren't for my magic. So when I say I can spot a predator a mile away, I'm dead serious.

The Douche sniffed at her. The cute little thing stiffened

while folding her hands in her lap. At that, my stomach began burning. He doesn't acknowledge me glowering at him. He leaned closer, "and another of whatever the cutie is drinking."

I look down to see the shy blonde's response. It bothers me that I need to see her give this guy the cold shoulder. And if she doesn't, I have no control over what kind of hell I might unleash.

The blonde shrank back from the Douche. He holds out his hand, "I'm Joel." The blonde takes his hand but her movements are stiff.

"Cory," she says, with a hint of dismissal? He shakes her hand but then something happens, her body goes rigid and she looks at me quickly with something in her eyes.

What the hell does that mean?

She watches me for another second, which is the longest she has ever looked at me. I have no idea what she is looking for in my eyes, or what she's trying to convey but what I do know is that I can't look away. It doesn't make sense, I feel stuck but not because of a spell, I would know. My brain is currently fighting to break the connection but at the same time, I want to know what that look means and I can't figure it out.

What does she want? Is she asking for my help?

The blonde breaks our connection and turns back to the Douche. The burn in my stomach is making small progress to filling my body with fire. It's in my veins; it's what I am made of. Fire.

If I don't calm down something bad will happen, because the fire raging in me, needs a focus point to release it. Right now my focus point is the Douche, but burning someone alive at a bar may be a little frowned upon. I am not used to feeling whatever it is I am feeling, for anyone, so that also puts me at a disadvantage.

I put the beer bottles on the bar, pop the caps, and push them in front of the Douche, harshly expecting him to take my hint.

He nods at me while tossing a few bills at me to cover the charge. I take in a long breath. I need space but I can't seem to get my feet to move away from the blonde. The sweet looking thing is just perching in her seat, twisting a white opal ring over and over on her middle finger, attempting to hide her feelings while her face is the epitome of calm.

I don't like it at all.

With impeccable timing, her friend with windblown, dark brown hair, chestnut brown eyes, and an "I will bury you in the desert" kind of look, walks in. Tonight she is wearing a tan leather biker jacket, cream colored scoop blouse, and dark jeans that rock an impressive sized belt buckle.

I blew out my cheeks, unaware I had been holding my breath. I tender the Douche's order but watch in the mirror as the blonde avoids his question about where she is from, by asking a question of her own.

The Douche took an involuntary step back, narrowing his eyes at the blonde with a new look of calculation. The step back allows the brunette to step rudely in front of him and cut off visual communication. He's mere inches from the brunette's heated glare.

The brunette looks back at the blonde. "Couldn't wait, sis?"

Sis? Sisters?

They look nothing alike.

"You said five minutes," the blonde answered nonchalantly, lifting her shoulder in a half shrug. "I came early to get us seats."

The fire inside me subsided, knowing the little cutie is safe. Wiping my hands off again, I walk away from what most certainly is about to happen. The Douche is about to cut in and look like an even bigger ass getting between an over-protective sister and the young bombshell.

"Hey, Cory? Why don't you come back with me? I have a seat saved for you back at my table," the Douche says, trying to look around the brunette.

I roll my eyes.

"Really guy? You think my sister would be interested in a guy like you?" I hear the brunette say condescendingly, even though I am halfway down the bar.

"Hey bartender." I hear from the north side of the bar. The bar is a big circle, so I tend to walk around in circles all night which is irritating on any given day, but since the summer time was bringing in more people it was pushing my limited patience. Later I will have to restrain myself from pummeling several young, dumb, pansies when it gets hectic and everyone is shouting for my attention from 360 degrees around me.

I walk to the next patron. He's leaning on an elbow, covering his mouth with his hand. The mammoth sized man has wide shoulders, with high, tight, short black hair. He has a five o'clock shadow and is wearing a red, gray, and black plaid button-down. The guy lost me at the thick leather cuff around his left wrist, adorned with two additional small brown and black bead bracelets that look like mini claws. Nickelback poser.

"What can I get you?"

Before he answers I hear the Douche on the south side of the bar yell, "Your smart mouth is about to get you in a world of hurt, girly." I search the back door hoping the bouncers have caught this little interaction. Nope.

Figures.

The Nickelback poser in front of me has zeroed in on the scene and left me with his twenty dollars in hand. He rounds the corner, and I follow suit, half because I am curious and half because… I have no idea.

The brunette is face to face with the Douche, with her shoulders squared. "Oh yeah, flea bag? You wanna teach me a lesson?"

The Douche opens his mouth to respond at the same time the Nickelback poser grabs his shoulder and spins him around. Stunned at the ferocity in the Nickleback poser's face, I step back so that I am closest to the blonde, just in case something happens. The vibes between the two males is heated. So much so that I can feel them.

I shouldn't be able to feel vibes.

I look down and notice for the first time that the Douche's hands are misshapen. His nails are dark black, and his hands are covered in long, gray and black hair. I should have known.

Werewolf.

I hate wolves.

The Nickelback poser holds the wolf with one hand. His eyes are glowing amber and locked in a death stare, almost like he was mentally berating the Douche.

Another werewolf? *Ugh.*

The werewolf Douche flinches forward and then sways back, averting his eyes. The movement is barely perceptive, but I have a knack for the details. And I am pretty sure that they just had a stare down for who was more dominant, and the Nickelback poser won.

The Douche tries to pull away but the poser squeezes down harder on his shoulder. The Douche lets out a resentful breath while he tilts his head slightly in ultimate submission.

"You were going to fight a girl, pup?" The Nickelback poser asks with a curled-up lip. The Douche kept his head bowed. The Nickelback poser points at him, then says in a tone that rumbles deeply, "Get your pack, and get out." Stiffly, the Douche takes a few steps backward, keeping his eyes on the more dominant wolf, then he gives the brunette a deathly stare promising some sort of revenge as his eyes begin to glow.

The Douche is quiet for a few heartbeats before he says, "Your little girl has a smart mouth. I would teach her some respect because next time you might not be around for when she needs a lesson in manners."

The poser doesn't miss the fact that the brunette has opened her mouth ready to add her own two cents. However, attempting to help defuse the situation, I clear my throat drawing her attention. Her eyes widen as if to dare me to chastise her. I want to, but I am a professional .

"Ready for that Shirley Temple?" I ask, tossing the dirty rag in the laundry bin under the bar and picking up a new one. The brunette eyes me with venom. I want to laugh at her because I am taking away her tough girly vibes by suggesting a childish drink, but truly, she drinks Shirley Temples or Cherry Coke when she sits at the bar with her sister.

I finally smile at the brunette who is still scowling at me. In my periphery I can see the poser fixing his attention to the brunette.

"I will take a Bud Light, as usual," the brunette lies.

I ignore her little lie about a Bud Light being her usual, however, I don't turn down the order. So, I turn around, grab the beer, twist off the top, hand it to her and wait.

She turns to her sister, the shy blonde who looks utterly bewildered, taps her lip-gloss marked martini glass, and says, "Cheers to your last night." The blonde coughs, holding back a laugh at what apparently is an inside joke.

I noticed the brunette's hesitance when she puts the bottle to her mouth, it is pursed tight so when the liquid hits her lips nothing flows in. The sweet blonde, Cory, sets down her martini and licks her lips slowly as if she knows I am watching. And again, I am. Then again she must know I am watching because she shyly looks up at me then turns away as her cheeks blush pink.

Little tease.

The Nickelback poser and I watch the Douche walk up to his buddies, say a few words, which in turn causes them to tug down their drinks and leave, glaring at all three of my patrons. I wish I were impressed at how quickly that was dealt with, but I truly wouldn't be surprised if they retaliated later against the Nickelback poser or the brunette.

So long as they leave the blonde out of it. Groaning to myself for that stupid thought, I look to the roof momentarily, hoping for some semblance of normalcy to get back in my brain. I don't like people, I'm not the nice guy and I never look twice at a human female. And I definitely do not get emotionally involved in the lives of others. Ever!

The poser taps the bar, "I'll take that beer now."

I reach over to the small beer refrigerator when the brunette whirls around and hands him her beer, "You can have mine. I didn't drink out of it." Then she looks at me before the guy has a chance to protest, and says, "I'll take that Shirley Temple now."

The poser pushes the beer bottle back toward the brunette. "Thanks, but that's okay," he says, eyeing her with a look I can't pinpoint.

The brunette gives him a quick once over and says sarcastically, "Afraid I have cooties, Wolfy? I thought your kind doesn't get cooties."

I have to force myself not to smirk. Yeah, she does have a smart mouth.

The poser grabs her drink, and before he takes a swig he sniffs the top. I watch his jaw flinch and his eyes close halfway as he drains the bottle. He drops the bottle back on the bar after a long swig and says with a sneer, "You must have backwashed your cooties. That tastes like shit." And then he walks away.

The brunette's jaw drops and the blonde is covering her mouth, but her eyes are smiling. I fold my arms waiting for her to pay her charge and also enjoying her humbling moment. She pulls out a card and tosses it at me. I am surprised she didn't ask to check out, by the way she is looking right now, it's clear that his words stung. They shouldn't have, I mean who cares what some stranger thinks, but apparently this chick is easily offended.

"Hey, bartender!" Echoes from the north side of the bar, and I use that as my cue to leave.

CHAPTER TWO
BETH

The bartender, in all his male bravado, finally leaves after almost sloshing my Shirley Temple in front of me.

Jerk.

Cory watches him walk away, and I wait impatiently for her attention.

"Cory!" I hiss. "Stop mentally undressing the jerk." She turns around with a mixture of embarrassment and irritation. "I don't mentally undress people, Beth," she says pointedly. Cory sneaks another look at the bartender before taking a small sip from her martini.

Liar.

"Anyway," I begin drawing her attention, "let's first talk about why that fleabag was practically humping your leg when I walked in here." I tilt my head accusingly, even though I know she would never have instigated anything. Cory is the quiet and shy type, most of the time. But if you push her, she becomes a mountain, unmovable and hardheaded. Oh, and heaven forbid you ask her personal questions.

Cory exhales dramatically and shakes her head, "I'm an idiot." I watch her closely because she and I both know she is closer to a genius than an idiot, so I hope she explains herself instead of leaving that statement up in the air. "The bartender heard me tell that guy my name was Cory."

It takes a few seconds for those two little points to click. I put a spell on her driver's license. The spell was initially made to protect her. When we were in college a dirt bag had stolen her driver's license and credit cards from the school lab. He hasn't been able to get near a computer since. If anyone read her driver's license it would read Charlene Davis, but her real name is Cory Kamp.

I try not to click my tongue in that motherly way to joke with her, she seems a little on edge, plus, joking would hardly get her to explain why that douche was sniffing her from head to toe.

The driver's license thing is hardly a big deal considering who I am and what I can do; plus her new driver's license came in the mail today and I don't plan on renewing my spell.

Cory usually is the girl that adheres to all things moral, for the most part. Okay maybe not all things moral or even most things ethical, I mean she did blackmail me a few times when we were kids. But, she hates looking foolish.

It's not in her to be wrong about much, considering she is the closest person I know to being a microbiologist genius. So the driver's license having the wrong name on it bothered her as soon as I made it.

"He probably won't even notice," I say, hoping she lets it go. Cory rolls her eyes and purses her lips, clearly upset but not wanting to verbally say it. She takes a sip of her martini and her eyes fade out, giving me the ultimate cold shoulder. Great. Just great.

I pinched the bridge of my nose.

Usually I let her play in her head, but we were out to have a good time. And truth be known, she is the one who wants to come here every Friday night. I have no idea how she heard of this place. It's a human bar but obviously there are wolves in here. Not the safest bar for Cory. She may be super smart but she falls short when it comes to practical matters.

I am going to give Cory ten more seconds before I poke her in the ribs and make her talk to me.

I take another sip of the Shirley Temple. I turn the glass around with my index finger and thumb a few times, rehearsing my weak moment to order something I knew I wasn't ever going to drink. It was stupid to even pretend that I would drink it. I never would. I have seen drinking cause too many problems in my life and I just don't feel compelled to drink. Not ever. But of course I did it so that I didn't look childish in front of *him.*

The one person on the planet that could make me feel like I was the most insignificant person in the world had to walk into this bar tonight. He makes me doubt myself with his snarky comments, and of course he did it with little to no effort.

I can't believe he's actually in this bar right now. I sneak a peak in his direction, hoping he won't notice. I never thought I would see him after high school. Hell, I never wanted to see him after high school. I never wanted to have to smell his tangy scent that draws me in and makes my cognitive function blow a stupid fuse. Why! Why now and why tonight? I mean, why did I have to see how utterly amazing he still looks after all this time?

A familiar heaviness settles on my chest. Ugh! I can't let him get to me again. Not again. He doesn't deserve it and I refuse to go down that bleak rabbit hole again. I was in hell all day every day for years until I graduated and left that small-ass town as fast as I could.

My biological parents showed up after 18 years of absence, offered me a chance to live with them, and I took it. I wanted out of that forsaken town and they had my one-way ticket, plus they had the answer to why I was different, why I could do magic and no one else could.

Noticing Cory was turning her glass too, I ask, "Hey, you see that guy that was just over here? The one I gave my beer to?" I look over to him, the tall, stunningly gorgeous man with bronze skin, coffee brown eyes and hair, wearing a red, black, and gray plaid button-down with a dark grey shirt underneath. He is looking away from me at the moment, but even from this angle he looks just as heart-stopping as he always did.

Cory takes a sip of her drink, looks around the bar, then shrugs and returns her eyes to me with a blank expression. She probably doesn't remember because it's been ten years since I graduated high school and seven years for her.

"Remember? The guy from high school who was mauled by a bear?" I wait for Cory to nod that she remembers, but again she shrugs and I fear I'm losing her to whatever is going on in her head. "He was in a coma for almost a month," I add quietly, hoping those stupid wolf ears can't hear me from the other side of the bar.

My sister takes another slow sip of that nasty dirty martini and shakes her head absently.

"Are you serious?" I ask indignantly. How could she not remember that? She has to be lying. Or maybe she doesn't care. I mean she has a photographic memory for heaven's sake. So the odds are good she remembers. And I am not going to let her lack of interest in my story stop me from rehashing it with her.

"His name is Dar. He was in my grade. His younger brother had gone missing a few weeks after school started that year." I can't really explain why Dar always stood out to me in high school. Of course other girls thought he was gorgeous with his strong, silent brooding, but for me it was so much more. During high school I didn't shut up about this guy for four years. Every day was another great day because I saw him, albeit from a distance.

I was obsessed.

It was absolutely disgusting. Ogling and pretending that Dar would one day notice me, that kind of pursuit was beneath me.

That silly girl I used to be no longer exists; not since I found out that my last name, Carver, had nothing to do with my biological father's last name and everything to do with my bloodline being a multiple-magical bloodline.

I never got a straight answer from my adopted parents as to why their last name was Kamp and mine was Carver, even though I was their adopted daughter. It wasn't until my biological parents found me the night of my high school graduation that I understood why I still had the name Carver instead of Kamp. Carver was a title, not a surname.

A Carver, by their definition, had to have at least three magical bloodlines. And because magical blood doesn't mix well, we were some kind of anomaly.

They also gave me the Cliff's notes version of the supernatural world and the different species inhabiting the world. My parents explained that being a Carver was something to be proud of because it means we are more powerful because we are able to tap into all the good stuff from all the bloodlines.

The night of my graduation, my biological parents took me from my family, without so much as a goodbye. One moment I was watching Dar talking to a group of girls and felt almost out of control, when poof, my parents pop in next to me, introduce themselves and ask me if I will give them a second chance. That night I was in a house made of red brick and lots of stucco on the other side of the country.

I was far too brash that night and I shouldn't have left like that, but I was angry and stupid. I know that some adopted kids always yearn for the love of their biological parents, or at the very least want to meet them.

I was just like that.

I learned quickly that mine were jerks. They told me their sob story about how they were forced to give me up or the Magical Council would punish them. And then they gave me a history lesson that went a lot like this: when the Magical Council found out about Carvers, they went bat-shit crazy and tried to kill us all off because the Carvers then, like the Carvers now, can't be controlled by a pureblood, we are universally more powerful. A first-generation Carver with only three bloodlines would easily win a fight against the strongest pure-blood. Well that's their story anyway.

The council decreed that all Carver children were to be raised by humans for the first 18 years, in hopes that we wouldn't learn how to use our powers. Well the council messed up with me because, little do they know, I had used my powers before I started kindergarten. Their hopes to curb my abilities had failed long ago.

Then our little family reunion took a turn down the crazy street. My biological parents taught me the laws that affected Carvers. The Magical Council may not have been able to overpower us but they continued to make laws for us. The laws were so strenuous that if I was caught doing magic in front of a human, I could be sentenced to death.

As if I didn't know that being caught doing magic was bad. I grew up with humans! I knew how they reacted to those who were different and I was not dumb enough to get caught. But my biological parents added insult to injury by putting their fine touches to the rules. For example, I was no longer allowed to contact Cory or any humans, and not that I had any intentions of talking to purebloods, but I was forbidden to talk to them as well. For all their so-called parental guidelines, they had no idea what it was like to take care of a kid, let alone a teenager like me. If they did, they would know that I didn't take orders very well, or at all.

My biological parents informed me that the growing numbers of Carvers had set in motion some kind of war. The Carvers have been secretly rallying together so that we, I mean they, can stand as one powerful force against the Magic Council that has been making their lives hell.

Or at least that's what my parents told me the council did.

Then, after listening to all that war babble, I thought we might actually get to the part where we might get to know one another and start being a family. Oh wow, was I delusional.

My biological parents shipped me off a few weeks later to a place that Carvers gather to learn magic from one another. I secretly called it "The Carver Camp." I went to their stupid camp against my better judgment. I didn't speak to the other Carvers after meeting a guy who had an ego the size of Texas.

According to his ramblings, his adopted family gave him a hard time for being different. He didn't go into specifics, and I didn't ask, although he did make it clear he spent all his free time trying to make them miserable. But he wasn't like me, he seemed to only be able to control wind or the air. I made sure to keep my powers to myself. I still was not in a habit of showing others my abilities, regardless of their magical background.

The Carvers hated humans just as much as the purebloods. I never really had a problem with humans. My adopted family was normal according to what I saw growing up. My adopted parents loved each other even though they still argued every now and then. They wanted us to do well in school and have successful futures, which is why they pushed us to get good grades. If we did poorly, our chores doubled. We were normal kids. We did dishes, cleaned our rooms on Saturday mornings, went camping in the summers, and snuck out to go to bonfires and house parties in high school. All typical human stuff and I loved it.

I grew up with two sisters: Cory and Karen. Karen was the natural daughter of my adopted parents, and Cory was adopted three years after me when she was an infant. We were the three sisters who didn't look anything alike.

Thankfully, my adopted parents didn't shun me when they noticed I was different. They didn't let me get away with being different, either. I still had to do my fair share of chores. And if they found out I used my magic to do my chores, I would have to do everyone else's, too. Using magic was draining. One time I had to clean the whole house myself. After using my magic, I was so exhausted I slept for the rest of the weekend, unable to do anything else. Let's just say I learned my lesson.

My sisters were like any others I suspected, they were incredibly annoying, hysterically funny and amazingly loyal, especially Cory. That was my understanding of what a family should be like. It's what I based my perceptions on. And my biological parents didn't meet those standards. They didn't love each other and they didn't look at me like my adopted parents did-with affection and understanding dribbled with very high expectations. Something about the way my biological parents talked to me just rubbed me the wrong way. I really didn't like being talked down to just because I had no knowledge of the magical bloodlines.

My biological parents told me I was a fourth-generation Carver, which meant I had a mixture of every magical creature in my blood. The way my biological parents talked about the different generation Carvers, it was clear that they had been breeding to achieve a specific kind of offspring.

Both of my biological parents talked about the purebloods as if they were scum, weak and arrogant. I was raised to not be prejudice against others. I mean, technically I was the different one growing up and no one in my family judged me, so why would I judge others just because they were different. No, I judged others depending on who they were and what my gut said about them.

Needless to say, my parents expected me to be like them. Join their fight against the purebloods and such. In fact they would talk to each other about the man they said I would one day be matched – as in, creepy arranged marriage.

After that, I just wanted to go home. I wanted to forget about the madness that I had seen and heard. I wanted as far away from my parents as possible. I preferred to be around humans, specifically my sister Cory. I had never meant to leave her. That was my one big regret.

But now all that Carver war mumbo-jumbo is behind me. Just like Dar. All of those feelings are behind me.

"I don't remember him," Cory shook her head, bringing me back to reality.

I almost berated myself. I shouldn't be pushing this topic. He doesn't matter to me anymore. I shouldn't care if she knew who he is. Obviously, he still has no idea who I am, which only pisses me off more. So I should drop the subject.

Instead of dropping the subject I heard myself say, "I used to sneak out of the house and go to the hospital to see him." I continue to turn the glass clockwise. I really should drop the topic.

Her eyes twinkled, "Oh yeah." Then she smacks her thigh and points at me like she remembered. "You paid me twenty bucks so that I wouldn't rat you out to Mom."

I shake my head at her, "Extortionist."

I open my mouth, about to tell her more, but I stupidly sneak a look at Dar. His back is facing me so I can't see him, and it annoys me even though it shouldn't. I shouldn't care.

I don't care.

Cory waits for a follow up comment. I don't have one. Actually at this point I am starting to feel like being alone. Tonight would be a good night to go to Pike's Peak.

I watch Cory sneak another look at the bartender. I want to roll my eyes, but I don't. The only reason why we come in here is because she likes him, but of course she won't admit it. She never will. Cory has an aversion to sharing personal feelings.

I sneak another quick look at Dar. He is staring at me.

Of course he would turn around when I don't want him to!

I fix his glare, letting him know I am not intimidated. I lift my chin and then give him my back, "Finish your drink, Cory. I'm bored and I still have work to do when I get home."

Not technically a lie. But originally I had not planned to look over my work until tomorrow.

She looks at me with a whiny face, but she knows better than to argue. I am her ride home.

The bartender walks by, and I lift up my hand to stop him, "We're outta here." He looks us over and lingers a few seconds to glance at Cory. Then he nods and brings back our receipt and my card.

Cory slowly finishes her martini. Not sure if she is being slow on purpose, but now is not the time to mess with me. I can start to feel my blood tingling. Not good.

I am ready to spring this joint.

I refuse to let myself look in his direction one more time. Why did fate hate me so much?

Screw him and his beer drinking cooties.

Sneaking to go see him while he was in the hospital was the stupidest thing I ever did. It was also the only time I ever talked to him. Well, technically, I used my magic to talk to him telepathically because he was in a coma, but still. It was the boldest thing I had ever done.

I never told him my name even though he asked me several times. I don't know why I didn't tell him, but when I first said hello in his mind he freaked out a little. He asked me a lot of questions that I didn't understand, something about his moon or the moon. I still have no idea what he was talking about.

On the second trip to the hospital he told me about the bear attack. At first I thought he was joking when he said the bear transformed into a witch. But after he described what she did with a blunted curved knife, I believed him.

That's when I looked over his chart and saw that his heart was weak from being overworked due to his injuries. In fact, the chart depicted each and every stab wound. When I asked him how he was still alive after what happened, he didn't explain. All he said was that the witch must have poisoned the knife with silver because he should have been healed by now.

I didn't understand his comment about silver until my parents taught me about werewolves. Imagine my surprise.

I also remember how sad I was when he told me that he knew he was never going to wake up. He told me that he was going to miss his family and his friends. Then, like a little liar, he said he wished he could have gotten to know me. That was the night I spoke to him in French, my blood language.

I was very young when I first started speaking French. The words came to me as easily as breathing. I didn't know that speaking in French somehow triggered my magic. It wasn't said in a spell or clever ditty. The magic inside took my words and formed it based on my instincts I think.

I didn't know how powerful I was until that night with Dar. I never knew I could heal more than a few bruises or skinned knees. As a kid I never needed to heal someone from stab wounds. In fact I only used it once since then, on Cory when she was really sick and the doctors didn't know what was wrong with her.

That night, at the hospital sitting next to Dar I told him he would heal from his wounds. I told his heart to be strong like mine and to use mine when he felt weak. Then I told him to get some rest and I left. The next day at school I heard that he awoke from his coma.

I don't remember a time in school that I was more excited than that day. I started picturing and fantasizing about how Dar and I were going to get to know each other. Some thoughts, I am embarrassed to say, were not appropriate for a high school girl.

A week later he returned to school with all the pomp my

fellow classmates could cook up. I looked for him every time I walked to my next class and during lunch, but he was always talking to a group of girls or his friends and I was too embarrassed to intrude. So instead, I waited for him to find me and remember me and our talks at the hospital. All my excitement and hopes crashed after he had been back a month and he still had never even glanced in my direction.

I remember feeling crushed every time I passed by him and he acted like I didn't exist. Maybe it was my fault for not telling him who I was. Maybe things would have been different if I would have introduced myself.

Regardless, that's what happened. My heart never healed from my senior year. I remained hollow from that time forward.

Cory places her empty glass back on the counter, and I stand up to pull on my tan leather jacket. I glance at Dar one more time before we dash. He is talking to some chick that looks like a stick bug. I lower my eyes and think about making Dar's drink break so that it spills all over his shirt but I hold back, barely. He really is not worth it, he wasn't worth my time in high school and he isn't worth my time now.

Not that I would go back and not heal him, I would still heal him, but I wish I could go back and erase all those memories. My chest started feeling heavy and I knew that if I didn't get out of here now it would really start to hurt. Zipping up my jacket after two failed attempts, I am shaking. I really hate my own weakness. Hate it. Screw him and his arrogant ass! In fact, why wouldn't I get some pay back? Why wouldn't I ruin his night the way he ruined mine?

I looked at the beer bottle and the stick bug creature next to him pawing at his shoulder. If she just took one more step to the… Dar turns to me right then and bores his amber eyes into mine as if he knows what I am thinking.

Warning me.

Averting my eyes with a dramatic eye roll, I pull out my keys and walk with Cory straight out the door, at the same time breaking the blasted bottle that I had a firm mental fix to. The validating whine from a female took some of the heaviness from my chest away. Even a little goes a long way.

CHAPTER THREE
SHANE

The blonde and her sister just left. And the Nickelback poser's beer was knocked over hard enough to burst all over one of the bar bunnies. I pulled my rag out from my apron and headed over to pick up the broken bits. It's going to be a long, boring night; actually it's going to be a long, boring week before I see the shy blonde again.

The Nickelback poser has a steady eye on the back door where the two girls departed. I walk up to him and begin picking up the pieces.

"Another beer, and napkins," he says, in a dark timber. His displeasure, for some reason, makes me want to smile. Then I realize that as soon as the blonde left, I feel like my normal self again. Disconnected and patronizing towards everyone in equal amounts. I decide to ignore that realization to grab another beer, pop the top, and set the bottle in front of the poser.

I hand the skeleton looking bar bunny next to him a few napkins that she quickly makes use of. After she places the soiled napkins back on the bar she ignores me all together and leans in to the poser's ear to whisper something. Lazily dropping her arm across his shoulder while she reaches for the bottle of beer in front of him with her other arm.

After she takes a long drink from his brand new bottle she places it back in front of him, giving him the "let's get out of here" look. The poser looks her over and then narrows his eyes at the bottle like it offends him. The look was similar to the way he looked at the brunette earlier.

"Rum and coke," a small, pink haired looking pixie calls out from my right. I leave the disgruntled Nickleback poser to look at the frilly-looking girl who earns my appreciation for her pixie-like style. She bites her bottom lip playfully. I pick up the Captain Morgan and begin to make her drink.

I have a weakness for fairies. Humans are not supposed to know about the supernatural creatures, according to my real father. He said it's like signing a death warrant. If the Magic Council finds out you were the person who spilled the magic beans to the humans, it would be your ass on a slab being tortured and then killed. So with that warning I have never been friendly and close with humans since I was eighteen. I have never bedded a human, nor have I ever invited a human friend or acquaintance into my home. I keep to myself and I like it that way.

After a few rounds at the bar I seem to be keeping tabs on the poser. Irritatingly, he seems to be the only interesting person worth watching tonight. I watch him hold on to the beer in front of him tightly as if it's holding him upright, but his eyes are faded out as if he is thinking instead of listening to the bag of bones next to him. Then if that wasn't a little odd, his eyes keep lightening to amber every once in a while. At first I thought it was because of something the chick was whispering to him, but there were times when she was saying nothing and his eyes were still blazing.

I don't get wolves. I really don't, but there is clearly something not right with this one. He was so quiet that I almost missed his question when I rounded the bar.

"How often do they come in here?" The poser asks.

Taking in his mood and the vibes he was leaking out, I can tell he's pissed. His eyes are lighter but not glowing, and it seems as though talking is a bit of a strain. Everyone knows that when a werewolf's eyes glow, you want to be somewhere else. Everyone except me; I am not afraid of him. Just because I am a bartender does not mean I want to pass along gossip or information, specifically information that correlates to a person I have no intentions of talking about to anyone, ever. I ignore his question and keep walking to find another thirsty patron.

The wolf growls at me as if that is going to entice me to answer him. He has no idea who I am and I aim to keep it that way. The best offense is keeping your challenger in the dark. Telling him that I am a Carver, and that no one on the planet can touch me just sounds a little too cocky, even for me.

According to my biological father, I am the only fourth generation Carver. My biological mother is a third generation Carver and so is my biological father.

When they came to get me the day I turned eighteen, I found out that I was important, which is the exact opposite of how I felt my entire life. My adoptive parents were not decent, and their four boys belonged in hell, not jail or somewhere to talk about their feelings. The things they did to me and others made me into the person I am. And I am the person that took away their ability to hurt anyone ever again.

Of course I didn't know my adoptive family had been magically forced to take care of me until my biological parents told me. My mind told me not to blame my adoptive parents for being indignant, but I was a child and they never, ever, acknowledged me or helped me by keeping me safe from their sons! I had to take care of myself because they didn't.

My biological parents thought I was going to jump at the opportunity to be a part of a real family. They must have forgotten what it was like growing up with an adopted family, because I was not buying their crap. And they did a good job of feeding me their crap. Something about a war and how the Carvers were going to take over some kind of Magical Council.

At first I was happy to just be out of my adoptive parents' house. Yes, my biological parents were far more attentive and giving… at first. They tried to test me to find out what I could do. Maybe it was because I was uncomfortable with other people knowing too much, or maybe it was because there was something in my biological parents' attitudes that rubbed me the wrong way, but I couldn't become the show monkey they asked for. I did show them a few tricks, but the big stuff, like my fire, I kept to myself.

After they watched me show them the few tricks I knew they were disappointed, but by then I didn't care, nor did I want their approval. The next month they sent me to a stupid camp with the most arrogant assholes I have ever met. I grew up in Hollywood, so I know what an arrogant asshole looks like.

In their camp run by my dad, Rich, they tried to learn and teach basic magic and spells. It was so unbelievably easy. For example, to do witch - I mean earth- magic, all you had to do was to say the words or incantation that always made me think of Dr. Suess, because most of the time it rhymed.

Fairy magic was all about exercising the magic already inside of you and exploring all the little nuances that each fairy could do, in addition to their basic fairy talent. Vampires and werewolves didn't have any magic. They used their instincts.

Compared to the magic I did, I was floored with how little these other Carvers had. If I had a hard time believing my parents when they told me I was special, I wouldn't doubt them after going to that camp. It was clear that all the first and second generations Carvers were weak in comparison to me.

Weeks later my parents sat me down for another long talk. They told me that they knew I had a lot of potential and I needed to use it for a purpose. Annoyingly, they had decided what purpose they wanted me to serve. My purpose, according to my parents, was to find the family members of the council members to later use them as leverage. Oh and let's not forget my bride, oh, I mean, heart. A Carver's mate was called their heart. They said they knew another couple that had a very powerful daughter who would be my perfect match.

My father briefly explained a little bit about Carvers and their hearts. It's similar to werewolves, in the sense that a werewolf could breed with another wolf, but when he or she found their mate, they couldn't be with anyone else. For a Carver, we didn't have to bite one another to mix blood like the wolves, instead we offered our hearts – or better explained, our soul, to the other person in our blood language, and then poof, we were bonded for life! Two souls bound for eternity.

Not. For. Me.

Not to be too dramatic, but I can't even fathom being with the same women for a year, let alone a lifetime being bonded.

My father told me that he and my mother were not bonded. They had only come together to join their powers to make me, the most powerful person alive.

My biological father described how the Carvers planned to change the Magical Council to a Carver Council. In short, he planned to expunge the unnecessary rules, like having someone else raise your kid for eighteen years. There were a lot of rules for Carvers.

The idea of making the rules less strict was an idea I could believe in, but then they told me how I was supposed to use the Magical Council's family members as leverage. It was going to be a blood bath if it ever happened, and I truly hope it never does.

The Carvers had done their homework and watched almost every person on the council to make sure that when they killed the council member, their families and friends, no one, would try and avenge them or be willing to fight back.

I hated the idea of hurting someone who is genuinely innocent. I wouldn't stand for it, and if they pushed me I would stand against them. If the bride they told me about was going to sign up for butchering innocent families then she could join all the other people I cut out of my life.

I objected to my father's plan and he quickly lost his cool. So much so that I went flying into the opposite wall, dislocating my shoulder. My father didn't even blanch at what he had done. In fact, he was still trying to argue his point while my mother was calling for a healer to come pop my shoulder back in place. I never thought I would hate my real parents more than my adoptive parents, but it's true. The day he threw me into a wall using his power was my line. I was done.

I let him try and intimidate me. I pretended he convinced me of my errors, well I doubt I did a good job of acting convinced, but I said the right words anyways. I did all I had to do so that I could return to my room to gather my things, and then I teleported my ass as far away as I could.

I left everything from my life with my adoptive family in my biological parents' home, even my favorite yellow amber necklace I wore every day until that night. I was determined to start a new life.

One without magic, one without any ties to my previous life, and one where my father would never find me.

"Hey, bartender!" Some schmo in a pinstriped suit called out, trying to talk to a chick that looks like an eighteen year old.

I look around quickly. The werewolf is gone and deep down I know I am going to see him again. I am unsure what it was about the shy blonde's sister that he had an issue with, but there is definitely something about that brunette that doesn't sit well with him.

I walk to the schmo who called for me as three more people call out, "Hey, bartender!" The night is just getting started.

* * *

Finally the last patron leaves the bar. I watched Sal, the owner of Amber Line, exit his office. "Sal!" I call out. I catch his attention with a short wave.

"Hey, what's up, Shane?" He asks as he tilts his chin up to me. I am easily four inches taller.

"You need to hire another bartender," I say as lightly as I can, which isn't really casual at all. We have had this conversation before so I don't think I had to explain my point yet again.

"Hey! You know I like you kid, but don't tell me how to run my bar." Sal is a New York Italian and believes he runs the world because he has a lucrative bar that's still going hot. I don't apologize. I'm right. He's wrong. And we do need another bartender and I have been telling him to do this for at least a month. I am running low on patience and tonight was too heavy for one bartender.

I keep looking at him, waiting for him to simmer down and have a man-to-man conversation without him getting in my face about being disrespectful. He has an overly sensitive attitude and that is not my fault. "Yeah, well, I put out an ad. I'm going to do interviews this week." He eyes me waiting for my response. When he didn't get one he asks, "Happy, now?"

I untie my apron and fold it up. "Just make sure the dude has some experience. Teaching isn't my strong suit."

"Don't I always do right Shane?"

My mouth twitched. *No.* "Always," I answer, while covering up a yawn. I watch Sal walk to the back of the bar to get the cash register and receipts I already counted and had ready for him. Done for the night I head out the side exit.

The fresh night air is crisp and fills my lungs. It's at times like this that I am thankful I am not a vampire or werewolf so I don't have to smell every single person who has passed by here, all I smell is the damp earth from the light rain that must have fallen earlier tonight.

I walk to my car and click the remote to unlock it. I have to keep up appearances and drive like a normal working-class human, even thought I could simply teleport to my apartment. On the plus side of having to drive, I really like my new car.

I start it up quickly and peel out of the parking lot. At home I park my car in the parking garage, get out, lock the car and walk to the elevator. Once inside, I teleport to my loft.

Home. Mine. No one comes to visit, so I don't have to worry about someone stopping by unannounced or looking around and making comments about my lack of decoration and family photos. I pay in cash, and I don't make noise. And that's the way I like it.

CHAPTER FOUR
BETH

It's five minutes till four in the morning; I walk in the house tired and groggy from running the Bar trails at Pike's Peak. It's a 13-mile hike, one way. I'm exhausted. It's exactly what I needed to clear my mind from tonight's crap.

Cory is sleeping on the couch with her book on the floor beneath her hand where it must have fallen. My chest feels heavy. *She waited up for me.*

I grab a blanket from the laundry room and lay it over her. I pick up her silly Thumbelina bookmark, slide it in the back of the page before folding it closed. She looks so peaceful. I watch her for a few minutes.

Folding my arms to watch her shallow breaths, I conclude, yet again, how important she is to me. Cory has always accepted me, and I can't put into words how much that has grounded my life. Sure, she has also pushed the limits of my patience, but never once did she do anything spiteful. Cory is a good person with an amazing, good-natured heart.

Growing up having the ability to do magic is not as cool as it may sound. You always have to hide a huge side of you from humans who have a proclivity to kill what they don't understand.

Yes, my family loved me, but they also didn't trust me not to do something harmful. I know they were being cautious but it hurt, nonetheless. At the same time, I did a lot of stupid stuff as a kid and I did break a lot of stuff, some on accident, and some on purpose. I wasn't going to hide who I was at home. Magic is a part of me; I didn't want to lose that small part of me that made me unique.

Since I was a baby, if something broke I was the first one to be blamed. I admit that I was usually the one to accidentally break it, but it wasn't always my fault. My magic was new to me and I had no idea I could break stuff anytime I was angry or sad or too excited. I mean, come on! I am not a robot.

One time I left a human sized dent in the hallway wall because Cory jumped out of the bathroom screaming "raar". It was pitch black, and we had just watched Freddy Krueger! Seriously, she knew better. I responded to the perceived threat of a possible Freddy Krueger attack, at which time Cory was flung back really hard and the air was knocked out of her.

After I turned on the lights I saw Cory plastered against the wall, with her eyes closed and blue lips. She had stopped breathing. It took a few seconds to respond, and possibly a few years off my poor heart's life. By the time my parents came, Cory was breathing again and I got a two-hour lecture about learning to control my magic and was grounded for three months.

Once I tried using my magic to do the dishes and ended up shattering the contents of the entire china cabinet. I was grounded for six months that time.

Playing with magic wasn't always my cleverly crafted idea. Cory has a devious, sneaky side. She would create little silly games that we could play without our parents finding out. My favorite was Midnight Pictionary. It was pretty clever of her to think of making our markers glow in the dark but not be seen in the light. If our parents came in and turned on the lights they would never know. Sometimes I think Cory could have been a kingpin. You never really knew what she was thinking until she was already done with what she had planned.

On the weekends that I was grounded, and Cory was left to play by herself, she create a game I could play, even though I was grounded to my room. For example, she hid things from me and made me try to find them. At first it was super easy, I would call them by name and make them come back. By the next weekend, Cory upped the difficulty level. It got to the point that I couldn't find what she hid or where her hiding spots were. To this day I still don't know where my favorite toe socks and all my fluorescent toenail polishes are.

Cory is three years younger than I am, but you wouldn't know that looking or talking to her. She is smart, really smart. That's why I always worry about the quiet ones.

My adopted family was good to me, but after I left with my biological parents Cory was the only one I went back for. She was the one I wasn't going to live my life without.

I unzip my tan jacket, drop it on the arm of the couch and lie down. I didn't suffer from insomnia or anything like that, so staying up late was not natural. I'm tired. I want to crash out right here on the couch in my dry sweat and stinky bar clothes, but every time I close my eyes I see him again. So I am waiting for exhaustion to hit so I go from awake to a light coma.

I close my eyes and feel my whole body melting into the couch. The vision of Dar and his perfectly chiseled jaw and robust shoulder frame are slowly fading…fading.

"Hey. You sleeping?" Cory whispers.

Visions of Dar are brightening and now I can practically picture what it would feel like to run my hand down his chest.

Ugh.

Rubbing my eyes, I roll to my side and peer out with one eye. Cory is sitting up, which means I am going to end up staying up because I can tell she wants to talk.

Agh. Little sisters…

With my one eye still closed, I answer, "Yes."

"I was worried," she says quietly, even though we are the only ones in the house, and it's not like the neighbors can hear us.

Ignoring her comment and hoping to avoid the topic, I flip onto my stomach and nuzzle my face into the crook of my arm, "Happy Birthday, Cory. You're twenty-five. Woo… Hoo."

"You know the rules," I can hear the smile in her voice. "You are my slave today. You have to do whatever I want."

I can't help the smile that creeps over my lips. We had this rule growing up that no matter whose birthday it was, they never had to clean or cook *or* be grounded. For Cory, the extortionist, she took it a step further. She added that I had to do whatever she said, which always needed the addition of my magic. She never asks me to do anything malicious so I have always magically caved, so to speak.

With as little emphasis as possible, I groan. "I can't wait. What is your first wish, Birthday Master?"

The couch next to me creaks as Cory sits up. "Let's start with some coffee, nonfat with a drop of hazelnut cream." She is pretending to sound aristocratic, and failing miserably.

Summoning the fire inside me to force me off the couch, I finally get up. If the Birthday Master wants coffee, then she will get some coffee. Slowly moving one foot in front of the other I make it into the kitchen and open the refrigerator, pull out coffee grounds and reach for the creamer.

"Wait. Not that one!" Cory yelps as she jumps off the couch, bounds over to quickly snatch the glass canister with the coffee grounds.

I let out a slow breath, eyeing her wearily. I am unsure what coffee she wants me to use now because that was the last of it. I think. Thankfully, Cory can read my bewildered expression and answers, "Um, this is my newest concoction. I use it to feed my plants. Kind of like a fertilizer." Cory is holding the glass canister tightly.

Okay so she can't read my unspoken question.

Annoyed, I ask, "What beans do you want me to use?" Then my brain processes what she said and I narrow my eyes at my leery-eyed sister. "You put fertilizer in the refrigerator?"

I wish I could strangle her as she nods with a sly smile. Unable to muster any more energy to scold her, I turn back to the refrigerator to fish for the real coffee grounds. I find them in the back, labeled "coffee," of course. I grab the hazelnut creamer and slam the door.

"Um..." Cory hesitates without looking me in the eye.

Oh, for the love of everything that tastes good! "What?" I shout at her, exasperated and cranky. I push the bottle in her face and say, "It says Hazelnut Creamer!"

Cory winces, "I know. But…"

I am about to ask what it really is but she grabs it and takes both the fertilizer and the mysterious liquid in the creamer bottle up to her room.

"What is wrong with you, Cory?" I mumble while rubbing my forehead. She may be brilliant, but she forgets that our kitchen is not her laboratory.

I shouldn't be surprised, and in all honesty I'm not, she's been mixing weird stuff since my adopted parents bought her first chemistry set. I am just tired. I want to go to sleep and pretend that the last twelve hours didn't happen. But I can't and now I have to play birthday genie for the next 24 hours. I have no idea where I am going to find the energy, but I will make it through. But first things first, I have to find the real hazelnut creamer and not another mystery liquid.

Now that I am paying attention, there are several non-marked bottles in the refrigerator. I lean my body over the white refrigerator door and rest my head on the crook of my elbow.

Counting the nefarious looking bottles, I ignore the fire simmering in my blood because my mood is regressing. Five. Five creamer looking bottles, all non-labeled which means that they could be dangerous.

Cory's constantly creating odd concoctions, and I've learned that the bad ones she won't label. The good ones she does. To what end is she forever mixing and creating these things? I wish I knew. Although I suspect that she experiments at home what she is not allowed to do at work.

I don't know why haven't I stopped her. Probably because she has always encouraged me to learn more about my magic, and never once has she looked down at me for not being human. So I won't discourage her experiments, not that she ever tells me what she is experimenting on, but regardless, I support her.

One time when she wasn't home I drank a cup of iced tea, or what smelled and tasted like iced tea. I ended up waking up in my bed a week later with no recollection of what happened. To this day, Cory has not explained what I drank and why I blacked out for a week. Then again, I did take away her voice for a week in retaliation, so I doubt she will ever tell me.

Cory walks back in the kitchen fully dressed with light eye make-up, which means we are going out. I take a moment to think before I use my magic to change my clothes. A second later I am in flip-flops, green cargo pants, and a tan t-shirt. I can make any of my clothes transform into new clothes, a wonderful trick I learned in junior high after I sat in gum.

I gave her a questioning look as I placed a coffee liner in the coffee pot.

"How about we get coffee from the Tasty Pastry?" She offers. Then she looks me over and says, "I can wait for you to take a shower if you want."

"What? I don't smell good enough for you?" I ask, as if I am offended even though I would love for nothing more than to take a shower.

Cory scrunches her nose, "You stink. You really should take a shower. And it's not like you can magically do that."

With a snort I walk out of the kitchen and head to the shower. She's right about that one.

After a shower, a new set of clothes, and a touch of make-up, we begin the day. In the car, Cory is rummaging through her oversized purse. I focus back on the road tempting myself with the idea that if I freeze time I could take a nap and Cory would never know her birthday lasted an extra four hours.

I pull into the Tasty Pastry's drive-through and order a large nonfat café latte with hazelnut for the birthday girl, and a black coffee for me. I will need all the energy I can get.

I pay the lady at the first window and she hands me the black coffee first. I set it in the drink holder and reach out for the second cup.

"Ask for some napkins." Cory snapped.

So I did. When I turned around with the latte and a handful of napkins I see an odd expression on Cory's face, kind of like the cat who ate the canary. I narrow my eyes at her, warning her that now is not a good time to piss me off. The shady smile does nothing to comfort me. I plan on giving her the silent treatment until she tells me what is going on, but as soon as that thought is created it breaks due to the impatient jerk behind me. He has his hand hard-fasted on his horn.

It's far too early for this shit.

I mentally picture a horn in my mind and melt it. Milliseconds later the horn stops blowing and my shoulders relax. I smile and forget all about canary-in-the-mouth Cory, and take a sip of my coffee.

Right now a few things are very apparent. First, it feels like I just swallowed liquid nitrogen. It's so cold it burns. Second, my insides are igniting. The fire that usually lives in my veins is under attack. Third, I can't move. I am frozen in place. I can feel every pop and sizzle in my body with the addition of light pressure on my hand, as Cory tries to take the coffee out of my hand, but the cup won't budge from my death grip and my thighs are also on fire now.

"Oh crap!" Cory panics, looking at my legs to which I assume are covered in my black coffee by the feel of it.

Time has slowed down for me, and I can feel my insides battling between the rigid cool burn and the live fire. Then it feels like several million bubbles are swimming in my stomach. I feel it coming up and I burp loud. It tasted like exhaust, or something equally nasty and vile. The fire in my blood is attacking the liquid nitrogen, or whatever it was that I ingested.

As my body begins to feel normal again I try to focus on my surroundings. There is a tingling feeling roaming over my skin, including the dull irritation on my thighs. I can feel the paper cup with my left hand and I am gripping it for dear life. My heart is pounding like I am in a boxing ring, high on adrenalin, and ready to go toe to toe with anyone and everyone.

I grab the steering wheel. Before I can ask, "What the hell was that?" my light grab of the steering wheel turns into a hulk squeeze.

Crap.

"Was that liquid nitrogen?" I babble, still staring at the malformed steering wheel. “Did you just try and poison me?” I meant it to come out sounding harsh and threatening, but my voice was shaky.

“I thought it would help?” Cory said, while taking her coffee from the drink holder.

“What did you think would help?” I ask between my teeth chattering.

Opening her mouth to answer, a loud knock sounds on my window. Cory and I jump and she drops her coffee onto her lap and all over my passenger seat. I can hear the hiss when she inhales.

My fire begins heating in my chest. I turn back towards the window, glaring at the jackass who dared to get impatient with me.

My nostrils flare as I breathe against the driver side window. All this prick has to do is say one word, and he will successfully set me off, and I will end his world.

My look tells him to piss off and that is exactly what he does. He holds up his hands, backing away slowly.

I watch him in my side mirror as he gets back in his car. Satisfied with him inside his vehicle, and calm enough to drive, I slowly roll out of the drive-through and park the car.

Taking a few moments, I focus all my energy on Cory. "You have three seconds," I threaten her with both words and tone.

"I just wanted to help you feel better. You looked tired so I thought I could give the coffee a boost." She has pushed herself as far back into the crack of the passenger seat and door, with a worry in her lip and her eyes the size of saucers.

I want to strangle her. I want to pummel her without actually hurting her.

Gah!

"What did you put in my coffee?"

"Something I have been tinkering with," Cory looks away. I purse my lips at her, half because I want to strangle her and half because she is cowering to me. I would never hurt her.

Not really.

It's complicated. And a sister thing.

I take my tainted coffee in hand and open the driver's side door, to pour out the remaining drops. Then I take the empty cup in Cory's hand, step out of the car and slam the door hard, making sure that Cory has no doubt of how truly pissed off I am. I fix my clothes as I walk inside the Tasty Pastry for another coffee latte. I am not doing it to be nice and forgive her for that stunt she just pulled. I am doing it to calm the fuck down so that I don't say something I will regret later. I may not be ready to combust, but I am still pissed. And the fire inside me is not totally subdued. Thankfully, I have enough control over my magic that I didn't just have an accident.

Back in the car I magically change my car's upholstery, which is the closest thing I can do to clean the coffee stains. And then, at Cory's pleading look, I touch her shirt and pants and change them, too.

"Where am I going?" I ask in a deadpanned tone, not bothering to look her way.

Cory pulls out a folded paper from her purse and hands it to me. Hesitating, I take it and lean back to unfold the paper that I am sure is a list of her birthday wishes.

I shudder, "This is a job application for the Amber Line." I peer over at Cory, wondering what exactly she is thinking.

"I want a job at The Amber Line," she said, thumbing small circles on the lid of her coffee.

"You already have a job," I fold up the paper slowly and toss it back at her. The paper hits the window with a thunk before it drops into her lap. "A good job in fact, at the National Laboratory for Safety and Prevention, where you are paid a good deal of money to work on that micro stuff you actually studied in school!" My temper was rising and I knew I shouldn't be yelling but I couldn't help it. "So tell me Cory, tell me why you want to toss that good job out the fucking door to work at a sleazy bar for a quarter of what you bring how home now? Huh? Tell me Cory!"

If she really wants to work at that piece of shit bar I was going to actually shake her until her brain reset. I would slap her so hard she was going to fast-forward to next week. I would think of *something* to do to her to convince her how bad this idea was.

Hell, I spent hours with her while she used me to quiz her for her tests. She graduated high school early and was already attending Pomona University when I found her, after I left my parents. I moved in to her one-room apartment that day and said a few words in my blood language to become a new student. We both got Master's degrees. I got a job at Nat Lab while Cory started her doctorate in microbiology, specifically with research concentrating on carcinogens. My degree is in business management. When she graduated I had already lined up her job with the National Laboratory for Safety and Prevention, but we just call it Nat Lab.

Nat Lab is a good job with great pay and I get to work with my sister. But right now she was thinking of ruining all of that. I know it's not because she is really wants to change jobs. I know the driving force is none other than that rat bastard Shane, the Amber Line's bartender.

Not that I am against her dating, but there is something about him that doesn't feel right. I don't know what it is about him that rubs me the wrong way, but I knew there was something wrong with him the moment I saw him. Adding to the fact that her interest in him is pushing her away from her real job makes me dislike him even further.

Going to the bar just to watch him was borderline creepy, but this, this! I wasn't going to let this slide. This was stupid and this was so beneath her that I refuse to even think of it.

"You know Cory, if you want to get to know the bartender it would be a hell of a lot easier to just ask for his number. You do realize that, don't you?"

Cory's face turns cherry red. "No. I just want to work at the bar on the weekends. I could use the extra cash."

I eye her suspiciously. "You don't need the money, Cory." I said it, hoping it was true. I am not sure if she needs the cash but I was banking on my theory that it was all about the bartender.

"I do need the cash, my experiments are expensive." She tilted her head at me with a don't-doubt-me face.

She's lying. She has to be.

"What the hell are you experimenting with? Uranium?" As soon as I said it, I prayed she wasn't messing around with radioactive shit in the house. I could slap myself for letting this whole experimentation thing get out of hand. If she was gushing money on experiments then I should have noticed, right? There would be equipment and beakers and whatever else scientists used. Oh, lasers! There would definitely be a laser or something, I was sure of it.

Settled with the fact that she was fibbing about the experiments, I was one hundred percent not ready to entertain her little birthday wish to get her a part time job with her crush. Then again, maybe she needed to learn a lesson.

"Are you telling me you want to apply, or…" I raise an eyebrow to see if she wants me to use my magic to get her the job.

She chews on her bottom lip and I try not to roll my eyes. But then her cheeks get a little pink and I am amused with her shyness once more.

I wouldn't expect Cory to date like normal people, not when she was so socially clueless. I mean, she was actually cute and smart and had a good job. By all means she was a bloody catch!

"I want us both to work at The Amber Line on the weekends. I saw an ad and they're looking for waitresses and bartenders."

Everything paused for a moment. "You want me to give up my weekends? To work at a bar?"

Unbelievable. My sister must be drinking one of her concoctions.

Cory fumbles with the coffee lid again for a moment before she answers with more resolve than I ever have heard from the little trickster, "Yes."

My jaw drops slightly, "No. Hell no!"

Cory holds up her index finger as she raises her eyebrows. I know whatever comes after *that look* is going to be so bad I may end up taking her voice away for a week. "I did some research while you were out running last night. And I am pretty sure that my information is worth working a few weekends with me."

I lean back against the door and cross my arms over my chest, "Mmhhm?"

"Don't look at me like that. I know what I'm doing. I even know why Dar is in town. And I know that you will want to know." The charlatan took a small sip of the coffee, making a loud sucking noise on purpose. "In fact, I would say that you will-"

My nose flares as I get a clear mental picture of her vocal cords, and silence them.

"Nope. Nope. No. Not going to happen Cory," I say with my eyebrows raised in a perfect horizontal line. Cory touches her throat and I could hear heavy breaths rushing out of her mouth as if she was trying to yell, but no other sounds could be heard.

I had to take away her voice. I had to. She pushed me too far this time.

With lips tightly smashed on top of one another, turning them white as ivory, Cory puts her coffee down and starts fumbling through her purse. A second later she pulls out a small 3x5 notepad and pen. She holds up the pen and shakes it at me, as if she is threatening me.

I wiggle back on the door and close my eyes, longingly, "I don't care what you researched. I don't care what you found. And even if I were the tiniest bit interested, I wouldn't ask, so if this is your way of getting me to work on the weekends at a bar, you have crossed into delusional city."

I can hear her writing but I keep my eyes closed. I am breathing slow and even, so that she can't tell how much I am on edge here.

I hear the pad of paper whizzing through the air. The mini note pad hits the window with a loud clank, and then falls down the side in between the seat and door. I huff at my sister and reach down to see what she wrote.

You have three seconds!

I turned to her and I saw her holding out her index finger. Then added her middle finger.

"You don't scare me," I mocked.

She held up her phone, typed a message and pushed send, and then smiled maliciously.

"What did you do?" I swallow hard. *What could she do?*

Cory started appraising her nails and I could feel my stomach begin to squeeze with uncertainty. I gave back her voice and then waved my hand at her throat.

"Cory?" My voice was steady even though my insides were not.

"Are you going to get us jobs at the Amber line?" She said sweetly, as if she were not blackmailing me.

Carefully I answered her "I will get you the job at Amber Line. And I promise to be there every weekend, but I don't need the job. Now," I pause, waiting for her to look at me, "what did you do?"

Cory bites the inside of her lip and studies me for a moment before tucking a lock of hair behind her ear. "I'll tell you what I did if you work for a month, with me, on the weekends, and then you can quit. I just need a month." I opened my mouth to interject, but she cuts me off. "Wait. If you agree to work for a month and get us jobs, I will tell you what I did. And then I will promise that this is my last birthday wish for today. *And*, I will tell you what I found out for free."

I slap my hand on the steering wheel. "Why would I care to hear about someone who doesn't even know I exist?" I push back and rest my head against the headrest. "Why the hell would I care? He's nothing to me. He's just some guy I knew in school who I crossed paths with at a bar. It's nothing. It means nothing. He means nothing." I closed my eyes tight, begging for my words to come true, but the hollow feeling in my chest was still there like it has been since I was seventeen. "If you want to work at Amber Line, fine. But don't wrap me into your crazy schemes."

"You're wrong," Cory said lightly, as if she could make the words hurt less if she said them softly. "He does know who you are. I checked."

The knot in my throat would not let me talk with a straight voice, so I remained quiet not willing to show that kind of weakness.

"I'm sorry I pushed," she whispered. I felt her hand on my arm and I wanted to snatch my hand back, but the warmth in her firm squeeze made me feel connected. It made some of the rigidness ease. "I didn't know."

Then I heard the click clack of Cory on her phone. I peer over and watch her vigorously typing on her phone.

"What are you doing now?"

Her maleficent smile was creeping up her face. "Confirming with Sal that we can start tonight. And you can bet that he will be there tonight and I promise to make him pay for all the pain he has caused you."

"Who do you think you are, Lex Luther? You can't plot out my revenge. That's not fair," I said half-heartedly, amused and half grateful to her because I knew she meant it. And I knew that even though I was going to hate working every weekend for a month, someone has to look out for her.

"You're not going to kill him are you?" I ask while pulling the car into reverse.

With a light chuckle Cory answers, "Nope, it will be even better."

CHAPTER FIVE
SHANE

It's mid-day on Saturday when I walk into work. I like to arrive a little early before my shift so I can stock up on as much alcohol as I can. Saturday nights are busy and I don't like having to restock during my shift if we get slammed.

Danny, one of Amber Line's waiters, is wiping down a table when a soft female voice calls out, "Danny, I can do that. It's my area anyway."

Curious about a voice I don't know, I turn to see the shy blonde from last night. Intrigued, I watch her completely ignore me as she walks by and pats Danny on the shoulder, then wipes down the table as if Danny didn't just do that. Cory, that's the name she gave the douche last night, but her driver's license read Charlene. I didn't register her error until later that night when I was driving home.

Danny cleared his throat. He gives me the chin lift acknowledging that he approves of the new girl and her slim figure, with a petite waist, perfect legs, bending over the table. Her black button-up blouse was snuggly tucked into tight black jeans and she is wearing grey flats. Somehow the flats made her feet look so itty bitty that I swear it reminded me of a fairy. Noticing her lightness of foot, and the flittering way she walks to another table, almost has me flashing back to a fairy I dated several years ago. Cory even had a small dusting of freckles.

Inwardly I groaned.

Everything about her was calling to me and begging me to take notice. I did take notice. But I am not going to do anything. I won't. I have rules. No humans – ever. I couldn't even fathom more than a friendship with the few guys I knew, but I couldn't be friends with someone like Cory. It just wouldn't work. I would expose myself magically. I couldn't ever be myself around her. There was no point in getting into a relationship with anyone if I already knew it wouldn't work out.

That's why I only dated fairies. They were magical, and the only ones I could deal with that had the least amount of character flaws. Werewolves were far too rude and edgy. Vampires are too sensitive and have a tendency to wallow. Witches, ugh, don't get me started. I could spend all day listing what I hate about witches, starting with how they are pretty much humans that can do a few parlor tricks. They're not even immortal. They are like humans in the way in which they fall in love to marry, start a family, and die.

Fairies were polite and didn't ask too many personal questions. They do have a bad habit of keeping secrets and plotting your demise with a big smile on their face, but I can work with that. I mean come on, like I would date a person who didn't go out of their way to be my nemesis.

Also, fairies were smart and vegetarian. I am a vegetarian and so it just… works. Humans? Don't. Cory… wouldn't work out. And just because my body is hot for her doesn't mean I can give in.

I don't want to have to break it off later, after I grew tired of her. And I would, because after a while all the excitement of getting to know her would diminish. Eventually I would find that she really wasn't that interesting, and I would find something I couldn't stand about her. There is always something that I can't stand with everyone I meet. And Cory would only be a passing thing, but in the end it wouldn't be worth it.

I have seen it all; working at a bar really gives insight into how humans hook up and break up. So no, I am not interested in Cory. Not even a little bit.

I scan the room for Sal, the owner. Usually he is in the office or talking to the cooks about his new ideas for an appetizer, but when there is a pretty girl around, he can always be found near her, giving her the "I'll take care of you" talk.

I see him walking my way with *the* brunette beside him.

Oh hell.

I should have known. It's not like one thing in my life could possible go my way.

I rub my temple and watch as impassively as possible as Sal pulls the brunette forward, with his hand on her back and one hand extended to me. "And this is Shane. You'll be working with him tonight," he smiles up at me and adds, "this is Beth, our new, beautiful bartender. She will be working weekends to help out."

I hold out my hand to Beth, Cory's sister, "Hi."

She responds in the same unenthusiastic tone, "Hey."

I peer down at Sal and ask rhetorically "Want me to show her the bar? I can show her what to prep and the list of drinks." He nods and drops his hand from her back, telling her that if she has any questions to ask me.

We both watch him walk away, then turn to each other with a similar cold, calculating stare. I speak first, "Didn't know you were looking for a job?"

"I wasn't," she says, eyebrows raised.

"Then what are you doing here?" I fold my arms over my chest and make sure my back is straight.

Her face tilts to the side as she answers, "Does it matter? You need help, and I have the time," her tone is clipped, and she looks at the bar for a half a second before cutting her eyes to the other side of the room, where I know Cory is wiping down tables. Not that I am keeping tabs. I'm not.

"Are you always this cheerful?"

She curls her lips, still not looking at me. "For you? Yes."

I glance up to the roof wondering why everyone I meet I have to hold back the urge to stuff them in a trunk and leave it in the middle of a demolition site.

"Thanks Sal," I hear Cory call out and my eyes dart to see what she is thanking Sal for. Sal was fixing her collar? *What the hell?*

Beth asked beside me, "Did you just growl?"

I could feel my hands clenching into a fist. I'm not interested in her sister. She can trust me on that one. "I know she has a fake ID." I turn to Beth hoping to see her squirm. Even though it took me a month to notice the fake name, but that's beside the point. I should tell Sal so they both get canned and then maybe, just maybe, I can get some peace in my life.

"And yet you kept selling her drinks. What does that say about you?" Beth says in a tone I can't really decipher.

"What does it say about you? You're making your under aged sister work at a bar." I say accusingly, while leaving her before she has time to answer.

Beth jabs my shoulder as I step up into the bar corral, I almost stumble forward, which pisses me off. I turn around at the same time I feel the fire inside me begin to burn, bringing my magic to the forefront of my mind, waiting for me to give it a command. Beth narrows her eyes but does not move back or look in the least intimidated. The idiot steps up to me and now we are nose to nose. "What it says, is, that you're about to get slapped, open palmed, in the mouth, because Cory is none of your business." The muscle in her jaw twitched, "And, had you been a better bartender you would have noticed her fake ID a month ago, and if you were a better nosey-ass-bartender you would have found out that today's her 25th birthday." Then the smart-mouthed, arrogant, pain in my ass walks away, but not before she pushes past me with a shoulder bump and says under her breath, "I don't care who you are, or *what* you are. If you mess with her, I will kill you."

I run my hand through my blonde, curly mess and grab hold of the hair at the back of my neck and squeeze.

"You look tired." A sweet, soft voice spirals in my ears and my body responds favorably.

Calmer than before, I look down to the sweetest, shy girl blushing lightly. I rub my eyebrow before answering, "I've had better days."

"Want me to make you some coffee before your shift?" Her voice sounds hopeful. "Plus it would be great to get some practice before everyone comes in." Well how could I turn that down? I mean, she probably really needs to practice. She probably doesn't know how to do much, let alone serve people with a smile all day. Yeah, I guess I could let her practice on me.

"Sure."

The corner of her eyes crinkle as she says, "Okay, I'll be right back."

I watch her walk to the coffee pot and look curiously at the machine. Instead of doing her work for her, I wait to see if she will figure it out.

"Hey. Eyes off my sister," I hear beside me.

The pugnacious brat standing behind me with her arms folded in a silly attempt to intimidate me. I cock my head to the side. "First, you don't scare me, so acting like you are some bad ass, that only makes you look stupid and is irritating the hell out of me." I pause to accent my point. "Second, I am helping Cory to do her job so back up and go finish cutting the oranges and limes."

Beth's eyes burned with hatred.

I held her eyes and set my jaw.

"Here you go, Shane," Cory says.

Beth looks down and frowns. "What is that?"

"Shane looked tired so I made him – HEY!"

Beth had grabbed the coffee and tossed the paper cup in trash and pointed at Cory. "No!"

"Very grown up of you Beth." I mutter, because I had been looking forward to the coffee.

Beth ignores me all together because she lowered her head so she is in Cory's face speaking fast and low. Cory is speaking back in the same quick pissy-whisper thing girls do.

Beth leans back and holds out her hand. "Now Cory! I mean

it. Give it to me now or we leave."

Rolling her eyes, Cory pulls out a vile of clear liquid and places it in her sister's palm.

What the hell?

Cory looks over to me "It's caffeine mix. You know like the five-hour energy drinks?"

Oh.

Beth grabs the vile and stuffs it in her pants pocket and walks away mumbling something about strangling someone.

Cory pushes stray pieces of hair behind her ear. "I'm sorry, I was just trying to help."

She looks so sincere that I can't believe I am not about to yell at her for trying to juice up my coffee. I let out a slow breath in an attempt to at least look displeased. "Yeah well next time just get a regular coffee. Okay?" I can see her face lighten. It bothers me how much it affects me that she is smiling like that. I wipe my hands down my face, "I gotta go." And with that I walk around the bar as far away from Cory as I can get, which also means I am, once more, too close to her sister.

It's not like I need this job, per se. I just need something to keep me occupied. I'm a minimalist and I don't need much to be content. I don't need to spend money on traveling because I can do that anytime I want, and I have already seen most of the world. I don't make huge investments or worry about the stock market because I really, truly, do not care about money. It pays the few bills I have, but the rest I can use my magic for. For example, my new car was all magic.

I am not out to impress anyone. I don't want to be seen with a big belt buckle, shiny watch, or flashy chain around my neck. I don't need to have my hair slathered in gel or have my nails buffed and shined. I am a man, with little to no need for most of the materials the world has to offer. I wear dark brown boots that have scuff marks I put there, not purchased. I have faded jeans because I wear them in, not purchase them half-faded with holes. I wear plain, solid color shirts because the thought of wearing anything swirly makes me want to vomit. Yes my hair is curly, but it's kept short so it's not ragged. Yes I grow hair on my face and it looks like I have a five o'clock shadow four hours later, but I shave it every day because I have good hygiene. Yes I have hair on my body because shaving it makes me feel like a twelve year old boy whose balls have not dropped. This is how I am, and I will not excuse myself for it.

I will not dress a new way for anyone. I will not change who I am because someone has a problem with me. And I will not let anyone intimidate me. So with that thought, I decided I was not quitting at the end of the night. Instead I am going to push through, and if I am lucky she will quit, or better yet, get fired.

Beth smugly looks me up and down as I walk by. I choose to ignore her and continue to walk back to the stock room to fill the bar and get several white hand towels. I pass a few patrons who are here to start their night off early. A small group heads to one of the tables while two guys head to the bar. I probably should go and take their order because I honestly don't know if Beth knows what she is doing, but… letting her see that she doesn't know anything is also very appealing.

Shrugging my shoulders, I continue walking to the stock room. I take my time and look over the glass bottles of alcohol. I pull out a pad of paper from my back pocket and pen from my apron and write down the few bottles we are running low on. Then I do a little re-organizing and, lastly, grab a stack of towels for the bar.

I scan the bar and another group has grabbed a table. Cory is talking to them now. At the bar more guys have sat down and are calling out with their hands in the air to get her attention.

I leave the stack of towels by the cash register while pulling one through my apron belt. I head to the guy with his hand up but Beth gets there first.

"Hey hon, I've never seen you in here before. You new?" I look at the schmo trying to sweet talk Beth.

I resist telling the schmo how eating glass would be easier than trying to warm up to the spoiled brat, but I hold it in. Barely.

"Shane?"

Mentally ignoring how her voice is the sweetest thing I have ever heard, I look down at Cory with a light blush in her cheeks.

"Can I have three cosmos please?"

I like her politeness, a complete opposite from Beth. They must have different parents because they look nothing alike. I nod back at her then grab three martini glasses from the shelf below the bar. I can hear Beth in the background, yelling at someone. I need to hurry because Beth is the kind of girl you want to stuff into a trunk, wrapped in plastic because she's probably the one who threw a broken bottle at your face.

I place the finished glasses on the bar and Cory moves them to her black holder one by one with her small dainty hands. With a shy smile, she calls out a "Thanks."

"Look, guy, order something or I will hose you." I look over my shoulder, and Beth is holding the soda gun faced at the schmo in a business suit. I want to laugh, and yet, I shake my head to get rid of the mental pictures of her in my trunk. I walk over and calmly take the soda gun from her hand and return it to the holder.

I didn't miss that she let me do it with no resistance. Then I eye the guy in a pinstriped business suit.

"What can I get for you?"

The pinstriped prick looks me over with contempt, as if I am the problem. "Hey, I was talking to the lady," he whines.

Shocked, I look at him and turn to Beth who half shrugs her right shoulder. I pick back up the soda gun and hand it to her, knowing the chaos will ensure.

Seconds later I hear "Ahh! What the hell was that for?"

Unable to stop myself, I chuckle as I walk to the south side of the bar. I may have to reserve killing her until after her shift. She is definitely a volatile pain in the ass, and I absolutely will end up killing her if we work together for too long, but… she does have one redeeming feature. She does not take shit from anyone, which means tonight is going to either be highly entertaining, or someone is going to call the cops on her. I am hoping for the cuffs.

I looked over the multitude of bodies that have arrived over the past three hours. Some are dancing against each other on the dance floor, and some are sitting at tables watching the dancers on the floor. I scan the tables and stop at Cory, who is taking an order from a table with several women with fake smiles, shiny shirts, spandex pants, and big grey and white fur boots.

One of the girls with a black shiny tank top and matching fur boots is glaring at her. The nasty tramp with fur boots says something that I can't hear, but I can tell whatever she says bothers Cory. The sweet, shy smile has disappeared and she has her eyes locked on her little note pad.

My chest fills with fire. *Damnit Cory. Don't let them get to you.*

I watch as Cory finishes their order and walks quickly to the bar. I intercept her before she walks past me to Beth. I won't let her cower from them. She is ten times the lady than any of them are.

"Ay! Cory." I call out.

Cory tries to keep a half smile to appear friendly, but her eyes were glossy. The more I watch Cory struggle, the more irritated I feel.

"Do you need something?" She asks politely, hiding most of the sadness in her voice, but I can see it in her eyes.

"Yep." I lie, thinking of anything to say. "I need some orders. What do ya got?"

She places her drink holder on the bar and pulls off the top sheet of paper from her note pad having me read the order instead of her telling me, which I prefer. Taking a second look at the order, I contemplate messing with their drinks. It would serve them right the way they treated Cory. But I have not sunk that low since high school.

The last two drinks are dirty martinis but I didn't make enough. I clean out the shaker about to top off the drinks when I see Cory walking away.

"No wait!" I hold up my hand to stop her.

She slowly turns back around with a question on her face. I look at the drinks but all of them are full.

Which one was low? How did…

Shaking my head, "Nothing. Nevermind."

Cory drops off the drinks with a bright smile. One that looks genuine. Huh? Maybe she gets over things quickly. I know I should be answering the calls from a patron on the north side of the bar but I can't help but watch Cory.

She calmly hands out the drinks to the ratty girls at her table and walks away with a smile. Cory walks to another table of guys with white and blue button-up shirts, nice slacks, shiny shoes and loosened ties.

Shysters.

Big mouths, big games, and big time losers.

"Um, bartender?" I hear someone call out, and Beth walks past me with a groan. I watch her take the order before I return my attention to Cory. Cory is trying not to smile as the guys are saying something that is making her giggle.

I hate shysters.

I remind myself that it shouldn't matter who makes her laugh or cry. She isn't my business and I really don't care.

"Hi, Shane." Enora sat on a bar seat to my left, she used to be a waitress here and is full-blooded fairy. She left a few months ago after she finished her degree. Enora is one of the fairies that studied human psychology. She works with enforcers to find other fairies who break fairy law. Kind of like a fairy profiler.

"Hey, how's work?" I ask as I grab the towel from my apron and wipe down the bar in front of her. I mentally slap myself for possibly being caught by a very perceptive fairy, who may have noticed who I was watching a few seconds ago. Not that it should matter because I am absolutely not interested in the shy blonde, but the perception looked bad. Enora knows I don't date seriously and I never date humans.

"Good." She smiles her enchanting smile that has had me mesmerized from the moment I saw her. Her hair is long and light, strawberry red with dark-brown, reddish eyes. She keeps several braids in her hair with odd strings wrapped around it, like a hippie might. Her freckles are adorable and lightly splattered on her nose but nowhere else. I would know because I have seen every inch of her body.

"Has it been busy?"

I shake my head. "What can I get for you?"

Enora draws her lower lip between her teeth and gives me a knowing look. "I'll take my usual."

I try to smile, but I know the tension in my face is making it strained instead of friendly. Yeah, that's not going to happen. Her usual means she drinks vodka and Redbull until closing then I drive her home, then we continue to drink until we fall into her bed adding to the notches we have already put in her head board. A few hours later I drive home.

I shake my head firmly. There is no reason to even act like there is a possibility of that happening.

With a dramatically single eyebrow raised she says, "Fine. I'll just take a vodka and Redbull."

I grab the Grey Goose and begin to pour. "So, how is the new help?" Enora is looking behind me, giving Beth a once over glance.

"As expected. Just started today," I answer, keeping my tone as flat as possible. While she worked here, Enora became an expert at decoding my subtle tones and inflection. Or maybe it is because she is a fairy and they try to control all those little inflections to cover all of their unwanted emotions. They don't like to show their anger or sadness. With fairies you have to pay attention to the small slips and inflections to know how they really feel. Reading people's subtle inflections and body language is a learned trait. I can read normal humans easily, but fairies are better at watching their emotions and being incredibly polite, so reading them is difficult.

"Oh yeah? Who else started today?" She asks slowly while turning in her seat to scan the room.

I leave the glass in front of her on top of a small, white napkin and walk away. "It's good to see you Enora." She knows I don't explain myself to anyone. I don't plan to change tonight. And she *knows* she was dangerously close to stepping over the line.

"Shane!" I hear Beth call my name. I walk around the bend to the north side and find her face to face with the Douche from last night, with his fists on the bar glaring at Beth with glowing eyes. I let out a bemused breath and ask, "Four beers and a shot of whiskey?"

Hoping that no one else has noticed his eyes, I look around him to make sure. Not that I am their babysitter or a supernatural enforcer, but I just prefer to not exacerbate the issue by allowing others around me to skirt the rules.

The Douche is leaning into the bar, fixing his glare at Beth. It wouldn't take a genius to figure out what he wants to do. I jerk my chin to Beth, letting her know to walk away. Contrary to her angry demeanor, she walks away with a small snort of dismissal. Again I notice that she is not fighting me. Possibly another redeeming feature?

The Douche lets out an exaggerated breath. I pull out four Budweisers and reach for the whiskey. He leaves a card on the bar and says, "Keep it open. And," he looked over at Beth and points in her direction, "keep her on a leash." I try not to roll my eyes at the irony of a wolf demanding to keep a human girl on a leash.

I pick up the card as my eye falls on the Nickleback poser sitting alone at a small two person round table, staring at Beth.

Then I see Cory walk up to him with her black tray in hand. I can't help myself from watching to make sure he doesn't try anything.

Then I hear a loud crash from the south side of the room, knocking me back to my senses. The noise emanated from the table of girls that were wearing too much fur and glitter. All of them were lying on the floor . . . sobbing? I could see each one in tears, and two were hugging each other.

Stunned I watched as the bouncer and Danny, the other waiter, help all the girls up and out the door. When I looked back at Cory I didn't see any shock or surprise on her face. Not even a hint.

Dammit, that can't be good.

Cory turns back to the poser and holds up her pad and begins writing. Then she starts talking to him again, but he is not looking at her. She pokes him with her pen and I can see something flash in his eyes. Slowly, he looks at her and I can feel the tension in my blood begin to burn. I don't like the look he is giving her. Werewolves are unpredictable and Cory is an ignorant human who has no idea what she is poking. He nods his head slowly and looks towards Beth again.

I look towards Beth to see if she noticed. Oh she did. She is eyeing him like she wants to put a hot poker through his eye.

Cory finishes writing and heads toward Beth. The poser is watching Beth and I still can't identify the look he has in his eyes, but I cannot rule out that he looks unstable, and yet he looks relatively calm. The problem is, werewolves are tricky people to read. All that wild rage running around in their blood has some serious side effects.

"Hey, babe. How about a Corona and your number?" Some young, punk-guy asks Cory, as she stops at the bar.

"Sorry can't, bar policy." She says sweetly and way too politely. I let my fire free and imagine the man's bowel system and squeeze it. The man's eyes bulge out and he grabs his stomach tightly. I let go of the vision and push my fire back down. I watch as Cory ignores the guy next to her and gives Beth a strange look. Beth shook her head before reading the order Cory has scribbled down.

The guy probably turned twenty-one recently. He has a stupid, drunk smile, greasy, disheveled light auburn-brown hair, sporting an expensive diving watch and a golfing shirt. The rich and stupid I like to call yuppies. It was obvious that he was tossed.

Beth told the guy to sober up and Cory was ignoring his advances once more. Forcing myself to detach from Cory and the scene, I walk to two girls with platinum blond hair.

"Good evening ladies. What can I get for you?" I asked, as I wipe down the condensation from their current drinks that I didn't make.

The one wearing a red halter-top wanted a Bay Breeze and the other blonde, with a silky olive shirt that shows plenty of cleavage, wanted a Whiskey Sour.

I began making the drinks, doing a few spins and grins for the girls. As I top off the Whiskey Sour I turn towards the end of the bar and caught Cory watching me with her lips pressed together. She is ignoring Beth who was placing drinks on her black drink tray. I hold her stare for another heart beat before I winked at her. Averting her eyes, I didn't miss the blush creeping up her face.

Cory dropped off a few drinks at another table before stopping in front of the poser and sliding two bottles of beer in front of him. He picked up the bottle and took a swig, and spit it out just as fast. Cory didn't turn around and I didn't like the conspiracy that was starting to form in my mind.

I was going to have to keep a better eye on Cory. Not that she did much without me noticing. My eyes just found her easily. All night-long I kept a weathered eye on her. I noticed the poser left shortly after he paid for the two beers he didn't drink. I also noticed that her and Beth kept having little spats when they thought no one was looking. And of course I noticed every single time Beth threatened a patron.

It was a long night indeed.

* * *

The bar is closed. Finally. I wipe my hands on the white towel hanging on my apron and decide to take the trash out while Beth is sweeping the floor. On the way back in I wash my hands in the bathroom before I make my way to the bar to check on Beth. I pull the apron back over my waist and tie it off at the same time Cory walks into me. I see her about to fall so I grab her waist and hold her still.

Blushing, she says, "Thanks." But she is not looking at me. I would be a liar if I said she doesn't fit perfectly into my hands. I would be an idiot to not notice how good she feels this close.

I am about to let her go and walk away, but she looks up at me and I am struck once more. She is holding me with her eyes. It is clear how unsure she is, and yet, I also notice her eyes darkening.

"Hey Carver!" Louie, the bouncer, calls from somewhere behind me, "You forgot to lock the back door." I don't miss how tense I feel Cory go in my hands. I reluctantly let go of her waist, and apologize to Louie. Cory is standing like a statue staring at me, as if she is looking at me for the first time.

"Carver?" She repeated, in a whisper.

I smirk, "Shane Carver." Holding back the desire to pull her to the storage room and kiss that look off her face, because right now something is off. Something is different about her and the way she is looking at me, as if I have become her favorite meal. The look is causing a new burn, starting low and hot. If I was able to ignore the pull I had towards her before, I am not going to be able to ignore it now. Now I have to make a fully conscious effort to take a step back.

Louie walks up to me and grabs my hand in a half hug. It was a customary greeting for Louie. "Hey I saw Enora tonight. Are you still…?" He didn't finish the sentence, letting it hang in the air as if it might offend me he was asking about her.

I shake my head and notice that Cory is no longer in front of me. "Nope. Haven't seen her since she went back home after she graduated." Louie is human and has no idea that Enora is a fairy. She is not as stuck up as the other fairies that won't even look at another person unless they are the same race. Enora is free to play wherever she wants.

"Ah, so it's cool then, right?" He asks with a hopeful smile and looking past me. I don't have to see who he is looking at to know that Enora is there. And more possibly, she saw me with Cory. Not that we did anything, or ever would. It's just that I am sure she saw what I saw.

"Yep it's cool. You know I don't hold on to anyone."

"Alright then. See you around." Louie gave me another half man hug and walked off. I turn around to look for Cory.

Something is wrong. Every table is cleaned and the chairs are flipped up. Nobody cleans up that fast. I walked to the bar to see what else needs to be done and find everything clean, stacked an organized. This is not normal. This looks a lot like magic.

I looked around and try to reflect on what I knew. First, Beth knew I was something else but didn't flinch. Second, Beth also was not afraid of werewolves. It's possible that there are a few humans who know about the other supernatural races. If she is a hunter she would have already tried to kill the wolves and me, so she wasn't that either. Third is that when Cory said Carver, it was not really a question of curiosity, it a question of validation. I know enough pure bloods when I see them so I am confident that Cory and her sister are not true pure bloods. If by some chance Cory is a Carver she wouldn't be so freaking shy. All the Carvers I know act like me… and… Beth?

Beth!

Beth must be a Carver. That's why her sister would know what that means. That's why they look nothing alike. That's who cleaned the tables and bar, that's why she was not afraid of the werewolf from the other night; and that's possibly why the poser was keeping tabs on her tonight.

Wait a minute. Enora was here tonight, too. She wouldn't have been able to leave home again unless she was given permission. The fairies don't leave home without permission and a good reason, furthermore, they don't get involved with anyone else but their kind.

What the hell was Enora doing at the bar then?

* * *

Sunday night, jazz night with live bands. Cory is going out of her way to avoid me. If it were anyone else, I don't think I would have minded, but Cory is different. It is almost as if she is trying to force herself to stay away from me, even though I know the pull I feel for her goes both ways. I know why I wasn't giving in to the pull, but I couldn't imagine why she isn't giving in. If her sister is a Carver, then she would want me even more. Right? I mean, we are on the top of the magical food chain.

Maybe that is the reason she is keeping her distance. Although I didn't get the vibe that she is scared of me. I bet she thought she knew all about Carvers because of Beth, but she knows nothing about the amount of power I carry in my veins. With one word I could turn her world up side down.

"Hey," Beth says, as she walks past with a case of beer.

"Hey," I call back, as I cut up the rest of the oranges for the girly drinks and wheat beer.

I am not one for beating around the bush and I figure it is best if I just call out the truth between us. I walk up to Beth as she is putting the bottles in the small refrigerator, "You're a Carver."

"So are you," She says in a bored voice.

I was right. Cory knows what a Carver is, and she ran to tell her sister.

"Might want to cut down on the magic. No one cleans up that fast," I warn.

Beth finishes putting the bottles in the mini-refrigerator and stood with the box cutter in hand. For a minute I wonder if she is threatening me, but then she began cutting the empty box. I shook my head that she was wasting time breaking down boxes the long way. I touch the sanitizer water and heated it up. I did the same to the soapy water and then wash the dirty glasses. I heard Beth mumble, "At least when I do magic I don’t do it in front of a bar full of people." Her words are clipped.

Still not looking back, "I didn’t." I have no fear of her accusation, and if she is referring to herself as “the whole bar” then she has more issues than I originally calculated.

"Yeah right," she puts the box cutter in her back pocket and held onto the flat empty box.

"How about you try to get through the night without hosing anyone? Huh?" I say disapprovingly, but wishing I hadn't said anything at all. It would suggest that those were the only things she did wrong.

Beth's lips flatten. "Stay on the south side and I'll stay on the north, that way I won't entertain thoughts of strangling you."

I almost laugh at her. It is like a mouse threatening a Cobra.

Beth continues, "Oh, and stay away from my sister. I've met enough of people like you and she is not going to have anything to do with you or whatever crap you're into."

I could see her eyes lighten to green. I smile inwardly. *Maybe all Carvers could make their eyes glow different colors.* I was told mine were arctic blue when they shine. Vampires eyes turn white when they are emotional, like really hungry, really horny, or really pissed. Fairies and witches didn't have anything like that.

Regardless, I am unimpressed that this little Carver is threatening me, with all her first or second generation's bloodline swarming in her veins. I couldn't help myself. I laugh cynically.

Beth hooked her hands on her hips.

"Beth," I say condescendingly. "You know nothing about me. So don't threaten me unless you want to find out."

She stares me down so I let her feel the fire in my veins. She flinches obviously aware of my superior power.

"And about Cory? I don't date humans."

"Beth I need a Jaeger bomb, Coors light, Cape Cod and a shot of Tequila." Cory's voice rings out, breaking my concentration on Beth. I look down at Cory who tosses her hair behind her shoulders and looks at Beth and then back at me, and forces a smile. Whatever. I leave knowing that Beth was going to take care of her. So I walk back to the stock room to grab another bottle of white wine.

When I return, Cory and Beth are hissing to each other yet again. Cory is holding her apron in her hand. At some point she has taken it off and I wonder if she is about to quit. I am hopeful and unnerved at the same time.

"Checking out?" I ask, eyeing her with a look that said I hope so. Cory scowls at me, and Beth's eyes say they want to tear me to pieces. It is like watching a little kitten with her hackles raised, trying to look scary.

Cory threw her apron on the bar, "No. I am headed to the top room tonight." I stop walking. I know I heard wrong.

The top rooms are for VIP's, and not the good kind either. The dirty kind, that has lots of money and has a tendency to do a lot of iffy things. The few waitresses that quit were all because of the VIP rooms. I shake my head, "No. Not going to happen."

Cory's eyes rounded, but I wasn't going to let this happen. It wasn't because I don't like her out of my sight, or the fact that I have no idea who is in the VIP room tonight. No, it is simple, it is all for safety reasons. I don't think she is experienced enough to take on guys like that, and to be honest, no one should have to take on guys like that.

Sal, the boss, should have put a stop to it. The few times a waitress named Denise complained, he had the guest and waitress explain what happened. After that chat, Sal said the girl misunderstood what the guest wanted. The next weekend the waitress never showed for work. She sent him a text about moving back home and that's the last anyone heard from her.

And that's when I started keeping tabs on the waitresses,

specifically making sure they made it to their cars at night. Thankfully I did because some girls attracted some really bad attention. One girl I walked out to her car was being stalked by a vampire named Niko, who I noticed was in the VIP room that night. He would have taken her and drained her, if I hadn't teleported to the waitress' house, and killed the bastard that tried to break in minutes before she was going to pull up in the driveway. The girl never new how close she got to becoming his dinner.

Cory only started yesterday and she is novice to the clients Sal lets in. I want to say something. I can't let a silly, shy girl walk into a VIP room not knowing what kind of people are looking for special treatment. It's one big room with velvet couches and chairs along the walls with a small dance floor and an eight-person table. Sal had lots of contacts, some were shady with sketchy appearances and the others were well dressed shysters with heavy pockets.

"That's what I said," Beth spat out.

I look at Beth hoping she understands my expression, *you don't even know the half of it.*

"I am not a child Beth. I can take care of myself," Cory folded her arms over her chest, "and you, you're not my boss. And if you try any of your Carver crap I will know. I am all *too* acquainted with Carvers. If you do anything, I promise you, you'll regret it." She ended with a sharp look to her sister.

Cory is just as bad as Beth. I take it all back. Politeness my ass. She is soft in the brain, like a marshmallow. She has no idea what a Carver like me can do. My fire is building low and dangerously close to out of control as Cory walks away from me. I wait until I couldn't see Cory anymore before I turned to her sister, who I was about to lecture, when I noticed she was mumbling something under her breath.

I waited until she was done before I asked, "What did you

do?" I know she must have done some magic but, being a Carver, I couldn't tell how much or what she did. That is the most infuriating thing about Carvers, their magic is practically undetectable.

"I just put a mirror of her heart in mine. That way if something happens I will know right away. If she is nervous, scared, or calm, I will feel it." I nod with approval. Very nice. I have never done anything like that. In fact, I didn't know we could do something like that.

"How did you learn that?"

"If wolves can feel the hearts of others, why can't I do the same thing?" She ran her hands down her sides twice.

Wolves are known to feel the emotions of their mates. Or was it they could hear each other's thoughts? Crap. I forget. But, it looked like something she had done before.

I walk back to the bar and try to put Cory out of my mind. Beth has a mirror of her heart, and that will let her know immediately if something is wrong, so I shouldn't worry. Actually I shouldn't care. I don't really care. I am just a responsible team player. It's important to make sure everyone on the team is safe. So technically, it wouldn't matter that Cory's up there instead of Danny. I would still want to make sure they are okay. The words don't feel true, but I don't want to analyze it further.

On the north side of the bar, Beth The Terrible was taking an order. So I turn back to my south side where I plan to stay because it has a perfect view of the VIP box, and the stairs going in and out of it. That way if anything happens, I can be there first.

"Long Island, please." I look down and see a girl with short, shoulder-length messy blonde hair, and glowing orange eyes. Glowing as if she doesn't have a care in the world, as if it were totally normal to show that side of her magic. Her lacy black tank top shows her neon-green bra that made her look horribly trashy. She has no dark black eye make-up on, but she looks the type, instead she does have a considerable amount of bright orange lipstick slathered on her small bitty lips.

No. Hell no. I'm not putting up with another Carver. I already have Beth's magic issues to work around, and lets not forget the wolves that come in every night, so no, no more magical creatures.

"Dim the lights in your eyes or get out," I warn, dropping the white rag in my hand to the bar, and fold my arms.

The Carver didn't dim the lights in her eyes. Instead, she smiles and I bring the fire to my chest, waiting for her to make the first stupid move. I'm ready, poised to teleport this chick to the top of Pikes Peak and leave her ass there. Right after I knock her out and shoved her in the trunk of someone's car.

Magically, a glass appears in front of her, then it fills with liquid that looks a lot like a Long Island Ice Tea. The Carver puts her gangly hand up and grabs it slowly, then takes a sip. She then leans to the side as she flicks her nails and says with a smug smile, "Richard says 'Hi.'"

My father. My fire instantly roared in my stomach. That rat bastard can rot in hell. And if this chick is with him then she can go to hell, too. I can't think of one redeeming quality about my father. Then the thought occurred to me, this girl better not be the girl my parents told me about. The one they wanted me to mate with.

"Get out now." I sneer as my fire builds even stronger inside of me. I know that if I don't calm down soon I will end up teleporting out of here to let some of the fire out before it consumes me. My fire almost has a mind of it's own. I have yet to figure out why it reacts differently depending on my emotions, and who I am around.

The trashy orange-eyed Carver sips her drink loudly. It's like nails on chalkboard. "I don't think so. I am enjoying my scenery." She scans the room quickly, "I can see why you like it here, so many creatures infesting the place." She sniffed the air. "Never thought I would see Richard's son slumming it with the same creatures who would kill you the second they find out what you are."

I swipe my hand near her glass and mentally teleport it to the trash. "It's time you left."

The trashy Carver pulls out a tube of gloss from below the bar and applies it slowly. "Do you really want to make a scene, Shane?" She slides a finger over her lips and smiles nefariously. "I'm willing to play, but are you?"

No.

Holding in my fire, which is still building and becoming very distracting, I take a hold of the rag and squeeze. "What do you want?"

Her orange eyes narrow as she leans in, letting her boobs practically fall out of her shirt. Not that I looked, but I could tell in my periphery. "Stop fraternizing with our enemy and join the fight. Find your match! Sitting on the fence is for pussies."

Hearing her tell me to find my match should have lessened the fire I felt, especially now that I know this chick wasn't here to share hearts and all that load of crap.

"I wasn't born to bump the bed post with some other Carver because some crazy witch thinks she knows the future. And even if there is such a woman, I can tell you right now I would hate her. I haven't met a Carver I would dream about drilling all night, let alone sharing a part of my soul and those are my two main qualifiers."

She slapped the bar with her right hand. "She's your perfect match! Richard knows her parents and they worked very hard to get you two together." She let out a harsh breath. "In fact, I doubt you would be able to stop yourself from falling into her bed the second you see her."

I look around to ensure that no one is paying attention to this before I answer, "I'm not getting into this with you or anyone else. So why don't you go back to *Richard* and tell him I'm not interested in being the slut boy or the knight in shining armor."

Her eyes narrow, she leans back and folds her arms under her breasts, making them an accent, and yet again I didn't look. She is trying to use her body as a distraction. "Oh, I'm sure I can find something to get you to come back, Shane. That, I can promise you."

Pursing my lips smugly, "You don't scare me."

She coughs in her closed fist where several shiny bracelets are jingling. "That's because you're too stupid to know better."

I wipe my hands on the white rag, "I think it's time you left."

"I think it's time you realized that you don't actually have a choice." She tilted her head, as if to mark her point.

I turn towards a patron with her hand up, "Alright, well thanks for the chat, Orangey?"

"Fennel."

I snort. "That's a horrible name. I almost feel sorry for you." And then I left, hoping more than expecting that she would leave.

I gave the next patron a warm hello that is a complete farce because as soon as I am done with her I am going to have to go into the storage room to teleport somewhere to let go of the excess fire inside of me. If I don't, I won't be able to focus. The fire will consume all my thoughts and take over.

When I was young that almost happened. It was the scariest thing I have ever experienced. My skin was so hot I think it melted, and all I saw was white. It was like I was fading away and becoming only a living, breathing, fire. Of course now I know that I am made of fire, but still, it can escape me and take over if I don't keep it under control.

"Merlot," the lady says, without looking up from her phone. I quickly pour the drink and tender the order.

Finally able to leave, I hastily walk away, not checking to see if Fennel, the trashy Carver, is still sitting at the bar. Once I shut the door, I teleport to Mount Katmai in Alaska. It is virtually uninhabitable, which is perfect for when I need to let out my fire. It's a volcano that blew its top and caused a large crater at the top. In summer the snow melts, turning the crater into a lake, and then freezes back up in winter.

I take off my shoes quickly and walk into the freezing cold water. I can hear the ice shuttering and sizzling as I step out into the lake. I walk out until my calves are under the ice-cold water. I concentrate on only letting the fire out of my feet. I dig my toes into the rocky soil.

I close my eyes tightly, struggling to pinpoint where my fire can leave. The pressure is causing the blood to rush to my extremities. I can feel little tingles running all over my body, similar to when feeling returns to your limbs after you have been sitting awkwardly for too long.

Flexing my power, I try and rein it in. My chest is burning and I know if I just keep focusing on holding a mental lid, my fire will eventually give up. But it's not giving up without a fight.

I roar, but all I hear is gurgles.

I open my eyes and they begin to burn, as if I am submerged in acid. I swim to the top of the lake and scramble out, letting my fire clear the toxins out of my eyes and all over my skin. My clothes are gone and I am naked sitting in the snow, on top of a volcano.

I teleport to my apartment for a whole new set of clothes and then teleport back to the stock room wondering how much time has really passed.

I look down to my watch . . . *dang.* It's gone. Must have melted along with my clothes.

I walk out of the room and Enora is perched on a stool at the bar. She waits until I am close. She smile slyly, "Hi Shane."

I wash my hands at the bar sink and grab a clean, white rag. "Enora? What brings you here again?" I try not to let her see how distracted I feel. Right now all I want to do is march upstairs, grab Cory, and make sure she is okay. And maybe kiss her so fucking hard she can't breathe. That might help actually. I mentally shake my head at that thought.

"Ah, you know just visiting." She flips her hair back with another wistful look. That look always got my attention, but now, it didn't even make a dent.

I look down at her and fold my arms over my chest, curious that she no longer had the ability to excite me. "Right. So what are you really doing here, Enora?"

Her eyes squint then narrow, "Visiting."

Rolling my shoulders. "Sure, you can keep saying that but we both know you're lying. So spit it out."

Immediately she bows her head, and unfolds her legs on the

stool, "I can't."

"Can't? Because you are afraid the fairy courts will find out you told me?"

She looks up with big round eyes, but I wasn't buying it. "They'll know if I lie. I can't tell you. But don't worry, it has nothing to do with you."

I've known Enora long enough to know she is not worried about me. I swear if her arrogance were a stick, it would be the stick that was so far up her ass you could taste the wood in her kisses.

"I'm not worried about me," I respond.

"Clearly." Her friendliness melted. The ice in her eyes is back and I am talking to the real Enora now.

"What is that supposed to mean?" I try to hold back my pleasure of getting her to talk.

She cleared her throat. The kind of response that makes every living being want to smash someone's face in. "Only that you seem to have lowered your standards."

Thankfully, I have my fire so far submerged that her little attitude was not going to cause me to burn this place down. But earlier she might have gotten to me. "Did I? And what makes you say that?"

"You know what they say about the company you keep."

I want to roll my eyes, but I held back. Barely. It really is a girly thing to do, and yet I constantly find myself doing it. "Don't say stupid shit like that, just tell me what you mean, be up front for once in your stuck up life."

"I'm not stuck up." Her eyebrows drew together.

"Enora. Get to the point. I really don't have time for this."

Obviously put out, she swings her arms in the air as if she is Vanna freaking White. "This place has really gone down hill, Shane, and you know it. There's always a pack of wolves in here, not to mention the other Carver you were just talking to, who looks like a slut, by the way. I mean come on Shane, you can do ten times better than her."

Jealous? I am not going to respond to her accusation. Although I would enjoy letting her know she was so far off base it was laughable. "Is that all?"

"Oh is that not enough?" She stands up abruptly, opens her purse to look for something, then thought better of it and finished, saying, "You want to talk about the vampire upstairs in the VIP? Or maybe we should talk about the fairy who is going around putting stuff in people's drinks. Or maybe we should talk about you. The Carver with no loyalty for anyone but himself. You're the selfish one, Shane. At least I stand for something?"

I use my tongue to clean my top canines looking as board as possible. Inside I'm laughing mirthfully because she spilled. "So that's why you're here. To bring back a fairy who's been using their magic without the fairy council's permission?"

She stills for a moment. Her eyes jet down for a micro second before she recovers. Pulling her purse over her shoulders, she says, "I'm not discussing it with you."

I smirk disdainfully, "You just did."

CHAPTER SIX
BETH

Shane just showed back up after taking a thirty-minute break. I am about to tell him to give me a heads up next time he steps out, when he starts chatting with a red head with a face full of freckles. I watch carefully, looking at his reactions, waiting to see if he shows any interest. If he is, I am going to let Cory know he's either a slut or interested in someone else. Actually I had told her that she was stupid if she even attempted to talk to a Carver, let alone want to date one. The brat acted like that was a good thing. It isn't. It is bad. And I don't like the idea that she is interested in him. All the other Carvers and purebloods I have meet are grade-A assholes. She doesn't know them like I do because I try to keep that stuff to myself.

The magic world is not her world and I don't want her in the cross-fire of the war my parents talked about.

With Cory's heart in my chest I can feel that she is nervous. I look over and see her walking down the stairs. She looks around, trying to hide that she is looking at Shane. When she looks down to the red-headed girl she probably doesn't realize she frowned.

When her eyes find mine, I lift my chin. She did the same thing back and walks to me.

"How's it going in the VIP?"

She looks away before answering, as her eyebrows scrunch, "Weird."

Not the answer I was hoping for. I fold my arms, "How so?"

She places her drink holder on the bar and shrugs. "I don't know. Just weird."

A little more frustrated, I ask, "I am the definition of weird. So why don't you try and explain it to me?" I grab the paper she holds out with her next order of drinks.

I am going to pretend that the breath she exhales is a relieving breath, instead of a defeated breath. "Well, I'm not sure, but I think a few people up there are not like me or you."

Please be wrong about this. I know werewolves come in, but that is the only supernatural kind I ever saw in here, well other than Shane, I guess. "What does that mean?"

Swallowing hard, she says, "Um, I think there are people up there that are not human, you know?"

"What do you think they are?" I lean down so I can hear her better. The paper in my right hand is crumpled tightly now.

Before she answers she scans the room, and whispers as best she can in a loud bar, "There is a black lady with long, thick braids that I think has fangs."

I stand straight. We are quitting this bar. That is for damn certain. "You think there is a vampire up there?"

Cory tries to give me the look that says I'm a big girl, but then her lips press from right to left. "I don't know. But keep your voice down just in case she can hear you."

I don't remember learning they have that great of hearing. It is the werewolves that do. "Doubtful."

Cory pointed at the small paper in my hand reminding me I had a job to do. "But there was also someone who I thought I saw in the corner one moment, and the next second she was gone. It was creepy. She had glowing, orange eyes. But no one else seemed to notice, so I don't know what to think."

Yep, we are quitting this place tonight! She doesn't know it, but I am not going to let her work in a bar with so many creatures. "Uh, I do. You're not going back up there."

"What happened?" Shane asks, while holding a white rag so tightly I can see his knuckles start to pale.

I scoff, "None of your business, Shane. Go back to your side."

Shane's eyes glow a light creepy blue for a split second as he looks at me, then they darken back to his natural color and he turns to my sister. I can tell that he is focusing all his energy on her. When Cory tells me mine glow it is always when I was dangerously upset. "I know something happened by the expression on your face, so spill it."

"You don't know my expressions." My head juts back, disbelievingly.

"I was talking to Cory," he says, snidely, not bothering to take his eyes off my sister. And worse, I think that just made Cory even more interested in him. Instead of looking at him like he is a loon for saying he knew her expressions, she tucks the stray hair behind her ear and asks, "How would you know my expressions?"

And just like that, his hard expression softens as he leans in to say, "I will tell you how I know if you tell me what's wrong." His voice was a little softer and I'm sickened to admit it might have been soothing.

Biting back my words and getting pissed off that they are having this little conversation without me, Cory continues, "Nothing's wrong."

Shane's mouth lifts on the side as if he knows she is lying. She is, but he shouldn't know that. "Did you see anything up there?" He pokes his finger on her hand and damn it if she didn't blush a little. I feel sick.

"Uh," Cory stutters, not looking away from Shane, as if he had her in some enthrall.

"What did you see?" He asks in velvety baritone. Oh my gosh what am I seeing? Is he hitting on her?

I push Shane away and make sure that my next words come across as clear as possible, "It's none of your business Shane! Worry about yourself."

Shane holds his hand out to Cory pleading a little. "Cory? Please."

"I think I saw a vampire. I saw fangs and her eyes turn from reddish brown to white while she was yelling at another guy in the room. And then someone popped in the room and then back out in a matter of seconds." And just like that she folds. Shane really is a smooth bastard. I seriously want to hit him with a fireball.

"Why don't you stay down here and I will send Danny up there." His words are still smooth, but I can tell they are forced. He is not happy with what she said. HA! That's what he gets for putting his nose in someone else's business. But he may be right to send Danny up there, so I am going to hold my tongue for a second.

Pouting a little, Cory says, "They are not doing anything to me and I doubt she even knew I noticed her."

Shane's lips flatten to a razor-straight line, not letting Cory's eyes move from his. "I don't care. In fact, why don't you point her out to me so I can hurl her blood-sucking ass out."

Oh hell ya! Shane is crazy, but I think I respect him a little more knowing he is willing to toss out the blood-sucker.

"What? NO!" Cory protests with her arms folded. This is probably the first time I have ever seen her whine to anyone but me. It's totally an act, though.

Shane shakes his head, not buying it. "Vampires are not allowed to draw too much attention, Magic Council's law."

"Then I will make sure they stay in there where no one else will see them!" Cory grabs the black drink tray and brings it back to her side.

I can't hold it in any longer. "Amber Line may be at the cross road, but they all can't just show up and go fanging people."

Cory didn't look at me. She's still eye-locked with Shane. "That's bullshit and you know it. There is no reason to kick people out when they haven't done anything."

Shane shrugs his left shoulder. "That's only because the owner has no idea there are even such creatures. He just thinks they don't like people outside their social groups. Think about it Cory."

"So if he really thinks that, then he won't like you throwing out his customers for no reason." Cory points her finger at Shane as if she just won the argument.

I shouldn't be rooting for Shane to win, but, I am.

"I won't be throwing them out for no reason. You said their eyes were white. Vampire's eyes glow white when they are pissed and dangerous. I won't allow those creatures to hurt… anyone." Shane backs up a step.

"Creatures? My sister is not a creature and neither are you, so don't say that."

I want to smile at her for defending me, but now is not the time for me to butt in. I mean, I call other magical people creatures. It really doesn't bother me.

"I'm flattered." Shane says, with a sharp tang to his voice.

"It wasn't meant to be a compliment," Cory hissed.

I bite down on my lip to keep from laughing. Cory is trying to sound ferocious, but instead she pulled off "the toddler that was being sent back to their room, even after they just gave the argument of their little lives."

"Where are you going?" Shane tries to reach out and stop Cory from leaving.

"To get more orders," She says over her shoulder.

Shane walks quickly along side of the bar, parallel to her. "Cory stop. Come back here." He tries to reach for her as the bar bended around to the south side, but Cory is too far away. "Cory!" Then he hit the bar. "Dammit."

I slowly walk up to his side and ask, "Why do you care about her so much now? You don't date humans remember?"

"Shut up Beth." He was still watching Cory with unreadable eyes.

Rolling my eyes, I scan the bar and see Dar's eyes are on me. I still can't believe he's here in this town, and worse, here in this bar.

Dar is sitting at a table outside the dance floor. Yesterday he watched me like a creepy stalker. I ignored him as best I could but it's hard when I swear I can feel him looking at me. It is a shame that he didn't drink whatever Cory planted in his drink. I am not sure what it was, but I could tell from his reaction that it was something he could taste. She really is scary with all those experiments she makes.

Now he's talking to some guy at his table. I don't know if his guest is a wolf, too, but the odds are, he is. Most wolves travel together. I assume it's a pack thing. Sometimes I envy that they can hear so well. Yes, I am nosey and I want to know what Dar and that guy are talking about because they are both looking in my direction. What if I try to use my magic?

I focus on my hearing and said a few words in my mind, specifically imagining Dar's table. I am not sure if it worked because now I hear everyone as if someone turned up the volume too loud. I cover my ears to a bar full of people talking, glass clanking, feet stepping, and a compendium of other bodily noises. Gross. To my dismay, Dar and his buddy have stopped talking. And worst of all, Dar is giving me a smug look.

Jerk.

I retract my last spell and my ears feel better now.

You know, sometimes I really think he can hear me or maybe he has an uncanny knack for knowing what I am thinking. Some people were just like that, they could tell what you were going to do before you did it. Not in the gypsy crystal ball kind of way but in the cold, logical deduction kind of way.

I focus my thoughts to my sister's heart. Her heart is at a

regular rate, I think. Or maybe I don't know the difference between calm and a little anxious, because had she not told me about the possible vampire, I wouldn't have even known she saw one. Her heart just seemed to lull by as if it was perfectly content.

Dar still is not talking, but he did nudge the guy next to him with a silent command and the stranger shrugs then heads to the exit. Dar stands and walks towards the bar. Avoiding him all together, I head to the south side where Shane was making an order. I grab a clean rag just to have something to do, and hope that Shane takes Dar's order. Shane looks at me with a question in his eyes. Thankfully, he dismisses me and asks Dar what he wants.

"Tell her to stop hiding like a child and get over here."

I instantly regret walking away. I am being a child, and to be honest I'm amazed he even wants to talk to me, considering he still doesn't know my name. Shane gives him a glance over before he calls out my name.

I don't look yet. I grab another bottle opener before I slowly make my way to stand in front of him with my arms crossed. "What can I get you, guy?" I call all the male patrons "guy" because it lets them know they are all the same to me.

"Two beers and shots." He said, in what looks like a scowl.

"Yea no problem." I answer back without looking at him. I give him the drinks and he throws me a few bills and adds, "I hear you've been stalking me."

Not sure if I heard him right. "I – What?"

Dar's expression is giving nothing away. "Someone has been pinging all my online accounts and calling a few people I know. Why don't you cut the piss and tell me what you want."

Stunned. "Wow. Just like that huh?"

Dar's eyebrows rise a little. "Stalking is illegal and a few of my friends were able to track it back to your home."

Squeezing the rag in my hands I say, "Huh. So you know where I live? Who's stalking who?"

He leans forward. "You're stalking me! I did the reverse to find out who it was, and your name was on the fucking lease. Don't try and play games Beth."

I slap my thigh with the rag. "I'm amazed! You do know my name."

His mouth twisted, "Are you serious?"

"Are you?" I ask, letting my hand drop to the bar, getting in his face.

Shaking his head and leans back, "Is that what this is all about? Your stupid high school crush?"

I smack the bar in front of his face, and stand back up. "Fuck you. You mangy, pansy-ass, flea bag."

His eyes were lightening a little. "I'm giving you right now to ask whatever it is you want to know, and then I am going to get a restraining order."

Restraining order? Douchbag. "Okay, sure. Here's my question. Can you… take your pathetic ass out of my bar and never step back in here again? In fact, why don't I extend that question to include the whole bloody state of Colorado?"

Amazingly, his tone darkened even more, and there was something that flashed across his eyes. "Don't threaten me Beth. You won't like the outcome."

Awe, the little puppy was trying to threaten me. Well that was not going to fly. "Puleese. You think I'm scared of a pup like you. Not in a million years. And if you really think I would put time into stalking you, you're dumber than I thought you were. In fact, I'm going to have to cut you off because you seem drunk-bucket stupid."

I took the drinks and trashed them, barely escaping Dar's hand as he reaches out for them. I pick up the bills and toss them back at his face as I walk to the other side of the bar.

There is one thing that can make me go from zero to one hundred and that is when someone thinks they are better than me. The fire in my veins started to vibrate. I watch Dar walk back to the table and a new guy was already there, waiting for him. The new guy hands a bottle to Dar.

My insides are past vibrating. Seconds tick by and I can't let loose what Dar said. I have not had an accident in so long but tonight, right now, might just break me down. Years go by and the first thing he says to me is that I'm stalking him? Unbelievable.

My own insides were squeezing together. I didn't look into his anything. But, I couldn't say someone didn't. Cory was pretty confident when she said she researched him.

I need him to leave. Now.

I take a deep breath and try to keep in the feelings of throwing every bottle in the damn bar at him. I want to hate him and make him feel the hollow blackness that has been in my heart since I left him that day in the hospital.

I need to calm down. I want to strangle him and watch the light leave his eyes. I am on the verge of imagining it. Not sure if my magic could actually do it without me touching him, or more importantly if my magic could do it in front of all these people without anyone noticing. I need a distraction.

For heaven's sake I'm a Carver and we can do anything. All I have to do is figure out how to cut the emotional response.

I let a few ideas pop in my mind but none sound good, so I start thinking about altering my memories. I hear a growl but I don't look up to see what happened. I don't care. I am busy strategizing how to erase Dar from my memory.

Still fiddling with the idea, I head to the stock room to get more beers. I leave my rag at my station and exit the bar. I walk through a series of men looking at me and trying to show me with their eyes that they are interested. I feel one hand brush my butt and I turn around and stare at crystal blue eyes, large shoulders, impeccable chest and a whole lot of everything I need to take my mind off everything. The blue eyes were smiling at me.

"You like that?" I ask, seductively.

"Oh you know I did," he says back with a devilish smirk.

"How so?" I ask, with a glimmer of amusement.

"Come here and I'll let you feel for yourself." He grabs me by my waist and I let him pull me in and… wow. He's good and ready. "Wanna play?" He whispers.

I smile and hold up the keys to the stock room, "Let's play." My heart is pumping against my chest and I can feel my magic start to swirl around me. I grab the door to the dry storage and opened it slowly, letting the big guy walk in.

He still has his hand on my waist and he pulls me to him. I let his lips touch mine. My fire rose up from my stomach and I could taste it in my mouth, waiting to be exhaled. My lips tingled and I could have sworn they felt as smooth as snakeskin.

Let it burn, I thought, loving the smooth feeling of my skin. Except the man I was kissing had stopped. I open my eyes and see the guy's eyes are blood shot. He teeters back on his heels, face ash-white. He looks down at his hands, as do I. They start shaking and then he is clenching his mouth falling into a seizure.

Oh crap… I think with a sparkle of relief? I can't stop watching and the longer I do, the more I feel lighter. As if kissing him caused me and my fire to erupt because it was so. . . wrong? I laugh out loud because I know I'm going crazy. Kissing strange men is frowned upon but not bad, not that I've ever done anything like this before, but I really needed the distraction. I watch him convulse for another second then I am blown forward as the door knocks into my back.

Dar kicks my legs out of the way and shuts the door.

My eyes narrow to him. He looks at me then peers at the other man next to me. He folds his arms over his massive chest and just shakes his head.

My emotions are all over the place - anger, anxiety, and guilt. I had no idea what was wrong with the guy who is now curled up in the fetal position. I just needed to get rid of the added pressure of my fire to think clearly.

I push up off the ground, feeling the fire inside me shifting as I move. It felt odd, like it was changing its structure. I just need to calm down, but with the look Dar is giving me I didn't feel safe.

"Sorry no pets allowed back here," I say with sardonic pleasure to an even more pissed off Dar. His eyes are full blaze amber. My fire changes from solidifying under my skin, to its original free-flowing state. My hands curl up into fists…at the ready. Except my fire is no longer building like it was a second ago, instead it continues to flow, I feel it slip out of my pores. My jaw drops, it's never left me like this before. It's never disregarded me like this. I can't even tap it down and it's seems to want to head straight for Dar.

My skin is crawling with what looks like millions of small red scales leaving me. The fire is slithering on the ground towards him and the idiot either has blown a brain fuse or has no self-preservation. He looks awed instead of worried. I shake my thoughts and try and pull it back before my fire reaches him. Yes, I was mad at him, more so a few minutes ago than now, but I couldn't let my fire touch him in its raw state. It would kill him, which is exactly what I would expect from my fire because, in all honesty, I was sure it had an intelligence of its own, and it's vengeful.

Dar's eyes dim to his regular hazel eyes. He watches my fire begin to spiral up his legs. I can feel his skin even though I have not moved. Everything feels like it is not real, even more crazy is that the fire is not burning him. He's just standing there, impassive.

My fire is not burning him?

It's practically massaging him. What the hell? I feel betrayed. I remind myself that Dar does not care about me, let alone acknowledge me until a few minutes ago when he threatened to get a restraining order against me! My fire should have begun building in heat. Angry heat. But it wasn't. Fire or no fire I would show him what a Carver is made out of!

Dar's eye watched me. When I took my first step to challenge him it felt like his presence doubled. I could practically taste the fury he was giving off. It is taking up the entire stock room. His eyes bore down on me. I take aim at his massive chest and lunge to push him through the door and out of my life forever.

I scream as magic abruptly swirls in the room. I see him look behind me with interest. The side of his lip curls up as he looks at me like I am the most pathetic person in his life.

I shake internally, wishing everything still and silent. I need to think! I need to get rid of Dar forever. Feeling my fire burst around me but not inside of me like usual, I struggle to get air into my lungs. I open my watery eyes. It takes a few blinks to understand what I am looking at. Small glass shards standing still in my face, I look around and everything is still. There is shattered glass everywhere, hanging in the air. It's as if a bomb exploded and it was halted mid-explosion.

There is frozen red liquid in the air, too. I look at Dar and he says, "I think it's clear who needs to leave."

I ignore him and close my eyes. This night has been my least favorite in my entire life. I am never going to fix this mess if I don't push him out of my mind.

First things first, it's time to check on the big guy on the floor. He looks frozen or passed out. I reach down and touch his skin, he does not have a pulse. I hope that means he is frozen. I let my magic enter him but I can't feel my magic move.

Oh crap. Did I deplete my magic?

I try and think about what I did because I have never been depleted of magic, and it's been a long time since I got tired after using it. I need to see if anyone else is frozen.

I side step Dar but he stops me with a quick hand. "I'm serious Beth. I've told the Magic Council about what you've done and they asked me to tell you to leave. If I were you I would try some place less populated." His tone sounds almost pleased to be passing along their message. I let his words pass over me. I forget them as soon as I hear them. I try to push past him but I can't. I can't use my magic to get past him and I can't feel my fire. It's like the fire is no longer a part of me. "You have been a pain in my ass for too long," he says, as an after thought.

I look around trying to get a thought, some kind of anchor to hold onto, to figure this out. Then his words filter in and I stop.

Damn him.

I took in a deep breath and move back. He is just standing there, looking high and mighty.

How is he not frozen?

If there is anyone that should be frozen, it's him. Well, technically he should be a pile of ash. I concentrate on trying to find my magic to take down the storage room guard dog. I feel his hand before I see it. The massive ogre hand wraps around mine, "Your fire is in me, if you want it back you have to promise to put everything back and leave." His tone is still arrogant and has a level of authority I have not felt before.

I watch his light-amber eyes glow at me, but it felt as though I was obligated to hear and answer. I could feel my fire on the outside of my skin, waiting to return to me, "Answer."

My body buzzed. I bite down hard on the inside of my lip. I can see my fire-scale things thrumming between my wrist and his hand. It is horrible. I want my fire back. It is mine! How can he keep it from me? I look up with a renewed hatred. "Give me my fire back and I will make sure everything rights itself."

"And you'll leave this… place." I'm not sure why it sounds as if he wants to interject a different word for "place," but I don't care.

"I'm gone," I hiss.

It feels as though my fire-scales are seeping from him back inside me. The fire is responding to the contact of his hand on my wrist. His body heat is branding my skin. His hand tightens around my wrist harder and I barely hold back the scream. It hurts. It feels like something foreign, or maybe shards of glass are ripping in my veins.

My voice breaks as I say, "Let go of me".

Everything has to be set right! I don't know if that was my voice, or his. I don't know if I screamed that or if it was in my head. My knees buckle. The only thing keeping me up is his tenacious grip.

The shards of glass or whatever they are entering into my veins are trying to make me stand up. It is as if a force was making me do as he wanted. I can hear his words repeating over and over in the back of my mind. I am turning into a slave of pain. The shards are slowly melting into my body and I scream again.

My wrist drops to my side at the same time I fall to the ground.

"Shit!" I can hear Dar say. But it sounds very far away.

My eyes stay closed. I don't want to see him. I can't face him, not after that. Not when he literally overtook my power. The realization hit me like a wrecking ball.

He has authority over me. How?

Faint words echoed in my mind. They were my mother's words about Carver's mates. We claimed our mates by giving our hearts, to the other, and vice a versa. It blended us and made us one.

I feel Dar put his fingers to my neck checking for a pulse. I can't stand his hands being on me so I flinch and smack his hand away fiercely. I refuse to open my eyes. I need space, my own space. I envision being cocooned and I instantly felt my stomach drop, letting me know my magic has responded. There was a buzzing in my ear as if everything was silent. Eerily silent.

I look around and I am surrounded by a white haze. I don't have to move to know that everything is going to feel soft and gentle. My chest rose and fell with rapid breaths.

I never gave Dar my heart. I only spoke to him three times while he was in the hospital. My chest tightened as I remembered my words at the hospital, I told him to use mine. But I didn't think that really constituted as the same thing. Did it?

What the hell did I do? I was so young. I didn't know any better. I let some time pass before I press a hand to the haze and picture the storage room again, taking away the shell I created for myself.

Grabbing my upper arm, Dar picks me up until my feet touch the ground. I stand with shaky knees. He points to where the guy once was, "You really messed up Beth. That guy remembers everything up until everything exploded. Now I have to fix your stupid mess so that enforcers and hunters don't find out." He is so enraged I almost missed that he is acting as if he is going to help me.

I back away from him and look around. All the bottles are whole again. I back up and turn to the door, and leave him in the storage room. I don't need his help and I am not in the mood to even discuss it.

Heading back to the bar, everything looks just as it should be. I look for Shane to see if he notices, but he is watching the VIP door. I look to the VIP door and see Cory walking down the stairs next to a tall, thin, ebony lady with long, thick braids down to her butt, wearing a light blue shirt with a low scoop and tight black pants with strappy black heels. She is adorned with several large pieces of jewelry and holding a glass of red wine.

Cory leans in to say something; as she leans in I can tell immediately that the lady is a vampire. Her teeth show and I take a step in her direction, but a hand wraps around my arm halting me in place.

"I thought I told you to leave," his voice whispers tight and menacing.

My heart is beating desperately in my chest. I can't shake the need to obey him, but I know that my little sister is way too close to a vampire. "Cory," I whisper, and whimper at the same time.

I can't leave without her.

"Nothing will happen to your sister. But something will happen to you if you don't leave. Now." His voice is stern but his hand softens on my wrist. Was he trying to be gentle? Yeah right. "Now go." His voice hardened at the end.

I feel his hand leave, and I try to get Cory's attention as my feet walk to the back door. She hasn't looked at me and my heart is practically breaking because, for the first time in my life, I am scared.

When I push the door open I feel Cory's heart start to jump and I turn, worried that someone is hurting her or maybe she finally saw me. But she is not looking at me. She is looking at Shane.

I hold the door open and hear Shane ask, "Hey. You okay?" I let the door close as I pull out my phone, and text Cory.

Me: Not feeling well. Had to go.

A few seconds later,

Cory: What do you mean? Are you okay?

Me: Had a run in with Dar. Tell you about it when you get home. Can you take a cab?

Cory: Yep.

I start my car and pull out of the parking spot, but the need to obey Dar leaves. I don't feel the need to go anywhere anymore. I drive down the street and park my car so that when she leaves, I will be here to drive her home. I can't leave Cory, and to be honest, I am worried about her and the vampire. I don't trust Dar at all. In fact, if he wasn't able to do what he just did, I would probably kill him for making me leave when my sister needed me.

I lean my seat back, text Cory and tell her to text me when she clocks out because I will pick her up. Then watch the back door to make sure that no one is laying in wait for her. I figure she will walk out in two more hours so all I have to do is bide my time.

A short time later the big guy I gave a seizure to walked out the back door. My heart pricked up. This is my chance to fix my mess and try out my theory on memory manipulation. I begin the words in my mind and whisper them, even though I know no one could have heard me. My stomach drops and I know my magic took hold. I am hoping that the spell worked. To test my spell I wait until he gets in his car. I run to the end of the street and jump out in front of the car.

He breaks hard and swerves. He jumps out and runs to me, "Are you okay ma'am?"

I act shaken up, "Yea. No. Yea. Oh my gosh. I'm so sorry."

He holds my shoulder, checking me over himself. I shrug away, "I'm fine. I promise." And then take off in his opposite direction. He yells for me but I keep running toward the trees with a big smile on my face. It worked; he had no idea who I was.

I wake up with a start as Cory opens the door. I'm pissed I fell asleep and now I'm curious how she saw me. Cory feigns an uneasy smile as she sits down.

I start the car and pull it into drive. My sister looks over with a curious smirk. The last thing I want to do is rehash what happened with Dar. Instead of letting her ask the question, I ask her, "Why the hell were you chumming it up with a vampire, Cory?" I don't hold back my contempt for the blood-sucker.

Cory raises her eyebrows as if I am the one being ridiculous. I'm not. She could have been hurt and I wasn't there to protect her. She should know better than that. Not that we talk much about other magical creatures. We usually just talk about me and my magic, and I don't usually let that conversation go on for too long because, when it came down to everything, there were some things I didn't know.

Huffing, Cory says, "That was Patra. She said she was an enforcer for the Magic Council."

I can feel Cory's heart stammer and I remember that her heart is mirrored in my chest. I say a few words in my mind. *You're safe Cory, therefore I release the mirror of your heart.* But our conversation was far from being over.

"You do realize that vampires are dangerous, right?"

Quick to snap back, she argues, "You do realize that Carvers are more dangerous, right?" I could see her searing me with her eyes in my periphery as I drive.

"I would never hurt you, Cory. That, is the difference."

Cory let out a breath and shakes her head, "And Patra can't hurt me, she's with the flipping Magical Council for heaven's sake."

I slam my hand on the steering wheel. "That means nothing. And you shouldn't think that just because she is in a position of authority that she does not break the rules. They all do."

"Just because you don't trust anyone does not mean I have to be the same." Cory checks the heater and turns it up to full blast.

I turn the heater up in temp but down in flow because I hate it when air rushes at my face. "You trust her? You just met her!"

Cory turns it back on full blast, "No, I don't trust her. But I don't go around slighting people because they are different from me. You treat everyone as if they are beneath you. Even other Carvers."

I quickly turn to point at her. "Shane is an asshole. I treat him like an asshole," I defend.

Folding her arms, "If Shane is an asshole, what does that make Dar?"

Ugh. She would go there. "That was quick. Didn't know it would take you this long to bring him into the conversation."

Unzipping her jacket, "I wanted to give you a chance to just tell me, but you didn't and now I'm tired and just need the cliff notes version so I can go to bed."

Somewhat pricked, I ask, "Are you asking because you really want to know or because it's the polite thing to do?"

Her jaw tenses before she lowers her hands to the vent. "Don't be rude. I ask because I care. You are the only one who asks about stuff to be polite. Which is really annoying, by the way."

Ugh. I squeeze the steering wheel wondering why tonight feels like the longest car ride of my life. "I do care, Cory."

She leans back and flaps a hand at me almost like she is shooing me. "Yeah? Prove it. Tell me what happened and then let me help you."

I was not at all inclined to tell her what happened, "I think you've done enough."

"What does that mean? Are you saying I'm incompetent? Or you don't want my help?" She adjusts her position so that she can look at me directly. And I can tell I hurt her.

Biting the bullet, I mumble, "Dar came to talk to me at the bar to tell me he knows I have been looking him up, which I haven't, so that was real fun to hear, oh and he is getting a restraining order against me."

"What?"

"Yeah, your background check must have alerted him." Against my original thought, I am not as angry after confessing that.

"It shouldn't have. I was very careful, but what do you mean a restraining order? That doesn't make any sense. He is the one coming into the bar you work at, you are not going out of the way to go to him." Cory bowed her head and her eyes glossed a bit. She's crunching the information.

"I know! But yeah that's not all." I am trying to keep her from getting caught in her thoughts so she can hear the rest. If I lose her to her head I don't know how long it will be until she comes back out again.

"Crap. What else?" She asks, but she is still looking away from me.

"When I went to the storage room he followed me in there. And my magic turned on me when I… lost it, kind of. It, my fire, went inside *him* and then made me obey him."

Cory sits up straight and looks excited. Ugh. "Oh whoa. What did you have to do?"

"Unfreeze everything I had frozen and put it back together. But the point is, I was a slave to him. It was awful. I was in so much pain I can't even describe it. So unless you know what to do about that, then I doubt you can help."

Tilting her head to the side she says, "You're a Carver. You can do magic that confounds everyone else. I'm sure your magic can fix it, but, I am also sure it's going to take me to figure out how."

I can always trust my sister to have complete faith in her abilities, "Is that so?"

"You hide from your magic, Beth. Don't try and deny it. If it wasn't for me, you wouldn't know how to do half the stuff you can do," she says in a matter of fact tone.

I turn down the heater because it feels like we are in the valley of suns. "It's still my magic. And it's my ass if I get caught."

Cory flaps the air near her ear. "Puleese. Have you been caught yet? No. So just trust me for once."

I hit the steering wheel again. "I have trusted you from the beginning! Don't act like I don't trust you and let you pull your sneaky little strings."

Squishing down a smile I see at the tips of her lips, she says, "Let me help you. Please. I know I can figure this out."

Relenting, "I am not telling you that you can't help, but I also don't think you can fix this."

Pulling into the driveway she shrugs, "Well if you can overlook the restraining order, then I should be able to figure out how to break his ability to control you and your magic."

"I hope so." And I really do.

"I know so." She confirms as I turn off the car and get out.

Unlocking the front door with my magic, I push it open, "You sound like a Carver."

I can hear her scoff. "I learned a lot from you growing up. I realized early on that your magic is infinite, but that does not mean you know how to use it. That's how I was always able to fool you. You limited yourself and your magic to the boundaries you give yourself. You didn't push it, so I pushed you. You should really thank me."

"Is that right?" I laugh and it feels purifying.

"The words you are looking for are 'Thank you Cory for always forgiving me for my outburst and rudeness, you have been instrumental in teaching me how to use my magic, I will worship thee forever.'" Her tone was light and she had a finger in the air, with her eyes closed for dramatic effect.

Rolling my eyes, I threw my jacket on the couch. "Worship thee? You're nuts, you know that right?"

Cory walks past me with her chin lifted high. She walks in the kitchen and points at the ground. "You should probably be on your knees and bowing to me right now."

Shaking my head and letting out a small chuckle I say, "There is something wrong with you."

Feigning a mocked face of shock she says, "You are being very disrespectful to your goddess."

I pour myself a glass of water and walk out before her craziness spreads. "Good night Cory."

Cory remains in the kitchen, but I can hear her say, "Hmm. You are dismissed servant."

I love my crazy ass sister.

* * *

I am so tired when I leave work at Nat Lab that I can honestly say,

I am not sure what I did all day. Cory and I are driving home and it's quiet in the car, not the creepy quietness but the kind where you didn't even notice it was quiet until you were already home.

We stop at Gino's Bar and Grill to get dinner since neither one of us planned on cooking. I was not even sure if I was going to eat or sleep first.

I don't bother to use the key to open the front door, as usual. I unlock it using my magic and push it open causing it to slam against the wall. Walking into the kitchen with a paper bag wafting the sinful Swiss cheese mushroom burger in my nose, I freeze mid-step because someone is standing there in the dark. I can't see perfectly in the dark like werewolves or vampires, but I know a dark silhouette when I see one.

I hold my arm out, keeping Cory from passing me, and I pull her back behind me using my magic to make her invisible. Then I use a few words and freeze her so she can't move from the corner of the front door and the living room. I slowly shut the door behind me and hesitate.

The kitchen light flicks on and I see that black lady with long, thick braids is in my kitchen. With Cory safely behind me I call my fire up and let some of it out of my palm. I roll it around like a crystal ball, hoping she's not so dumb to misunderstand my threat.

"Council member or not, breaking and entering is still illegal." I am trying to keep my voice calm, but this fang-er just broke into my house. And that is not okay. I am going to have to put a few spells on the house to make sure this never happens again.

Before I take my next step towards the kitchen, I remember that vampires have a keen sense of smell, too, so I mumble something else in my mind to close off Cory's smell.

The vampire is frozen behind the kitchen counter. I must

have frozen her, too, when I froze Cory. Deciding to roll with it I let her speak but that's it.

"Release me!" She says through her teeth. I haven't really had a chance to fine-tune my magic so even if I was inclined, which I'm not, but if I was, I couldn't release other parts. I learned how to freeze voices really well because I've done it to Cory loads of times.

Instead of snarling I breathe through my nose to keep myself calm. "You're in my home unwelcome and uninvited. I don't see a problem with my reactions."

I move slowly to the other side of the kitchen counter where there are three bar stools. I sit on the one closest to the door.

I can see the strain it takes her to talk. "Let me go or I will consider this an act of aggression against the vampires and the Magical Council." I know she is trying to sound threatening but knowing that she is trapped, makes her threat less motivating. I hope Cory is hearing this. This was why I don't trust the Magical Council or pure bloods.

"You broke into my house," I say, matter of factly.

"You violated the law," the vamp is still trying to break her frozen state. I have not met anyone who could counter my power. I couldn't help but smile as she continued to struggle. To show her that I'm not afraid, I let her go with a dramatic eye roll, and a less dramatic hand wave. If she did anything to my sister I would kill her. If she tried to attack me, well I would kick her royal ass and probably kill her.

I am also proving a point to Cory. I was the one being reasonable, this creature wasn't. But then again she might have been sent here because of what Dar told the council. "I was not stalking Dar, so whatever crap he told you is a huge misunderstanding." I say, a little miffed the council was even getting involved in this.

The vampire glares at me as she wipes down her dress at her hips. She is acting like she's wiping off my magic or something just as ridiculous. I peer behind her and notice that several glass bottles all with odd words in Cory's handwriting are on the counter.

She's not here because of Dar.

I stand to get a good look at the bottles, and to distance myself from the predator that is rifling through our stuff. "What exactly are you doing here?" I ask, meeting the vampire's creepy light-white eyes.

"We want to know why you have a refrigerator full of potions, specifically, fairy based potions." And then she picks up my old school book with several papers sticking out like note tabs, that I know I didn't put there. But I had a sinking feeling I knew who did. Oh I was really going to strangle her later. Her damn experiments weren't work related, they were magic related. My fire didn't see a problem with this, which pissed me off some, but I had a huge problem with this. Bad things happened to humans who dabble in magic.

I shrug, making it clear that her finding the potions didn't bother me. Even though it did. "I didn't know I needed permission to do magic," I say smugly.

The vampire's nose scrunches, "Don't pretend like you made them. These bottles are written in Cory's handwriting. And I happened to take a quick peek at some of her experiments at work and noticed similar fairy based formulas in her research."

I chuff, "Look at you, super sleuth. Not only did you break into my house, but you admit to breaking into a government facility. Perfectly acceptable actions from the Magic Council. Clearly, above the law."

Not a hint of remorse, "I enforce the laws, not break them, Carver."

Lifting my chin with a sneer, "Whose laws?"

The vampire has not moved much since I unfroze her. It was seriously unnatural. Her tone was self-important. "Ours. And our law states that you may not do magic around humans. The fact that fairy magic is being used in front of humans is unacceptable. I am here to gather the fairy potions and report them back to the Council. Because whoever it is doing this magic, is going to stand trial."

I lean my hand down slowly on the bar, making sure I am level with the wild-eyed, toothy bitch. "Get out of my house before I turn your blood-sucking ass to ash."

The vampire didn't seem enthused by my words. Carvers were always something to be feared, so her lack of fear offends me.

"I heard you were temperamental, but I didn't know you were stupid. Touch me and find that you have personally brought the war to your door step." Her tone was flat, without a hint of fear.

Am I going crazy or did she completely side-step reality? She is in my house, threatening me to bring a war to my doorstep? A war that I have no influence in, or interest. All because cures were being created with fairy magic? Oh and one more thing…

"There is no such law against Carvers doing magic in front of, or around, family members." I eye her to make sure I have her full attention. "You know the one I'm talking about right? The law that punishes any Carver who wants to raise their kids like normal people? The law that says you will kill them if they do? But of course you guys are so fucking thoughtful you allow the parents to reclaim their kids once they turn eighteen. Right after the kid has lost all hope of ever having their real parents come and claim them back with one fantastic apology!" I am seething, and I am sure my eyes are glowing because the vampire takes one step back.

But the toothy vamp recovers quickly, "Carvers were never meant to exist. You all are an abomination to all magical kin. So don't try and guilt me into treating you like you actually have a shred of humanity in you. You don't. None of you do. But some, not me, thought to give you the right to live, so of course we had to make restrictions to ensure the safety of all purebloods and humans alike."

I hope Cory is getting an earful. If not it would be a pleasure to retell this oh-so-fun scene later.

"I know the laws inside and out. I would be a fool not to, considering over half the laws are written to subdue Carvers." I point at the bottles, "Those were found in my house. They are mine. The fact that Cory wrote the label is inadmissible. The cures are based on logic and research because Cory is a genius, not because she is doing magic. The fact that there may be some fairy concoction that resembles similar elements is coincidence. Fairies don't create new concoctions, but humans do, so it would be logical for humans to evolve their science that parallels fairies. But in the end it's all hearsay. Unless you catch me in the act, it can't be proven. So now that we are clear… get the FUCK. OUT. OF. MY. HOUSE!" My voice is breaking and, I am not sure, but I think I was exhaling smoke. Ugh. Yeah, that was smoke. Tastes awful.

The vampire straightened, "I am confiscating these." She waves her hands over the bottle in front of her. "To find out who made them. All fairy magic is used with fairy energy or fairy blood, and if I find out that Cory has been illegally doing magic, I will have to report it."

Water. I tell the bottles. I picture the bottles in my mind and want every last one of those bottles to be filled with distilled water.

In my mind I said the same thing in every way possible I could think of, in my blood language, to ensure that there wasn't any evidence that Cory made them. Which she did, and I fear she may have been using her blood to create fairy magic. Not that is should have worked because she's a human, but she and I will talk about that later.

"Sure. Take them, but you have to find your own containers. Those have sentimental value." I was going to do everything possible to make this difficult for her.

"Don't be petty," she says with contempt. Then she picks up the bottles and slowly walks past me, and out the door where I hear a car door open and shut.

The car drives away and I grind my teeth ready to scream at the top of my lungs and maybe break some shit.

I am pissed.

Extremely pissed. I hope that my magic works for those bottles, but I'm not 100-percent sure. But now, I also worry that there might be some listening devices in the house. Anything the magic council could use against me, or worse, Cory. I need to keep in my anger for Cory's sake. I don't want them coming after her. If I accuse her of making those potions and using magic that she was absolutely not allowed to work with, they could use that as my confession. I would be punished and Cory would be right there with me.

I walk over to where I left Cory and made her visible again. Then I surrounded us in a white shell that I accidently created in the bar's storage room so that I can talk to her without the possibility of being heard. I wait a few more seconds until I unfreeze Cory. When I do, I am expecting some kind of apology, or long drawn out excuse. Instead Cory looks pissed, "Was that necessary?"

My jaw drops.

"Yes, you pain in the ass! A VAMPIRE broke into our home and ransacked it like she was a cop looking for anything to pin on me," I pound my chest for emphasis, "and I am the one acting out of line after defending your little experiments? You astound me Cory." I am shaking my head, trying not to let my fire out.

"Oh now it's our home?" She says, coldly.

"Oh come on! That's what you remember from that conversation?" I clench my fists.

"Oh, I heard her. She was needling you." She said with small dash of attitude.

"What!" I yell.

"It means to provoke!" She answers, shaking her head as if I am the dumb one.

Fuming, I bellow, "I know what it means Cory!"

Ignoring the fire that is coming out of my mouth in small spurts, she says, "Calm down. She won't find any traces of your blood or mine in those bottles." Cory rolls her eyes like she was not worried at all about what had just happened. Her ability to act like this is not a big deal is beyond my understanding. I drop the shell and Cory walks right into the kitchen. She pulls out the coffee grounds and a bottle of hazelnut creamer. She pops the top and smells it and then smells it again and narrows her eyes at me.

"Patra is going to be pissed," Cory says, with a half smirk. Then she holds out the bottle of creamer and says, "Fix it."

“Fix what? Cory! Are you really going to ignore what just happened? That suck-face just threatened to take you and me to jail!”

"She said trial, but that's not really the point I am trying to make."

Wow, she really doesn't get it. "I know, but it's the point I am trying to make!"

"I know that you're scared. I am trying to show you why you shouldn't be." She pushed the bottle of creamer in front of me again.

"I am not SCARED. I'm angry!" I ignore the creamer.

"Same thing," she shrugs.

I close my eyes and breath. I am so angry my fire is starting to swirl in my chest, not because it's angry but because it's worried. Damn her for being right.

Cory slowly tilts the bottle towards me. I grab the bottle sloshing the insides and peer down. It looks clear. I smell it and I didn't smell creamer.

Shaking my head I say, "I don't get it."

"I felt it when you messed with my stuff. As crazy as that sounds, I just know that you ruined it. It was like a piece of me had been cut." Cory says.

My stomach drops. "What are you telling me?" I sit down on a stool, unable to think or reassure myself that this can't be happening. I am holding the bar because it's the one thing keeping me steady.

"I am telling you to turn this water back into hazelnut creamer."

I spread my hands wide. "No I mean what do you mean you felt it? You shouldn't feel connected to your experiments."

The brat shrugs it off. “I don’t know, I just do. Now change it back, I need some coffee.”

"I don’t know how to do that." I say defensively, with my eyes in my palms. Then again I did just try and turn all those things into water so maybe… "I'll try, but before I do I need you to tell me what kind of experiments you’ve been doing."

She sniffed, “After you turn this into creamer.”

Shaking my head, I try to let my fire drain from my mind so I can think clearly. When it moves down to my chest I begin to think of hazelnuts and cream. Instantly the bottle I am holding feels heavier. I open my eyes and peer down. I see brown spots in the water. I twist off the top to expose several hazelnuts floating in the whitish water.

Close enough.

I grab a mug and pour in some of the waterish cream and hazelnuts. Then I think of Cory's hot coffee with two sugars and a quarter cup of hazelnut creamer. I know exactly what it tastes like and how it's suppose to look. I say a few words in my mind and I open my eyes, look down at the cup and see the coffee exactly as it would look if I made it from scratch. I hand the mug to Cory. Without any hesitation she takes it, sniffs it then takes a sip.

"I knew you had it in you," she takes another sip with a smile. "We should have tried this years ago. It would have saved us a fortune."

I grab a glass from the cabinet and fill it up with tap water and think of a cold, sweet, and fizzy Coke. When I refocus on the glass it's full of a dark brown liquid with several small carbonation bubbles. I take a sip and to my dismay it tastes horrible. I pour it out in the sink and grab a mug, fill it up with water and think of hot chocolate with marshmallows. Then I say it in my mind like I am ordering it from a coffee shop. When I refocus on the mug it looks and smells divine.

I grab my hot chocolate and take a sip. Cory is watching me closely. I nod at her when I put the mug down, letting her know it's perfect.

"All those experiments you have been creating are from my old school books aren't they?" I ask, knowing the answer but knowing that we can't just skip over what happened.

"No. None of those bottles were potions from your school book." She answered as she pulled a chair from the kitchen table so that she was sitting opposite to me instead of next to me on a bar stool.

"Then why is my book filled with notes in your handwriting? And why can you feel when I turned all your experiments to water?"

"I copied the formulas from that book years ago and have been tweaking it ever since. I've never had to use my blood in any of my stuff. Plus, the only ones that needed blood were the big ones, like binding potions." She answers while she is watching the liquid in her coffee. I don't know if it was guilt, shame or remorse, but at least she wasn't doing actual magic.

I nod at her, not really knowing what to say about the potions anymore, but I do want to address the vampire. "That vampire is dangerous, Cory. If you see her again, you call me." I say, heading to out of the kitchen. "Oh," I turn around and point at her, "and for the record, I will never trust them. Any of them. So be prepared that if one more person breaks into our house, I will kill them." Then I turn back around and go to my room.

* * *

A heavy pounding on the front door woke me up. I didn't even check the time before I bound down the hall and press my hand to the door, making an invisible barrier so no one could walk through. Then I open the door. To my shock, Dar was standing there in a plain, black t-shirt and dark blue jean, with dark black boots.

"You're an idiot," he says in a tired breath. He leans back and shakes his head. "Patra came to the pack land to find out about the huge misunderstanding you mentioned." He didn't look pleased at all. "Now there will be a formal complaint filed against you, from me."

Putting my fisted hands on my hips, I cough out, "You told me you were getting a restraining order. So when I caught that toothy suck-face in my home tonight, I thought the *only* reason she would be here was because you sent her."

"I didn't tell her anything," he says, as he puts his hands in his pockets.

"Because you didn't get a chance yet?" I fold my arms under my chest.

"No." He takes out one hand and scratches the back of his head. "I let it go when I noticed you weren't lying. So someone else must have been looking into my stuff."

"Is that a wolf thing? You just knew I wasn't lying because you know me so well, or is it something else?"

He lets out a breath and looks at the door, as if he just realized I had not asked him to come in. And I wasn't planning on it either. "Yeah it's a werewolf thing." He stops looking at the frame and asks, "What did Patra want?"

A little uneasy with his total 180 from how he treated me at the bar I say, "Don't act like you care."

He growled lightly and I see something pass by his eyes. He turned around and walked away, "I don't."

"I know," I mumble to myself.

He turns back to me, eyes glowing, "You have no idea what I have been through because of you, so drop the fucking attitude."

"Oh by all means," I step back and push the door open behind me. "Come and explain it to me. I'd *love* to know why I'm the problem."

He hesitates and looks at me as if I have set up a bunch of booby-traps for him. Then he looks at the door and says, "Take it down."

I smirk, and mentally take down the barrier I put up, "Done."

He walks back to the door slowly and steps away from me as he walks in. Already regretting my suggestion for him to come in and talk, I walk to the kitchen table and pull out a seat. Then I walk to the cabinet, open it, and pull down a mug. "Do you want some coffee?" Not that I wanted to make him some, but I didn't mind showing him the cool trick I learned tonight.

"No."

I put my hands around the mug and think of some more hot chocolate, but without the marshmallows. I don't think marshmallows were practical for the conversation I am about to engage in.

Dar sits down at the head of the oval kitchen table and puts one arm down in front of him. "Before I start, I just want to know if you are planning on leaving again. I know I told you to get out of here, but I just want to know if you are going to or not."

I sit down next to him so that we are far enough away, and yet close enough to have a conversation. "What do you mean by again? And no, I am not planning on leaving."

"You left after we graduated." He was not looking at me. He was looking at the mug.

"How did you know I left?" I couldn't help the intrigue and excitement I feel to actually have this conversation.

"I couldn't feel you as clearly as I had before. Not that I could feel you much. I could only feel your emotions, but when you left the bond weakened." His tone sounded dark and I adjusted my feet as a result of being uncomfortable.

"You can feel me?" *Bond?*

Dar narrowed his eyes at me. "You know exactly what I am talking about. You figured it out when your weird fire went inside of me, which was the most uncomfortable thing I have ever experienced, by the way."

Didn't look like it was painful in the way it was when it went back inside me. "I wanted to help you back then, but I didn't want to be…" I stop myself from saying "mate" because I'm not sure if he saw it that way, or if he even knows about the way Carvers mate.

"Werewolves can hear the thoughts and feelings of their mates. I couldn't hear your thoughts when I woke up in the hospital, but I remember talking to you in my mind, I just didn't remember what you said. But I could feel your emotions. So that was the first tip-off that I was mated."

So he did consider me a mate. "So you did remember me?"

"I knew I had a mate. I knew your voice somewhat and I could feel your emotions, but I didn't know who you were. I didn't even know your scent so I had no way of finding you." He took the mug in front of me and drank the rest, "Not that I tried."

Be still my heart... you rude bastard.

He looked at me with a knowing look. But he continued, "It was kind of a big shock to take in. One moment I am worrying about midterms and dealing with crap from my father because my brother had just been kidnapped. At the same time I was mauled by a bear wielding a knife, which is still unexplainable, oh and blacking out because I was dying, then miraculously being healed by your mate who I didn't even know, or had met."

"You didn't know it was me who healed you?"

"Nope," he said, with a pop on the 'p,' "I could feel when you were close, but by the time I had returned to school where I knew you were, I wasn't really interested in finding you. I kind of ... wanted to pretend you didn't exist."

I regret asking him to come in now. This conversation sucks. "Why?" I said, taking back the mug and filling it back up with hot chocolate.

"Because... of a lot of reasons." He looks at my mug and shakes his head. "Can you make it coffee with sugar no cream?" I push the mug forward, putting in the order in my head. He takes a sip and nods, "That's a neat trick." But it doesn't sound like he thinks it is neat, more so an oddity, and unnatural.

I am not sure, but I am starting to think he is bipolar or something. "I have spent years thinking you didn't even know me. I think you owe me some kind of explanation."

"You're not the only one who deserves an explanation, Beth." He takes a sip of the coffee and then downs it after that.

"What does that mean?"

"Why weren't you there when I woke up? Or better yet, why didn't you come find me? You want to put all this blame on me, when you were half the reason for all this bullshit." He pushes the mug to me again and taps the top.

"Me?!" I almost slam my hand down on the table but halt just before it made impact because Dar grabbed my wrist with a finger to his lips. Telling me to be quiet. Ugh. Acting responsible, and an asshole at the same time. Was that even possible? He tapped the top of his mug again and I hated myself for wanting to fill it for him. I filled the mug again promising myself that was the last time.

"I had no idea WHO you were Beth. I had no idea how to find you. I didn't know your scent and I didn't know…" When his words died off I was unsure if it was because of what he was saying, or if there was something else I should be aware of. They did have an excellent sense of smell and hearing.

"What?"

He lifts his eyebrows almost like he is warning me that I am not going to like the next thing he talks about. "I didn't know you weren't a werewolf. That's whom I had been looking for, trying to sniff out all those years ago in high school. I was looking for my mate, who I thought was my kind."

"Oh." Could this get any worse?

"It took a long time to come to terms that you might not be a werewolf. Then when you disappeared, I was even more angry at you." He drank the last of the coffee and thankfully he didn't ask me to fill it up.

"Because you couldn't feel me or because I left?"

"Because I realized you are a Carver." His tone and words make it perfect how he feels about Carvers. He doesn't like them at all.

"How did you realize that?" I make myself ask, even though I think I am breaking apart on the inside.

Dar looks me over curiously, but then looks away. "Do you remember my brother Cort?"

"I remember hearing he went missing."

He nods, "He was kidnapped. By a Carver. He told me about her the night he was taken. He said that he knew who his mate was. That it was a Carver. I didn't think anything of it when he left to go meet her. I didn't say anything when my father showed everyone the note the Carver left on his desk the next morning, announcing his only heir was dead. It said that they were punishing my father for passing a new law that would give the council the right to sentence a Carver to death if they were found doing magic in front of humans."

I tilt my head forward, grab the back of my hair at the nape and hold on for dear life. No wonder Dar hated me. He was one of those assholes who thought I was an abomination. "Your father passed that law?" My voice shook a little, but I figured that it wouldn't bother Dar considering he was totally apathetic to me.

"He was one of many to support it and agree to it." His tone is souring and I would have looked further into it but he didn't deserve it.

"That's a shitty fucking law. And complete bullshit, you know that right?"

He gave me a skeptical look, "I know that Carvers are dangerous. But can you see my point? My brother had just been killed by Carvers, and I found out a year later my mate that had been avoiding me, was one?"

I can't stop myself from defending my actions and who I was as person, not that it would change his mind about me, "I'm not like that, I'm not like them."

"I didn't know that. And you didn't give me a chance to find out because you left."

Yeah right, like it would have made a difference. "I didn't know that Carvers gave their hearts to their mates. And to be honest I didn't think I gave you my heart in the hospital. I thought I loaned it to you when you needed it. Actually, that all sounds dumb now that I say that out loud."

"I am figuring that out. But I also know that I would have died if you didn't." Then he shrugged as if that made it okay. It was okay to have saved him but he wasn't happy with being mated.

"That's why I did it."

He nods again. "The thing is, I don't know if you are my true mate. I have heard so many stories about how werewolves just know their mates the second they see them. But I never had that with you. I never felt like my mate was close or that I was going to school with her."

"What are you saying?" I really hate this conversation.

"I don't think you are my true mate. I think your Carver magic overruled the werewolves mating rites by giving me your heart."

A knot starts forming in my throat, "I didn't…" I can't even finish my words.

"I know. I just wanted you to see my side."

"I do and I am really sorry. I don't know how to fix it. I was told that once a Carver gives their heart to the other, there is no taking it back." I felt like crawling up in my bed and never coming out. I have never felt so horrible. Did I really fuck up his life? Did I fuck up mine by accident? How could I feel so many things at once?

"Yeah, I heard that too." He seriously sounded sad by that. As if I really did take his future from him.

"Damn. I'm really sorry."

"Me too."

"Do you think you if you found your true mate it would fix this?" I ask hopefully, wondering if he might know how to fix this. If he didn't then I was going to ask Cory to help me. She might have some ideas. If not I would find someone. There has to be someone that would know.

"I don't think so. Once a wolf has a mate, he can't be with anyone else. Literally. I can't physically be with someone else, even if I wanted to. Nothing works for anyone but my mate."

"Oh wow. So you haven't?" How did he transition to this topic? Why are we having this conversation? I really didn't want to know his equipment was . . . eww.

"Nope."

"Oh wow."

"Yep. But it seems like you were able to get around that."

I what? Miffed, I say, "Me? I haven't been with anyone."

His eyes are amber again, "I have felt it Beth. I can feel it when you . . . get excited in that way."

"Oh my gosh!" I covered my mouth and wish I could cover the blush that is burning on my cheeks.

"Yeah, imagine how I felt," he says darkly.

"That's not what I meant you sick fuck." I take a few relieving breaths and shake my head at him. He doesn't know shit.

"I know what I felt."

"Obviously you didn't because I have never been with anyone. You didn't feel me with anyone. You felt me take care of myself." I can feel the blush burning on my skin but I am not going to hide from this. I am being honest and his vulgar ass can just deal with it. I was never able to even date because every guy that I talked to just seemed wrong.

"What?" He sat back in the chair and looked at me. Really looked at me.

"Yeah, uh. Yeah." I pull back the mug and fill it with hot chocolate and take a sip.

"Humm."

Not looking at him I ask, "Can you not? Uh. . ."

"Yeah I can do *that.*"

"Oh. Well uh, good?" I sneak a peak at him and he might be blushing, I am not sure. It is not really bright in the kitchen. I had kept the stove light on, but nothing else.

"Yeah, I guess."

"So do you want me to see if maybe finding your true mate can fix all this?" I ask.

"Like I said before. I have no idea if I would even be able to recognize her now because my wolf sees you as his mate."

"Oh. Uh. Well, uh. Maybe there's a way. With Carvers we can

do magic that is not explained or even possible. So, give me a chance to fix it."

"I'm not going to hold by breath." He takes my mug and downs the hot chocolate.

Pity.

"I can hear you by the way. Once I saw you in the bar that night, I have been able to hear your thoughts and see the things in your mind."

Crap. I can feel the squeeze of my stomach with the fact of all I had thought of while sitting here.

"Yeah imagine how I feel."

Pissed, I say, "Look, I didn't do any of this on purpose so I will take my share of the blame, but I am not taking it all."

"Didn't think you would take any of it," he says arrogantly, and taps the top of the mug.

"Wow. You really are a dick. You must be an alpha." I fill the mug with more hot chocolate. Wondering if I was obeying him or if I wanted to share my hot chocolate with him.

"What did you just say?" He tilted his head, confused.

"You. Are. A. Dick."

"No, the other thing." He waved his hand slightly as if he could rewind the conversation.

How interesting he shrugs off my calling him a dick. Maybe he's called that a lot. "About being an alpha?"

"Yeah."

"I know you are an alpha, Dar. I know your father is an alpha and you are his first born."

"How do you know all this?"

Hiding the smile inside, I say, "Cory told me. She is the one who was looking into you – behind my back. I only just found out, so don't worry, she won't be doing that anymore."

"Your sister told you I was an alpha. Or that I was the first born." This seems to be important to him because his eyes are holding mine, making sure he doesn't miss a word.

"Why is this a touchy topic for you?"

"Because it is. Now tell me what you think you know."

Hot and cold. He is one moody bastard. "Okay…your father runs the pack. You are his first-born son. Your brother is a half brother, born to a different mom. You never went to college but you do have a lot of investments, and you own a construction company with all pack members as employees."

He holds my eyes for another moment and I hate that I feel I need to lower my eyes to him. He is not my alpha, per se. Or is he? I am not really sure, but I don't bow down to anyone, including him.

"My father was with my mother and accidently had me. She was an alpha female, but not his true mate. When he met his true mate, he told my mom about it. She told him to leave and take me with him."

Uh. That's shitty.

"Try not to think anything while I tell you this. It's distracting." He waited as if he was testing me.

I roll my eyes and take back the mug for a sip.

"My father mated with Cort's mother, so Cort is the only heir he claims. But when Cort died his mother wanted to go after the Carvers. When my father told her not to, she went anyways. Told him that he wasn't a man if he wasn't willing to fight for their son. Ophelia never came back, but her body was found a year later. My father changed when they took Cort, but when he learned his mate was no longer just missing, but dead, he shut down.

"He spends most of his time at the council headquarters. He only shows up once or twice a year, if that. But because he has not told anyone I am the next in line, the pack is divided. Some tell me to challenge him and take over. Some tell me that I am not fit to rule, but they are. It's a political mess. I help out where I can but the pack is restless and breaking at the seams."

"What is stopping you from challenging him?" I shouldn't be asking, but I am curious. Not that I am going to be able to help him, but whatever. I am just curious.

"I don't know if I want to be alpha." He takes back the mug and finishes it. Then he stands up and says, "So that's it. That's my side and now I know yours."

I stand up after him. "Fair enough. But this talk didn't resolve anything." I grab the mug and place it in the sink.

"I know," he scratches his head and looks at me with something in his eyes I didn't understand. Then his eyes glint.

Oh yeah, he can hear me and know my confusion.

I walk to the front door and open it, "Thanks."

He walks out the door and turns around with his finger in the air. "Oh and Beth? If you can, try . . . and watch the things you think about."

My stomach tightened as I remembered what I had done last night in his name. Shit.

"Exactly."

CHAPTER SEVEN
SHANE

Last night Cory's sister bailed on the bar and left me hanging. Only demons would understand the level of anger I felt towards her last night. I wasn't sure if she left, or if something happened.

Beth had been gone for an hour before I accepted she was not coming back. That was also when I started looking for reasons of why she would have left. Her and I had not fought, the douche wasn't in the bar and the one vampire I knew was in the bar had not touched any of the patrons. So there was no reason that I could see as to why she would have left.

That was until I looked over to the Nickleback poser. He had a soft spot for Beth. And when I say soft spot, I mean he looks at her like he wants to stuff her into a trunk and go off-roading.

I noticed the poser was on his phone but keeping a withering look on Cory. That was why I broke my own rule to stay out of other people's business. In those few micro seconds I had not only decided to make sure she got to her car okay, I was going to make sure that the poser didn't try ambushing her when she left. I was also going to find a way to keep an eye on her round the clock, I mean if Beth was always taking off like that, someone had to watch over Cory. She would become a target if Beth ever pissed off a pure blood. And the first pure blood that comes to mind is the darkly pissed off wolf.

The best I could think of right then was to slip a locating bug on her, and when I say bug I mean a coin from my pocket that I put a spell on quickly. I reached into my pocket and pulled out two coins. I got them in Panama when I was about twenty. They had the Conquistador on one side and I always liked the look of them. I carried them around just in case something happened. I'd like to think that my self-motto was to always have a backup plan.

The spell I put on the coins was a combination of fairy and witch magic, and completely genius if I say so myself. If I held the coin in my palm I could see in my mind everything around the other one. That way I could use it to teleport. I can't teleport anywhere that I have not seen. So this way I could always teleport to Cory no matter where she went.

I slipped one of the coins into Cory's pocket. I thought I was slick but she noticed. She pulled the coin out and looked at it, then up at me incredulously. "Um, what are you doing?"

I made a stupid excuse about it being a tip someone at the bar gave her. She didn't buy it. Before she put it back in my hand I grabbed her wrist. "Please Cory. Keep it. There are more special kind of people here than there has ever been, and I have no idea where Beth is or why she's not here. So, just this once, do me a favor and take it." I can remember her hesitation. But thankfully she nodded and put the coin back in her pocket.

Smiling, I pulled out a piece of paper that I already had written my number on and gave it to her. "The coin will let me know where you are, but this is for emergencies or whenever."

Cory huffed, "I'll be fine. I promise." She tried to give back my number, but the look on my face made her stuff it in her pocket. Then when I didn't move, I told her I was waiting for her to agree to use it. Instead of agreeing, she pulled out a small note pad from her apron and scribbled her number down and handed the paper to me. I took the sheet and punch it into my phone right there. I wouldn't put it past any woman to give me a fake number. I called the number and I heard a funny tune from her pocket. Her jaw tensed and she blushed a little.

"Now I have your number." Secretly pleased my plan worked out even better than originally planned.

* * *

I throw my pillow at the wall. I have no idea what time it is, but I can't get my damn mind to shut the hell up!

One time. Why can't you try a human? The dark side of me asks.

I don't want to. I answer, even though I know it's a lie. I do want to try her, I want to know how she would feel underneath me.

Then do it. You can always take the memory later. I refuse to respond to the dark part of me that thinks I would ever do something like that.

She works at the bar and if it went bad, or better yet, when our bedtime relationship went sour like they all did, it would be awkward. I learned my lesson with Enora.

I can feel the coin in my pocket. I want to check it again. But this time it wouldn't be to see if she got home, she already did that. It would be to see if I can catch her in the skimpy shorts and tank top again. I can't get that image out of my mind.

She would feel so soft and warm. A part of me is trying to tear down one of my unbreakable rules. No dating humans ever.

I could easily run my hands up her silky thighs right to her sweet spot, the spot I want to be in right now. Ugh. Visualizing it is making this worse, it's not like I am not already hurting from the pipe in my pants. And yes, maybe I could take care of it myself, but it would make it worse in the end. I would want her even more.

I leave my bed and walk to the kitchen, grab a water bottle in the refrigerator and down all of it. I grab another one and stuff it in my gym bag. I refuse to drown in my thoughts so I teleport into my car hoping the gym can clear my mind.

Two hours later. The gym failed me and I still can't close my eyes without her there. And worse I am letting my mind begin to plot, even though I am half-heartedly telling myself I will never go through with it.

You can call her and make sure she's okay. That wouldn't be suspicious and you do genuinely want her to be okay.

No. I know she's okay. I don't need to call.

What if she's afraid to call you? She's shy and someone has to make the first call. What's the worst that can happen?

Everything.

It's five in the morning and I am stiff as stone and I already broke down and took two showers.

Then just do it. Call her. No one's resisted before, and after each escapade you reset and lost interest. This has to be done.

She works with me. *No.*

Are you afraid?

No. I'm not stupid. This will pass. Maybe I can call Enora. She would let me over no matter what time it was. I look towards my phone and couldn't pick it up. The memories of Enora and all that we've done caused me to soften.

There has to be some explanation to that.

It is odd isn't it? We have to find out if it's Cory, or if there is something wrong with us.

I don't want to agree, but I do need to know. Thinking about sex with other women shouldn't make me lose interest. It should push me to call Enora and take my mind off the shy smile that is haunting me. But just the thought of being with Enora is making me feel sick.

And that has never happened before. I'm a man, thinking of having sex should never make me feel ill. Which means, I have to find out what it is about Cory that is causing this.

* * *

My eyes hurt as I open them to a sun-drenched bedroom. From my bed, I glare at my cheap window blinds that are useless against the afternoon sun. I grab my phone and see that I slept for about three hours. I fall back on my pillow, hating that Cory's long legs in short booty-shorts is flashing in my mind.

This can't be happening.

I pick up my phone and hold it tightly. Am I really going to do this? I tap my forehead with my phone and wish that I didn't want her so much. But I already decided. I need to know why thinking of any other girl made me lose strength. There was nothing natural about that.

I chuck my phone at the wall and hear the plastic shatter.

"Dammit Cory."

I pull a small scrunched paper from my black Dickies. I take a moment to admire her horrible penmanship. I call on my magic to fix my phone and bring it back to me.

I push my legs over the bed and hunch over. Before my thumb can push the power button I shake my head internally. I know this isn't going to be a hit it and quit it girl. I seriously want her.

Forever?

No. Not forever. That's insane.

Deciding that, I need to contact her so that I can get on with my afternoon breakfast. Even though I am tired, I am craving a peanut butter waffle sandwich.

The screen lights up and I slowly punch in the numbers making sure I get the number correct. Here goes nothing.

Me: U never text me when u got home. Rude.

She didn't text back right away. I gave her another minute, hoping she would respond, before I get up to take a shower.

After my shower I check the phone again.

Cory: You didn't ask me to.

Ignoring her comment entirely, I text: What u doing? I just woke up.

A few seconds later she texts back.

Cory: You're lazy. I'm at work.

Me: Ambers?

Cory: No. I work at NatLab too.

Me: 2 jobs?

Really? Wow I was actually impressed. And I don't get impressed. Ever.

Cory: Yeah, I figured I could pay off my school loans faster with two jobs.

She had a degree? Seriously, I am really impressed.

Me: What's ur other job?

Cory: I work in a lab.

That's a non answer. A little miffed she was getting vague I ask. Me: What kind of lab?

Cory: Carcinogens research.

What is carcinogens research? I quickly did a search on my phone. And now I am grinning. Cory's a biologist. Deciding against following up on this topic over the phone I decide it's time to play with her a little bit. Loosen her up.

Me: R u jealous I get to sleep in?

Cory: Nope. I like getting up early.

Me: Eh. Y?

Cory: Because I have stuff to do.

Me: Like?

Somehow this conversation was getting serious because I wasn't playing anymore. I really wanted to know what someone like her, a biologist by day and waiter by night did with their time.

I take my phone to the kitchen. I pull out a glass and fill it with water and drink all of it. I lean back against the counter as my phone chirps. I pull the phone out of my pants pocket, feeling triumphant with the answer that is bound to be very interesting.

Cory: None of your business.

Oh really? I smirk at how Cory is trying to act all secretive. I put the phone back in my pocket and push off the counter to pull out two frozen vanilla waffles from my freezer and pop them down in the toaster. After plotting how best to get her to go out with me, I pick my phone out of my pocket and text back.

Me: Eh. Fine. What r u doing tonight?

Cory: None of your business.

I smiled inwardly. She has no idea how persistent I can be. Me: Come out w/me 2night.

Even if she told me no all day, I was going to find a way to see her.

Cory: No more bars for me.

Me: I didn't say bar. I said come out with me.

Cory: No.

Me: Y?

Cory: Because.

Me: Because I make u nervous?

Cory: Yes

Me: I can fix that. Come out w/me.

Then she doesn't answer me. I take the waffles out of the

toaster and slather on some Jiffy creamy peanut butter. I take a bite and put in two more waffles in the toaster. Cory still hasn't texted back.

Rude.

I eat both waffle sandwiches and grab my bag for the gym. More than fifteen minutes had gone by before I text her again.

Me: Still scared?

Cory: Yes

I roll my eyes.

Me: I just want to go for a drive. No questions. No small talk. Just relaxing on a drive.

Cory: No talking?

Me: I'll put music on. What do u listen to?

Cory: Okay. Anything.

I laugh to myself. *Got her.*

Me: Have u been to 11 mile Ress?

Cory: No

Me: Good. What's ur address? I'll pick u up after work.

Cory: My sister drove us to work today, you can pick me up here.

Beth was a biologist too? No way. I wasn't going to dwell on how that little bit of information miffed me.

Me: I will pick u up from work.

Cory: Okay. I get off at 3:00.

I ask for the address next, and where was best to pick her up. I close my phone and my smile fades.

What the hell am I doing?

I really should not be doing this. Shaking my head, and once more going against my better judgment, I call Charles, another bartender, and ask him to work my shift tonight.

I teleport to my car, reminding myself that this is only temporary. Cory is only interesting right now but once I get to know her, the interest will fizzle out.

* * *

Cory walks out in a white dress, blue cardigan and matching blue flats.

My stomach tightens and I know, I just know, I am walking a fine line. I probably could have, over time, accepted all the dumb things I have told myself about her, and what a bad idea this is, and gotten over this little thing I had about her. I could have, I think. But not now, I can't walk away from what I am looking at.

All the comments, all the feelings about her that I have ignored, can't be denied right now. Right now, she is absolutely lovely as she blushes lightly while chewing the side of her lip.

I push off my passenger side door and stand straight so she can see me clearly. I wait until she's closer before I open the door. She's trying to hide a smile. She tucks her dress underneath her as she slides into the leather passenger seat. I take a good look at her sweet, soft legs and confirm once more this is the best and stupidest thing I have ever done.

I walk around to the driver side, open the door, and sit down.

I can see her nervousness, or at least I think I can. I promised not to ask questions so I keep in the few words that I have, wondering if they would have soothed her. We are just going to drive and relax. I turn up the radio, looking to make sure she is okay with my choice. She smiles with one side of her mouth, her hands are in a tight ball in her lap and I can't help but want to frown.

She can't be that afraid of me. I mean we do work together, right? I let my question go and pull out of the parking spot.

I take the back way, or better yet, the longest way possible, to Eleven Mile Reservoir. I can tell that Cory's stiff posture that she's uncomfortable. I want to say something, but I don't want to go back on my promise.

After an hour, Cory is fiddling with her phone and has her shoes off, sitting Indian style next to me. She must not be that uncomfortable anymore. Although I'm not sure what I did to change that.

I hate that I said we wouldn't be talking. It feels like she is ignoring me and there is a huge emptiness in the car that the music has not helped.

I look over and Cory taps the window. "Can we stop real quick?"

I slow the car and pull over. She opens the door quickly and gets out. I follow after her slowly, not sure what she is doing or if she wants me to join her. Cory makes her way down the small hill to the creek that runs along side the road. I stop walking the second I hear her camera phone snap a picture. I think she takes about two before she hits the thing and growls. "Gggggaaa! Battery died."

I walk back to my car and pull out my camera from the glove box. I haven't used it in a long time. I walk back to her and hand her the camera without saying anything. She takes it then she turns to the creek and snaps a few more pictures.

Cory half smiles as she reviews her pictures on the camera. Satisfied, apparently, she heads back to the car with me in tow. After five more minutes in the car she taps the window again, and asks to stop with a little more excitement. I smile and shake my head and pull over again.

She hops out and takes several more photos. This time I stop and rest against the hood of the car instead of following her all the way to the creek.

I watch her take snapshots and then I see her starting to review the pictures she has taken, right about the time I wonder if she will see mine.

Cory gasps. She looks at me with wide eyes. "Did you take these?" I nod at her but I didn’t say anything else, because apparently I am the only one who remembered the no-talking policy.

Ignoring the rules we preplanned, the little hypocrite walks back up to me and asks, "How long have you been into photography?"

I shake my head. "No questions."

Her jaw drops mockingly. "What? Come on! You just talked so the rules really don’t matter in this instance. Plus you only said that so I would say yes."

She’s right. I did, but I shake my head again and she frowns. Her forced frown is adorable.

"Fine.”

I open the door for her again and she gets in, folding her arms tightly across her chest.

I'm an idiot. I don't even know why I am enforcing this rule when I didn't like the rule to begin with. What the hell is wrong with me?

The rest of the drive is in silence and I worry I am royally messing this up.

Probably.

We finally arrive at Eleven Mile Reservoir. I get out and open her door, but she has her eyes cast down to her phone and didn't acknowledge me. Taking the rejection, I walk to the picnic table near my parking spot. I hoped she would follow me, but I have not heard the door shut. I turn around to see what's keeping her and I see her holding the camera in my direction, and then the distinct sound of clicking. I turn, giving her my back, casting my eyes skyward.

She's taking pictures of me.

"No pictures," I try to say without a growl, but I still growl.

"Too late," she says, with a little sass and, even though I can't see it, I can hear the shit-eating-grin.

Trying not to smile from her cuteness, I call out, "Delete it."

She makes a noise with her throat and says. "Um, no."

Then I hear her snap a few more pictures. I turn around and give her an annoyed look. She smiles at me like an innocent girl. "What? I was taking pictures of the lake."

I raise my eyebrows. I don't believe her. I stand up in an effort to get my camera back, when my phone rings. She backs up slowly with a smirk. She must think that my phone call will stop me. It won't. I continue to walk in her direction.

I hit the answer button as she holds the camera at me and I raise my eyebrows daring her to… she takes a picture. I shake my head in warning because as soon as I catch her I am going to take some very naughty pictures of her. I walk faster in her direction as she runs away with a girly laugh.

"Who is that?" Aaron asks through the phone. I look at my phone that I had yet to put up to my ear, and wonder why I even answered it.

"What's up?"

Aaron is a buddy of mine from the gym. He invites me to his bashes every so often, and I turn him down three out of the four times he calls.

"Party at my house. Stop by." He says, as if he is ordering me and not asking. But he is hopeful. He's in luck because if it gets me more time with Cory, then I'm all in.

"Okay." I agree for the first time in several weeks. I can see Cory on the other side of the boulders taking photos, but she is constantly looking back to make sure I am behind her. I stopped walking a second ago and now my plans are starting to change from just a drive to the reservoir, to something more eventful.

"Really?" He sounds shocked and pleased at he same time.

"Yeah."

"Awesome. See you later." I slide the phone into my pocket eyeing my prey.

I wait for Cory to finish snapping pictures and I teleport next to her. I grab her and the camera. Her girly laugh is rumbling on my chest and I am fighting myself not to kiss her.

I am not sure if she will be as soft and sweet like she was in my dreams last night but I am pretty sure that no matter how she tastes, I am going to like it.

I pull her back into my chest and touch her ear with my lips; she stops squirming immediately. In a low voice I whisper, "Now it's my turn to take your picture."

"I'm not very photogenic," she says, weakly.

I take a deep breath of her skin and see small bumps rise all over her neck. I brush my lips below her ear, "We'll see."

Cory arches her back and I can envision all her sweet curves that I want to get to know… intimately. I spin her around, grab the side of her cheek and make her face me. I want to see if she has the look, I have to see if she feels the same way.

Her eyes are guarded.

I hate that.

I let her go and take a small step back. I watch her as I hold out the camera in my palm. Then I telepathically lift the camera into the air, and she drops her jaw. Mentally, I connect with the lens, so it takes pictures of what I see through my eyes instead of through the lens. It's a neat trick I found several years ago.

I know she's guarded, but I can't help my need to touch her. I step back up to her and wrap my arm around her waist. She lets me. I lean down and brush my lips over hers. She lets me. I promise myself I won't push her… too far. I won't force her to do anything she doesn't want to do. Right now she needs to make a move. I have shown her my intentions, she needs to accept, she has to take the next step if tonight is going to go anywhere.

She moves her lips against mine, not exactly kissing me back, and yet not shying away either.

Confounding woman.

I pull back and see her biting her bottom lip. I take a picture. Then I look over her, adjust the focus in my eyes, and take several more. She has no idea what I am doing because the 'click' sound is on silent.

I push her light jacket off her shoulders and let it fall on the grass. She lets me, even though her eyes are asking me questions. I teleport us to a hip high boulder, to where the back of her thighs are flush against the smooth rock. I lean down and slowly guide her body down and back on a malformed rock, perfect for us to lie down on. I slide my fingers slowly over her skin, giving her more goose bumps and taking more pictures. I push her left knee away from me so that her legs open just a small degree.

Her chest is rising and falling slowly, possibly fighting with herself and what she wants to do, versus what she should do. I can see the tick in her jaw and how much she is trying to maintain a calm demeanor, but this is my art, this is my passion. To see beauty where no one else dares to look.

I lean down and smell her skin without touching her. I begin at her knees, and slowly breath in her soft thighs, lower belly, up past her arching chest to her neck.

I peer up at her eyes and they are closed. She is succumbing to her feelings. I smile and press a small kiss to just below her chest and then I back up to take another picture.

I move her several times and the camera is following me, so she must know what I am doing, but I am not explaining and she is not asking. For the first time tonight the silence is no longer a heavy weight of discomfort, instead it's a weight of physical intrigue.

I run my fingers over her shoulders and down her arm. I

swallow, knowing how her delicate skin might feel against my mouth. I push the thought away and focus on every picture I can take of her, without her feeling too exposed.

I see her pressing her right hand flat against the rock, her body is stiff and I can tell she is struggling internally. I finally get the picture I have been dying to get; I look over and see her hungry eyes. I snap my last picture.

I pull her up, teleport us to my car and open the passenger door quickly, knowing that I could have taken the kiss. I could have possibly made it into something more, but I don't just want her hungry for a small taste. I want her starving for me.

She slides in with a forced smile. I don't like being the reason she is uncomfortable, but if I kissed her right now, I wouldn't stop.

Cory isn't speaking. I am trying to keep my eyes on the road, but I can't stop the voice in my head calling me a lot of names that all boil down to being a world-class idiot.

I had her. *What is wrong with me?*

But I just knew, in my fucking gut, that if I took her then, she would regret it. I don't want regrets.

I look over and see Cory flipping through the pictures. She's biting her bottom lip and I think I see a small blush. Her slow, shallow breaths are the only indication of how hot and bothered I believe she is. It takes her a while before she stops looking at the pictures and pays attention to the road.

After an hour she unfolds her legs and narrows her eyes at the road, "Where are we going?"

I try not to smirk, but I can't help it. "Your penalty for not listening to me."

When she looks at the door handle I worry she might be thinking something incredibly stupid. I grab her hand and pull it to my thigh, doing two things at once- getting her attention and hopefully calming her down. "A friend of mine is having a few friends over. I told him I would stop by, we won't stay long," I made sure to keep my tone calm and soothing. I want her to feel comfortable with me, especially if my plans to have her later actually pan out.

But, if she really doesn't want to go I will take her home. I kept her hand in mine as she moves to face forward again. Again, the car fills with a silence, even though the music is playing in the background.

When we arrive I open her door, amazed she stayed in the car long enough for me to walk around. I am not an expert in dating by any stretch of the imagination, but it makes her even more endearing.

I hold out my hand to her. She takes it as I pull her up, and then she immediately shakes me off. No way is she getting away with that. I refuse to let her shy away from me, not after I saw exactly how she wanted me. I grab her hand this time and intertwine my fingers in hers. Leaning down to make sure she can hear me and feel my breath on her neck, "Give it an hour. After that just say the word and I will take you home." This seems to make her feel better because I feel her squeeze my hand twice.

We walk hand in hand to the front door. She rings the doorbell and we wait. If I had come alone, I would have walked straight in, but with Cory, she apparently isn't the type to do that.

A guy with dirty blonde hair, tussled like he just woke up, answers the door. His dark brown eyes are a little beady, and he has a scar on the left side of his jaw that starts a few millimeters from his left eye. He gives me a dismissive glance, "Hey, come on in."

I pull Cory with me, but to my annoyance the guy does not step back. Instead, he is standing right in front of Cory with a look I can't explain, but I don't like it. Right then I knew, I could feel it, but I have no evidence why this guy is all wrong. There is just something about him that makes me feel he is going to irritate the hell out of me.

Cory notices the guy staring, too, and pushes into me to walk past him. I hold her back and square my body to him. "Do your legs work?" He smiles but it's fake and he knows I know. And now I want to break the man's legs or kneecaps.

"My bad. I didn't even notice. I've been drinking since, like lunch time," he slurs.

I had no idea if Broken Legs' slurring was real or not, but again there was something about him I didn't trust, so I walk past him, making myself the wall between him and Cory. I pull her behind me, making sure never to let her out of my sight. There are more people here than I thought there would be. If Cory got away from me she could easily get lost in the sea of people. As a side thought, I wonder if she still has my coin.

I pull her up so I could speak into her ear. It's loud and I need to know, "Do you have the coin I gave you yesterday?"

She nods and pulls it out of her dress's pocket. I had no idea that dress had pockets. Nice.

I grab the coin and say a few words in my mind, turning it into a necklace. I round my hands around her neck and see the little chain she was already wearing.

"Take off the other necklace." Then as an after thought, I say, "Please."

Cory looks confused and then shakes her head, "I never take

it off."

I shouldn't push it, but I am. "You can put it back on as soon as we leave."

She remains still.

Whatever. I grab the necklace and yank it off and I ignore the gasp and guilt I feel. I can't unclasp the chain I was holding, to be honest this is a lot harder than it looks. When I get the stupid necklace into place I say, "Don't take this off." Then, at her worrisome eyes, I add, "What?"

"Uh, nothing." She is looking around as if she is seeing the party for the first time. "I need to use the bathroom?"

Um. Okay?

"Look, I'm sorry about the necklace, I'll fix it." I hold out my hand with the yellow amber charm I replaced with the coin but she doesn't look at me, or the charm. She looks lost.

"Are you planning on taking off?" I am pretty sure I am seeing a flight response to something.

"No," But her eyes are telling me a different story.

"Then what's the matter?"

I can see her trying to fight some sudden anxiety. I have no idea why she's freaking out right now. Taking it upon myself to sooth her, yet again, I grab her hand and she discreetly tries to wiggle free, but that's not happening. I grip her hand a little tighter, letting her know she is not going anywhere. I walk her to the bathroom, all the while slipping the amber stone into my pocket.

I wait outside the bathroom for at least five minutes before I knocked making sure she didn't sneak out the window. I begin doubting my resolve to actually go through with any of my plans tonight. She's turning this date into a babysitting gig.

When she finally opens the bathroom door I grab her wrist and walk towards the living room. Aaron calls out from the kitchen bar. He's the same height as me, dark mocha skin, dark brown-black eyes, with a bright, wide smile. Tonight he's wearing a red Chicago Bulls jersey. We grab hands, pull each other in for the bro hug, "Hey what's up?"

"You made it! I'm shocked." Aaron steps back to look behind me and smiles, if you can believe it, even bigger now.

"And who is this beautiful lady?" He holds out his hand. Cory takes it and in what I assume is her professional, friendly tone, answers, "Cory." She also found a way to get rid of my hand. She stuffs both her hands into her dress and looks around to play the shy routine again.

Seeing her close down bothers me, but not in the way it would have just ten minutes ago. Something is different about her. Something is way off and I have no idea what it is.

"Well Cory, how do you know my man here?"

I watch Cory as her whole countenance morphs from shy to polite. She shifts from one foot to the other, "Who doesn't know Shane?" She shrugs.

Aaron agrees with her and then begins to tell her how he and I know each other. Then, as if it were an afterthought, he offers her a drink.

“Water is fine,” Again she smiles at Aaron politely.

“Sure there are some bottles out back, let me take you there.” He tucks his hand around her elbow and tells me he will be right back. She's safe. I know Aaron, and he is a good guy. Probably a nicer guy to women than I am.

I grab a beer from the refrigerator and wait a few more minutes before I walk outside to the fire pit. I scan the people, looking for Aaron and Cory. They were laughing by the blue ice bucket filled with water bottles and soda. I sit my ass down on the stone bench next to the fire pit and watch the flames dance, as I run tomorrow's to-do list in my mind. Being around fire always calms me down.

Five minutes later I see Cory with a girl, and then later I see a different woman walking with Cory and the first strange woman.

Aaron dares to come sit by me without Cory and says, "Damn. That girl is smoking."

I nod.

"So what's going on between you two?" He rubs his hands together and I can't stand to look at his overly cheery face right now.

I look at him and give him a half smile, "She's a waiter at Amber Line. We're just hanging out."

That's when a few things hit me. Did I really bring Cory to my friend's house? Was I really thinking about sleeping with a human? How did this get so out of whack, so fast? I have lusted after girls before but this is different. I am actually in public with a girl.

I run my free hand through my messy-ass hair and desperately try to figure out how this happened. Nothing is going to happen between Cory and I, and I knew that to my core. So if I know that now, why the hell did I not know that earlier?

There very well may be something wrong with me.

Aaron laughs, bringing me out of my head, and then says,

"Yeah I figured. Well I am glad you actually showed up to one of my parties. How many times have I invited you?"

Too many. "You know I don't have many days off," I offer, ready to change the topic. I watch the flames in the pit ignoring the sick feeling in my stomach while I begin to dissect how I got to this point.

"Oh I know. That's your main excuse." He bumps my arm to get my attention. "You still hitting the gym?" He asks, looking me over as if I have not gained ten pounds of muscle and dropped some body fat since he and I quit working out together. I know he could tell.

I turn back to the fire refusing to rise to his jibe. "Yeah. I like to go in the mornings. Well my mornings anyways." I smirk knowing that my mornings were Cory's afternoons.

I laugh lightly, but then I am jolted from my conversation with Aaron when I feel someone push my shoulders back. I sit up straight and Cory plops down in my lap. My arms freeze for a second as my brain tries to process what is happening. Slowly, I put my free arm around her, not sure what to make of this. Then she grabs my hand and holds it against her belly.

This is interesting. But my gut is telling me something is off and this time it's not just me.

Aaron looks at me, then at her, and smiles even bigger. If I were watching this scene from the outside I would assume the same thing I believe Aaron does, but this not what it looks like.

I look around her back to see Broken Legs ogling her. He is looking her over, completely ignoring that she is in another man's lap. My lap.

An incredibly strong wave of protection washes over me.

Cory came to me when she was in trouble. I swallow and begin to plot. She made the right choice, if anyone was going to get this guy off her back, it was me.

She shifts on top of me, taking my thoughts to the gutter immediately. Damn her. "This is interesting," I whisper, holding her firmly in place with my hands. I don't need her rubbing down on me, I'm still a man and she's still tempting.

"Shut up," she quietly hisses.

My eyebrows raise at her sharpness. I guess she does have little claws. That's rather amusing. "The guy in the grey shirt with the scar?" *Who wants a pair of broken legs?* The guy was watching us and I wondered if he knew we weren't a couple and he was capitalizing on it. Cory may not be mine, but she was certainly never going to be his.

"Yeah," she whispers back, with an odd hitch to her voice.

I pull her back against me even more and say in her ear, letting my breath fall on her neck to make it look more intimate for the guy, "Walk into the house, grab me a beer from the refrigerator. Before you give it back, open it and take a drink."

She shifts, trying to turn in my direction. I assume she knows what she is doing to me as she shifts back and forth on my lap. "What?" She snaps and I can tell that she is thoroughly confused.

Okay well maybe she doesn't know what she is doing.

"It will make you look possessive. And will let him know you are not interested in anyone but me." I don't know why I even thought of this crazy plan. All she really had to do was stay here in my lap and the guy would give up. But a part of me needs to see something. I want to know what she is really feeling about me. I want to know how bad this is going to be when I drop her off tonight and never call her again.

I have no doubts that shy girls like Cory could become the stalker chick who was butt hurt because you never called again.

I can feel her taking in a shallow breath. Her heartbeat started pounding slowly and I am unsure if it is because of the closeness, or the fact that I am rubbing my mouth against her shoulder.

"Fine." She pushes me back and walks past the guy with her face forward. I watch the guy as he eyes her like a predator. I really don't like him.

He follows her inside. It takes everything in me to not take him out with my magic. He is a predator. I grab my coin and use the magic so I can see her and everyone around her. She goes straight to the refrigerator, opens it and grabs a beer. She lets the door close and the guy with a messed up mane is leaning against the counter next to her. Smug smile in place.

"For me?" He mouths.

She ignores him with an eye roll and walks to the back door. I let go of the coin now that I can see her with my own eyes. She opens the back door and walks through. She pops the top on the can and looks at me with a look I have never seen on her before.

She says something to the guy who is about to find himself with two broken knee caps. He's trailing her, even though her eyes have not left me. Taking a long swig on the can, the guy stops talking and looks at me. With my look and expression, I let him know to back off. The punk shifts his eyes and walks away with one more glance at Cory.

Cory pulls down the can from her lips and smirks at me. I try, in the manliest way possible, to smile without showing my teeth. Stepping up to me she hands me the beer and gives me the look to make room for her on my lap. I back up holding out my arms. She sits down and I wrap my arms around her pulling her closer to me, against my better judgment.

"He is still looking at me," she whispers.

I stop rubbing my mouth on her back, and ignore the question in my mind that is asking what the hell I am doing. I look around her to see that, indeed, messy hair guy is talking with Aaron, but keeps looking over at Cory. "I didn't say it would stop him from looking at you," I say in her ear, feeling her heart pick up again. "I said it would make you look possessive. And I wanted another beer."

She elbows me in the ribs. I squeezed her until she says "Ouhf." I nip her in the ear and warn her that it will be worse if she try's that again. She laughs thinking I'm playing. I'm not. I know this was all a façade for her, and for that I am truly thankful. But I don't allow people to try and hurt me, even if it is for fun. I just react to stuff like that. I can't change that about me.

A few minutes later, Aaron comes up to us and smiles with a knowing look. "Ready to play teams?"

"Play teams for what?" Cory inquires, while squeezing lightly on my arm that she was holding around her stomach.

Broken Legs walks up and puts his hand on Aaron's shoulder, "Pool." He holds out his hand to Cory. "Come on pretty girl. You can be on my team." Cory doesn't move.

I pull Cory up as I stand. "Nope. My girl, my team." The lie sounds real, as it's supposed to. I drill my eyes into the ugly, scared chump to let him know he is getting close to pushing my line. "Got it?" If he says one more thing to Cory, he and I are going to have a small talk about it on the front yard.

Without another word I pull her close to me, as I lead the way through the house and then into the garage where the pool table sat.

Cory grabs my arm as she chews on her lower lip. "Um Shane can you walk me to the car? I need to get my sweater."

Confident she didn't leave anything in my car but her purse I play along, "Sure."

"Hurry up it's your break," Broken Legs calls out. Ignoring him, we walk to the car and I look down at her with my arms folded.

"What sweater?"

Cory has pulled a nail into her mouth. If she does that again, I am going to tell her to knock that shit off, that doesn't work on me.

"Um Beth can make my clothes into...I mean, I'm cold and I would like a pair of jeans and sweater."

"Really?" I ask, clearly surprised and devious at the same time. Changing clothes. Damn Beth was a clever Carver. I have never thought to change my clothes with magic.

"Please." She begs, and I shake my head internally. She is driving me crazy with her girly begging. If I could get away from this party without drawing attention, I would probably do that right now.

I open my passenger door and let her get in. Then I walk around and get in on the driver's side. I let my magic out to ensure the windows darken so no one can watch this. Then I look at her hopeful eyes and trail my finger over her knee up her thigh and seconds later, after she inhales with a light gasp, her dress turns into a pair of jeans. She quickly wraps her arms around her stomach and bra.

Oops. Didn't think this one through, but I wouldn't change it now.

Then I slide my finger down her arm causing goose bumps on her and she is wearing my favorite sweater.

She looks over her clothes and pulls at the sweater. "What is this?"

"It's mine. It will look believable if you are wearing something I left in my car," I say casually, even though it was going to raise eyebrows regardless because now she was in jeans and a sweater instead of her summer dress. She holds out her bracelet and asks, "Can you change this into a hair band?"

I laugh and roll my eyes. "No. Hair down."

She scowls back. "Come on! I was practically naked a second ago, you jerk."

I shake my head and get out. She gets out flipping her hair up on a small plastic thing. With a frown on my face I notice that she took a pen from my car. I reached up to grab the pen and she jumps away from me, "No touch." She looks serious but her tone is playful.

I grab her hand and walk her back to the garage. Aaron notices the sweater. He gives me a knowing look that would suggest he thinks Cory and I are together. We aren't, it's complicated because I am doing this for her so that her party stalker leaves her alone. I look away and see that Broken Legs is looking over Cory intently.

"So what's your name?" I say to the guy who may be crawling out of here tonight. I want to punch him so hard he would fly around the world and become a new resident in Russia.

The guy looks me over before answering, "Brad." I smirk, Broken Legs Brad does have a ring to it. I tell him my name and leave Cory's out because I am not trying to introduce them. I am trying to get a grasp on the idiot that is making Cory uneasy.

We don't shake hands because I am holding the pool stick and lining up my break. I sink a solid and drop another one on my next shot. The bastard shoots after me and makes two in as well. Cory grabs the pool stick from my hand and leans over the table, lining up the shot like an expert, but while I am admiring her form, the pain in my ass is looking at her ass.

I scowl at Broken Legs Brad.

(Plunk)

Cory sinks a ball and I smile at her good luck. Then she slowly moves to the other side of the table, looking incredibly focused.

(Plunk) She drops another ball, and then another.

I am overjoyed to find that Cory can play pool. I am not saying she is good for a girl, I am saying she is good enough to be sharking people at pool halls. She dropped the eight ball and smiled at me before sitting down on a stool, looking humble. But… I know little Cory a little bit better than that. No one plays that well and doesn't feel like screaming inside after racking the table.

Next game Broken Legs made in almost all but the eight ball, but, I may have slightly slowed down the ball with my magic so that the ball didn't make it in.

By the end of game, I call it a night, but Broken Legs is now hot and heavy on the table. They had just won the fifth game and it was getting old.

"That's not fair, we are just getting started. How about first to ten," Brad says while trying to talk at Cory. Cory stands the pool stick against the table and says sorry to the idiot. Before he can say another word, Aaron holds his hand out to Cory.

"It was really nice to meet you, Cory. Come back next weekend with him, we are having a pool party." Aaron is being friendly and that is the only reason why I am not saying out loud what I am thinking about the pool party that we won't be going to.

"Thanks. I'll check my schedule." I have Cory's hand in mine now, and give a last look to Broken Legs Brad, who seems pretty disappointed to see us leave. So much so that he grabs Cory's hand and says, "Carver. Brad Carver and it was a pleasure to meet you… Cory?"

What did he just say? I narrow my eyes.

Aaron grabs Brad's grey shirt, but is pushed off quickly as a large gust of wind blows in the closed garage. Aaron stumbles back against the table and looks at Brad with a look of surprise. Air Carver. Someone's loosing his cool. I step towards him, tilting my head so only he can see my eyes glow. In turn, he narrows his at Cory. He snickers, "Soon, pretty girl."

If this ugly bastard thinks he is taking Cory anywhere, he's going to be extinguished faster than a birthday candle. I can feel my fire at the very tip of my skin. Cory leans into me with her hand on my arm and looks up at me. There is too much in her eyes for me to detect everything she is trying to convey, but I know that at least one of those looks is asking for me to calm down. I lean down and kiss her forehead, marking her mine. Hopefully he's smart enough to get my warning. "I know. Let's go." The fire I have has not receded a bit. And I wouldn't let it. That way, if Broken Legs wanted to play dirty I would be prepared.

Cory stays snug to my side all the way to the car. It's not totally annoying, but uncomfortable for me because I am not the snugly kind of guy. Once inside she keeps her head towards the window and remains silent. I had expected for her to keep up the snuggling bit when she got in, but once we pulled away, she dropped the 'act.'

I am definitely confused, but pleased at the same time. Maybe she isn't going to be a crazy stalker after all. The drive is mostly quiet because I forgot to turn the music on while I was plotting in my head about what I was going to do about the new Carver in town.

I pull up to her house. When she opens the door I lean over as she gets out, "Thanks for coming." She smiles and nods. She isn't giving me a chance to open the car door or walk her to her front door, like I childishly figure I might have to.

Annoyed at the ending to my day, I get out and put my arms on the roof to watch her walk safely to the front door. "Cory," I call out. Thankfully when she turns around her smile warms me, which also irritates me, "you looked beautiful in that dress today, but I think you look better in my sweater."

What the hell did I just say?

Her eyes light up and, even though it's dark, I am sure she is blushing hard.

"Thanks."

I pat the top of my hood, "Be safe, Cory." I whisper to myself and sit back down. I am numb inside, I don't feel drawn to Cory like I used to, but strangely the words feel true.

I reach over to grab my driver door and see two people I never wanted to see again in my life. My father, with his arms folded, looking disgusted; and the orange-eyed girl, wearing a short skirt and go-go boots, eating a licorice with an arrogant grin on her face. I watch as she pulls something out of her bra. The yellow amber stone charm that was in my pocket. How the hell did she get a hold of that?

Broken Legs Brad.

Keeping my face emotionless, I circled a few thoughts on what I would do if I saw Broken Legs again. Next, I let my thoughts discern what my father was up to, and who tipped him off that I was here because I know I blocked him from ever finding me. That way when I left I would know how to avoid him better. Lastly, he was seriously crazy if he and his trashy Carver next to him thought they could recruit me.

The trashy Carver looked up to my father and said something. When she turned back, it was impossible to miss the look that clearly said, "Gotcha."

CHAPTER EIGHT
SHANE

My father mouths the word, "Soon," and disappears.

I grip the steering wheel tightly. He always says that to me, reminding me that soon the prophecy will be fulfilled. I refuse to let my father and the prophecy dictate my life. I have been avoiding my father for so long that I almost thought that he wasn't my problem anymore. I shake my head. Just when I think my biggest problem is getting back my sweater from a beautiful blonde. Ugh.

I push my hand in my pocket and see Cory in her room, pulling books off her bookshelf frantically. I let the coin loose and decide to check in on her later when I'm not driving and I can find out what exactly she's looking for, and why the first thing she was doing after our date was look through her books.

My eyes close at a thought that dropped in my mind. She better not be looking for a journal.

I hit my steering wheel to bring my mind back to what's actually important. My father. He came here to make a point. He obviously knows I took a human on a date and he must be furious because I am supposed to be with some Carver chick. I slap the steering wheel again. I should have warded her house, like I've done mine. At the next stoplight I focus on the picture of Cory's house in my mind, and say a few words that will keep her safe. I feel my stomach drop and I know that, no matter what, my father's magic will never be able to harm her. Trusting my magic, I pull forward at the green light.

* * *

The next morning I wake with a start, as if something was wrong. I don't remember ever waking up in a panic.

I grab my phone off my night stand. No messages. I check my clock. I am not late to work, not by a long shot. I eye my jeans from last night and reach inside. My coin is no longer in my right pocket.

I give myself a half second to feel the dread that something may have happened. I rummage through my room to make sure I am not overlooking a single inch of the damn room, then I search the rest of my apartment, and lastly my car. I try and ignore all the thoughts that are buzzing in my mind, wondering if that trashy Carver somehow got into my house through all my spells. I trust my magic and refuse to let those doubtful thoughts take root.

I sit down on my bed and take in a few breaths and visualize Cory, then the coin. The words seem to come to me easily and I open my eyes as the coin floats from under the bed into my palm. Relieved, I close my hand around the coin.

I see Cory sitting at a big round table with two women on the other side. One woman I don't know, she's old and haggard looking with long, white hair. The other is a slim black lady with long, thick braids.

I don't hesitate, I make myself invisible and teleport next to Cory. The next moment I am standing next to her. I step behind her as she says, "So you asked me here because you think I have some influence over my sister and Shane?"

I can feel my jaw tighten down. I fold my arms over my naked chest and leaned against the pillar next to their table. Then, like I had done for Cory the other day, I use my magic to change my clothes.

Patra, the woman in braids, answered, "We think you are just the person to influence Beth and Shane."

Cory laughed arrogantly. Something I have not heard before, "You don't know them very well then. I have no say in what they do."

The old lady with her grandma voice said, "Dearie you're very clever aren't you?"

Cory made a noise that said she agreed.

The old lady continued, "Then you are clever enough to have noticed that you have two very powerful Carvers watching over you." Cory smirked. "So you can see why we would come for you, don't you?"

The vampire rolled her eyes. "Duretta's trying to be nice about it, but I'll be straight with you. I don't like Carvers and I don't like that you are covering for them. I know you've seen them do magic and I know that Beth showed you how to do fairy magic as well, but she messed with the bottles before I could get them analyzed."

The old lady sipped her tea, with a smug look towards the vampire. Obviously she didn't seem to agree with the vampire.

The vampire continued, "So with the council's permission," she sneered at the old lady, "I have brought you here to be tested."

Cory's shoulders are stiff. I don't know what her expression is, but I can hear her leeriness in tone. "Is that right?"

The old lady places an empty teacup on the saucer and smiles again like a sweet old grandma. "I tried to tell Patra and the Magical Council that no one who isn't fairy can do fairy magic. We invited you here –"

"–More like teleported into my lab and kidnapped me," Cory pulled up her arm, "and I go to lunch with Beth in one hour and a half so you better get me back before then, or she's going to flip out." I saw Cory point at the vampire, "And you know best how easy it is to piss my sister off. It's in your best interest to return me… soon."

Patra defends, "I was ordered to leave you two alive. Trust me, had I been allowed, you both would be dead." The vampire swirled her glass of wine in front of her smoothly, "and I would have become a glutton on your blood."

Cory picked at the sautéed vegetables on her plate, "Perhaps." She picked up a carrot from her plate and ate it, "Or perhaps not. But I can promise you, when the day comes to find out, it will be eventful."

The old lady's smile was so bright her eyes sparkled, "Are you a vegetarian? You have only eaten the vegetables from your plate."

Cory nodded once. Hmm, I guess we shared that dietary preference. I kind of like that.

Patra narrowed her eyes at Cory and scoffed. She shot up from her seat in an inhuman speed and was gone. I moved closer to the table. The old lady shook her head at the empty seat. "One day I hope to meet someone who believes what I say, when I say it."

Cory didn't look affected, "Care to elaborate?"

The old lady pointed at the plate in front of Cory. It had a large steak on it, "Care to tell me how you made all those potions?"

I looked at the old lady, and then at Cory. She was contemplating something. Her eyes moved from Duretta, to the glass of red wine in front of her. Cory's mouth curled slightly. "The wine. Vampires drink wine. I saw Patra drinking some at Amber Line, but that's all she drank. If I had vampire blood in me I would have wanted the wine?"

What? I've never heard of that.

The glass in front of Duretta was empty. Cory pointed to the cup, "And the tea is for witches. You said you are the seer, right?" Duretta smiles.

I'll be damned. That's her. The seer who told my father that I would end their war. But he told me the seer worked for the Carvers. I let my fire fill me. If my father sent the old lady to get Cory then I was obligated to finally take matters into my own hands.

Cory peered down to her plate. "The steak. Werewolves prefer meat."

Duretta was giddy now, "Exactly. Very good Cory."

Cory on the other hand didn't seem to appreciate the compliment. She was still looking around the table. Her lips were pursed. "I don't see anything for Carvers." Her mouth dropped as if the thought just came to her. "Oh," she rolled her eyes, "clever."

What did that mean? It took all my mental strength to remain quiet. Did Cory figure out the food or drink that Carvers preferred? If so, then she needed to explain that crap because I was looking at the table and the only thing I would have ate was the vegetables but she had already eaten them.

Cory looked around again and shrugged, "I get it, I do, but there is nothing here for fairies."

"You're right, there is nothing for fairies at this table, anymore. You ate it already." She stood up and held out her hand. I almost pushed Cory back in her seat when I saw who was headed to their table.

No Way! Antrom, the fairy's leader had left his world to come here. Dressed in a crimson red scarf, black wool jacket, dark blue jeans and shiny black shoes, looking like a disturbingly handsome European model.

Cory was biting the inside of her lip.

Antrom stopped sharply, bowed slightly, touching his right fingers to his lips. "Young Miss Cory. It is a pleasure to finally meet you." He raised his head and then held out his hand in a formal human gesture.

Cory's eyes closed slowly and bowed slightly, not taking his hand but touching her forehead, "It's my pleasure."

This can't be happening. She couldn't be. She must have read their formal greeting somewhere.

Antrom smiled, "Only a fairy would know the proper introduction when meeting another fairy."

Cory shrugged.

I flashed back to the day my real father told me who and what I am. I remember feeling scared, excited, and alone. I flexed my fingers at my side and decided to take a page from Beth's magic and mentally play with the words until I came up with a phrase to feel Cory's emotions.

I said the words and was hit hard with a massive weight on my chest. She was scared.

"Are you going to take me like Beth's parents took her?" She asked Antrom, politely.

Antrom's smile made me want to pound his face. On top of being the leader of the fairies, he also is a member of the Magical Council. His special skill is knowing what bloodline a fairy is connected to. If Cory is a fairy, he was absolutely going to take her back. If she is a half-breed like I'm guessing, he is going to have to con her to return with him, not because he wasn't allowed to take her, he was, technically, but like the old lady said earlier, she has two Carvers looking over her.

Antrom is a purist, so of course he isn't a fan of mine and he won't be a fan of Cory's either. My fire warmed inside of me, as if confirming this is where I am supposed to be.

"No. I am here to meet you, Miss Cory."

Cory didn't look disturbed by his decline. Inside she was reeling with anxiety, "And now you have. "

I smiled, even when she is drenched in fear she still was presenting a strong front. I admired that. "Would you be so kind and help me understand why you think I am a... fairy?"

Antrom flinched a little, "I suppose it would be difficult to believe that all fae refrain from eating the flesh of animals." Oh yeah, I forgot he likes to use the term "fae" instead of "fairy." Must be a testosterone thing. "Have you ever had something that was only yours?" Cory wanted to laugh at him now. Antrom continued, "Something that you didn't let any one see?"

She remained unmoved.

"Maybe a diary?" He was throwing rocks in the dark,

"Books?" He paused again waiting for some kind of response from her. He smiled like a little boy in front of a puzzle. Fairies *love* puzzles. They searched tirelessly for knowledge on all topics and especially on other supernatural kind.

"The fae," Antrom continues, "are very possessive of the things they claim." He was leaning down, speaking low in her ear. "Some covet knowledge. They search for it and then they never share it." He paused to watch Cory. Her emotions were right in check. He wasn't unlocking Fort-Knox-Cory.

The sly fairy with his devilish, aqua-blue eyes looked up and widened for a moment. His mouth opened in an O. "Some fairies don't have much to claim." Cory held her breath and I felt it. Realization. Antrom was on the right track.

"Those particular fae are very rare. They don't need much…" Antrom waited a second before asking, "Is there a room that only you go? That no one else has ever stepped in? Your lab perhaps? Or bedroom?"

Cory wouldn't look at Antrom, and he knew he struck home. I watched, along with everyone else, how his eyes sparkled with glee. Antrom held out his hand to Cory. "Must be a lot to take in, I imagine. Knowing that you weren't like your sister, but also not like the other humans."

Oh no. Hell no. Nope. Not gong to happen. He was word slinging all the same lies that my father told me. I made myself visible which took the two scumbags by surprise. Cory, interestingly, seemed to relax. I winked at her and she warmed even more. Oddly, I think I could get used to having that connection to her.

But priorities first, I need to make one thing very clear, "She stays here."

Antrom looked over at the witch, as if she had conjured me

up. Her brush off was perfect.

"This is the small problem you mentioned?" Antrom ran his hand through his thick brown mane. Then he laughed sardonically, "What is it with you and chasing every fae in your vicinity?"

Cory looked at me but, moreover, I felt her warmth fizzle to jealousy and hot damn it if it didn't slap on a glob of icing on my ego.

"I like freckles." I smiled, hoping to defuse the tension. Cory's jealousy didn't defuse.

Antrom held out his hand again, "Cory, would you like to come and see for yourself? A place made especially for those like us?"

"Cory," I warn, "if you go, he will never let you leave. Fairies aren't allowed to go anywhere without his permission."

I scowled. Cory was plotting. I don't know what she was thinking but I could feel the excitement for revenge. Okay now the connection with her is getting creepy.

And now her jealousy is moving smoothly into embarrassment, which means she is thinking about what happened yesterday. I will clear that little problem up in a second. So long as I can get her away from these master manipulators.

Ugh. Cory is bubbling with hope, and I begin to worry she is going to take Antrom up on his offer. I can't let that happen. It would be like letting her walk into a venus fly trap. "You're not a full blood, because if you were they would have tracked you long before now. You're what they call a half-blood. Half human and half fairy, and that's a very bad thing. It's against their laws to breed with a human." I tried to make my tone match my words, "Punishable by death, meaning, whoever breeds with the human and yourself are both in real danger."

"All lies," Antrom said calmly. Playing the gentleman's card, "If it wasn't for Duretta and I she would already be punished, or dead. It is because of me that she's very much alive."

Cory crooked her chin as if to say, "See."

Royal pain in the ass!

Antrom cleared his throat and Cory turned to him. Her emotions were solidifying again to stone cold. *Just like a fairy.*

Antrom sneered at me, "Shane and I have had years of disagreements. Don't let his prejudice influence you."

"She's not going."

Cory turned to me with fire in her eyes, "I am not an idiot Shane, I would thank you to let me make my own choices." Duretta snickered beside me. She obviously thought this was amusing. I mentally took a note to will deal with her later.

I had a second to change my game before Cory did exactly what I did when I met my biological parents. "No tricks. If she goes, she comes back," I know the words sound as if I am saying she can go. I still plan on keeping her on this side of the veil if I can manage it, but I figure she is a perfect candidate for reverse psychology. For all her brilliance, she is still a chick.

Cory narrows her eyes at me. Antrom lifts his hand to her shoulder. Cory side steps him before it touches her, "Only if she wants to come back."

Cory looks back at Antrom and said, "I appreciate your offer. I will let you know."

Antrom smiles and bows touching his lips again, "I would

expect nothing less." He holds out his hand, "It has been a true pleasure."

Cory narrows her eye at his hand then back at him, "You have been particularly persistent on taking my hand. Why is that so important to you? It's not a fae formality."

First, how did she know that? Second, how does she plan on getting in contact with him? Regardless of my two questions, I am pleased to see that Cory stumbled or, rather, acutely observed that something was different about Antrom's greeting. She probably had no idea that he can feel the magic in someone's blood and pin point it to a specific bloodline when he touches them. No need for DNA tests there.

Antrom watched her for several seconds before answering, "It will tell me what family you are from."

Cory nodded and smiled, "Thank you." She must understand how hard it was for him to tell her, "It has been interesting." She bows, touching her forehead with her fingers and walks quickly toward the exit.

I follow her out, a little miffed that she ignored me all together when she left. I pushed past the front door, didn't see her, so I pulled the coin from my pocket. She was around the corner texting someone. I teleported to her, forgetting I just did this out in the open where anyone could see. I looked around hoping my accident went unnoticed.

Cory was the only one looking at me. I knew it and felt it, "You're mad at me."

She opened her mouth and shut it. Then did that again.

I held up my hand. "You can be mad that I stepped in and told them you weren't going, but Cory, I know exactly what it's like to be on this side."

"What do you mean *this side*?" Her eyebrows were furrowed and if I didn't have a connection to her feelings I would think she was pissed but she wasn't. She was thinking. Hard.

"I mean the wrong side. The side where no one likes you, because you are not like them. That's the side you will be on. You are not a pureblood. You may not like it, but this is the one area I know more than you, and trust me, it's a place you don't want to be."

She pursed her lips. "You do know that Beth is my sister, right? I know exactly what she has gone through."

Contemptuously tilting my head down to her, "No you don't. Not even a little bit."

Her mock surprise was not lost on me, "You don't know us, you don't know what she has been through."

"You're right, I don't know. So tell me, did Beth's parents come get her at eighteen?"

I felt her surprise.

"I will take that as a yes." I know I sound like an arrogant ass but I also know that if Beth left with her parents, and is currently living with her adopted sister, then maybe Beth and I had similar experiences with our parents, meaning we both saw through a façade. "So you weren't there with her when she was introduced to what Carvers are and what a lot of Carvers want to do in this world."

At her confused expression I step closer, closing the gap, hoping I didn't totally ruin all my progress from yesterday. I need her to trust me, "Did she tell you about it?"

Looking down she shook her head slightly.

"Do you want to hear my story?"

Her emotions were all over the board, but the strongest was curiosity. I waited for her to answer. At her one curt nod I regurgitate my past in bullet points. She didn't look at me once. I could feel her sadness. When I was done I put my finger under her chin and lifted it up, "Don't pity me."

"I don't." It was a weak sentiment, even though her emotions were wavering. I let her chin go. I leaned down and touched my forehead to hers. I know there were people walking by us and all around but this entire time I have only paid attention to Cory, it was as if we were in our own world.

I couldn't take her emotions anymore and I closed off our connection with an addition to the spell, leaving the spell itself in place so if I ever wanted to feel her, I could.

"Please Cory, please trust me on this." I lift my head, pleased to know she let me touch her with ease, and yet not happy to see the resolution on her face. "You still want to go, don't you?" Biting her lip, she averted her eyes.

My fire flickered inside. I bore my soul to her and she was still interested in going on the other side of the veil. I pulled my arm around her neck and walked her to the alley so I could teleport us to her kitchen, a place I have seen multiple times through the connection in the coins.

She looks around after I let her go in her very clean kitchen. I wait for her to look at me before I blurt out. "I will miss you," I say softly, feeling the truth in my words, "when you leave."

Wait! *What the hell was I saying?* I had no intentions of letting her get caught up in Antrom's fairy web.

Cory shook her head and headed up the stairs on the other side of the kitchen wall. I followed.

The door swung open and Cory walked straight to her bookshelf that was literally the entire south side of the wall. I took a step into the doorway but halted, not sure if I should contaminate her sanctuary. Cory grabbed a book and headed back in my direction. She stopped as if she just remembered something. With a calculating smirk, she wrapped her arms around the book and waited.

My little minx.

I took in another step and crossed into Cory land. So much for her sanctuary. I walked to her bed and sat down with my back against the headboard. I folded my arms behind my head and made myself comfortable. "You could always just ask me what it's like there. I have been there a few times."

Cory huffed, "No thanks. I doubt you spent much time sight seeing." I pulled a pillow from the other side of the bed ignoring her chide, and put it behind my head.

"I am going to go," her words were there, but the declaration wasn't. If there was anything I could say to make her stay away from there, I would say the words. Hoping for the best, I grabbed her by the wrist when she got close enough, and slowly brought her to me. The best part is, her eyes are not rejecting this at all.

I turn her around and pull her back against my chest as she snuggly fit in between my legs. There was nothing more to say. I kiss the back of her head and take a drag of her intoxicating tropical shampoo. She stayed there and I felt content for the first time in my long life, all the while rubbing my mouth back and forth against her shoulders.

I don't know how much time passed because I had closed my

eyes. I felt her turn and helped her straddle my lap. She whispered, "Come with me."

She wanted me there with her? "As long as you come back with me."

She bowed her head and kissed my lower jaw. My fire was doing something funny. I almost felt light headed.

"Would you like me to give you a very good reason to come back with me?" I murmured.

I felt her unease. I didn't know I opened back up our connection but I was glad for it, this way I could navigate this moment better.

I kissed her sweet, soft lips lightly. Letting her get used to me. She leaned in for another kiss, but this time I held on to her neck while I kissed her deeply. I pushed up from the spot I was in so I could lay her down. She opened her mouth and I took the invitation greedily.

Laying in between her legs I ran my hand down her thigh and squeezed right under the curve of her pert ass. Cory bowed her back, pushing into my chest, and I rewarded her enthusiasm with a little nip to her neck. If I used my fire, I could warm my mouth, which, when I bite down on the crook of the neck, it sparks a flame, warming her entire body. I've been told it feels like a rush of heat running down the body totally relaxing the mind and lingering over the sweet spots. It is a little trick I learned and I've had nothing but compliments since.

I heated my mouth and bit down, not breaking the skin. I felt her nails dig into my back and heard a slow, breathy moan. I pushed my hand from her thigh up her hips and under her shirt. I leaned back to make sure she was still good with this.

Her eyes were dark, hooded, mirroring my feelings. I pushed her shirt up and saw her navy blue bra with adorable pink polka dots. I ran my thumb over the bra teasing the nipple underneath.

A loud crash sounded down stairs. "CORY!" Beth screamed. "You have two seconds!"

Cory stiffened beneath me. I glared at Cory's bedroom door. I watched as my magic closed and locked.

"Um. Don't take this the wrong way, but-"

I kissed her nose, "I got it. And keep your necklace on, and let me know when you decide to visit Candy Land." At her scowl I amended, "Fairy Land?"

She pushed me up so she could rearrange her shirt to cover her soft, light peach, naked belly. I held out my hand and pulled her to my chest. "When you confirm with Antrom, leave my name out of it. It'll be better that way."

* * *

It was ten in the morning when I dropped by to pick her up. She texted me at the unacceptable time of 5:30 in the morning. I didn't have to ask if she talked to Beth about it because I knew that had she, Beth would have objected.

Cory was all business. As soon as she told Antrom that she wanted to go, he set up to meet with her this morning at the butt crack of dawn. To Cory's redeemable thoughtfulness she told him she would meet him at eleven.

At the fairy gates, with Cory in hand, I was not surprised when Antrom's polite demeanor faltered as he approached. He greeted Cory in their silly fashion and I snickered loudly when they finished. Antrom scowled, Cory hit me her best scowl, so I kissed her on her nose. Cory blushed beautifully.

As a man, Antrom knew what I was doing. I was letting him know she's mine and he was going to have to go through me to keep her. And he did want to keep her, I just didn't know why.

The only way to get into Fairy Land was through the front gates. Or at least that was the only entrance I knew about. Their land wasn't on a different mystical plane. It was a huge chunk of land that they claimed and put a protective, invisible kind of bubble around it, which is why even the humans have no idea it's here. When you look at it from the outside it looks like a huge chasm. I don't understand all the specifics because at one point or another someone must have traveled to the other side, but I didn't care to investigate it.

Inside, you will immediately notice the way all men and women are properly dressed. No one really stands out from each other per se. For example, you will not see a punk rocker here, or some emo kids. The streets are clean; the buildings are well maintained. It's a really nice place if you are a clean freak.

Antrom decided to take the long route by making us walk though the botanical gardens. I hated every time she warmed inside with another rare flower. Seriously, how did she even know the difference in flowers?

The first real stop was a specialty potions shop. I rolled my eyes making sure she saw. *Fairies and their potions.* Cory tried their sugar free passion fruit tea. I declined all drinks and food. I always did. I always had a suspicion that the fairies put a little extra something in their food. I watched Cory like a hawk after she drank her tea. I wanted to make sure that they didn't put anything in it. I also wanted to hear everything Antrom said to her, so that he was not misleading her.

Second stop was their farms. I hate to admit that it was pretty interesting. Cory tried some seasonal fruit that I didn't know the name of, it was yellow though; I declined even though my stomach didn't agree with that decision. Cory kept her questions to a minimum. All the while, Antrom continued to ask random questions about her adopted family, her career, study habits, reading interests, and hobbies.

His smile, although it was smooth, didn't affect her. I checked. Which may be why he wasn't getting much in the way of good information out of her. She kept her answers brief and to the point. Of course he didn't look upset, but I knew that even though fairies didn't show much emotion on their face, you could see it in body language and words.

"Cory, are you interested in meeting your family?" His tone was light but the question was heavy for Cory.

I had opened up the spell so I could feel her emotions at the beginning of this trip. His question made her sad because she did, but at the same time she didn't. I knew exactly how that felt and there was no right answer.

Cory skirted his question and asked to see the library. Once we were inside, she told him that she wanted to spend some time alone to read. Antrom didn't leave right away, instead he watched as she flitted around from bookshelf to bookshelf. Whatever he was waiting for, it didn't happen because 30 minutes later he left, but not before he told her he would return in another hour.

I took a seat and watched her through the coin or with my natural eyes. I did notice that once Antrom left she immediately walked to the other side of the library and I watched (through the coin) as she ran her finger over the bind of several books. It looked like she was looking for something in particular.

After she opened and closed her fifth book I let her walk around without shadowing her this time. I put my feet on the chair facing me. A few minutes later, I was being shook awake. Cory pulled out the chair next to me and started flipping through a stack of books.

I must have dozed off. I rubbed my face and laid my head down on my arm. "Shane," she hissed in a whisper, "Shane."

I opened my eyes but didn't move, "Are we done?"

"I need a cup of tea. Can you get me one?" I blinked, surprised she woke me up to get her tea. Her eyes were pleading.

I took in a ragged breath and got up. I went to the front of the library and got a cup of hot tea they sold there. When I returned, she sniffed it, then drank most of it and scowled.

"Gross." She handed me the cup back and said, "Can you get me another one? Add three teaspoons of sugar to this cup." She tapped the rim twice. Her emotions were sky high on anxiety. I am not sure, but it looked like she may have dropped something in the cup, but when I looked in nothing was there but the half drank cup of tea.

I narrowed my eyes, letting her know I know something is off. She shook her head. I was going to go out on a limb right now and do as she asked, but she was going to explain this.

This time when I returned she turned the cup three times clockwise and drank all of it and asked for one last one but this time to bring back the sugar with me.

I brought back another cup of tea. And this time I saw her rub her fingers over the cup and a very small amount of powder fell into the tea, being absorbed quickly.

She motioned for me to sit down. Hesitantly, I did. Her timid smile didn't reassure me, in fact, inside she wanted to cry. Cory leaned over and kissed me. I knew she wasn't feeling affectionate, so I was mildly taken aback. But not enough to not kiss her back.

She kissed me harder and I felt a sting. She bit me! Then she used her tongue to collect the blood.

Hot little minx! Damn it. My fire inside pricked up and began swimming in my chest. As odd as that felt, I focused on Cory as she took another sip. I felt something tingle inside of me, something foreign to my fire.

What the hell did you do Cory? I asked with my eyes.

She gave me the cup that had a little red on the side. My blood? Then I saw her lip. It was bleeding. I looked back to the cup. Our blood? Her heart was pounding, my fire was starting to simmer and I couldn't figure out what she was doing, but it felt like this was going to be one of those moments, the kind you won't forget and possibly forever regret.

She was doing magic. Fairy magic. And I knew I should toss the cup. Instead, I took the cup and downed the rest.

Cory let out a relieved breath. I put down the cup. I felt different. I was unsure what just happened but I was not the same. Not happy about being in the dark about it, I looked down to the book in front of her and the writing was in a language I never have seen before.

"Young Miss Cory," Antrom called from behind us.

Perfect timing. We turned around together. My fire was rising. Something wasn't right. Antrom had his right hand out, "It's time Cory, to make your choice. You can do this willingly or not."

Cory moved to hold out her hand, I pushed her hand to stop her. Was she really going to do this? She moved past me and thrust her hand in his. His face was blank for seconds then stilled. Then slowly, his lips pursed into a tight circle.

"Bonded? You're bonded to this Carver?" He hissed. The true

Antrom I knew was showing his ugly head.

Wait. What? "Bonded?" My fire dipped low in my stomach.

Scumbag's eyes widened at me, "You didn't know?" His lips pursed.

Cory was amazingly blank faced. The disgust in his voice was unmistakable, "You can never be unbonded Cory. That was extremely foolish."

Bonded to me forever?

Antrom looked around and found the cup of tea. "You mixed a bonding potion right here? Impossible," His jaw was loose.

I looked at the deceiving cup and wanted to break it into a million pieces. I felt my stomach drop and a moment later the cup cracked breaking it in two, then into several pieces. Four heartbeats didn't pass before the cup had turned into sand. My fire was back with vengeance.

"Consider it child's play," Cory chirped. She sounded confident but the disgusting feelings of doubt, contempt, and regret were soaking inside me. My fire was flickering, unsure what to do with her saturating emotions.

"I'll consider this an act of defiance. Interestingly enough, it's a punishable offense." Antrom looked at the cup and then back at Cory. And his smirk grew, "An affinity for tonics and potions. Hmm. I should have guessed." He raised a finger and behind him several men in all black filtered out of the stacks from around us. We were surrounded.

Cory held her disguise of disregard but inside she was rioting. Damn her and her ridiculous girly emotions! It's hard to think with her emotions inside me.

My fire was starting to do that thing where it was thinking for its self. I could also feel the odd attachment, it didn't affect my fire, but it felt awkward as if I had an elemental leash that clipped inside me. I said a few words hoping that I could still turn off the emotional connections. I smiled proudly as her fears, doubts, guilt, and shame left. Priorities and all, it was time to get out of here.

Cory found her voice, "I hate to say this Shane, but, you were right."

Antrom grabbed Cory by the arm, "You are not leaving. I don't have to use my magic to know whose bloodline you descend from. Only one man in all the world could have made a bonding tonic in less than an hour. The same man who has been sitting in our cellars since he bonded the magical bloodlines."

Somehow my day keeps getting worse. The Carver Maker. I was bonded to the Carver Maker's daughter? Granddaughter? Wait how old was the Carver Maker? That would make Cory a descendant of a fairy, not a half-blood per se. I shook my head, pulling at the fire that was starting to attach itself to my skin. I could feel it radiating. Now was not the time to tip the balance of my control. I reminded myself that now was not the time to analyze her heritage. Although, I hate to admit, I do like puzzles.

I reached between Cory and Antrom, using my leg I wrapped it over his leg and pushed him back. He fell with a thud. I grabbed Cory, she was as stiff as a frozen log. I let my fire surround us, but it was difficult because it wanted to explode out of me.

Cory still had not moved a muscle, alerting me that someone had used their magic against her. I turned around looking for the culprit and the fairy behind me threw a knife directly at my chest. The iron in the blade was alive, soaring towards me, through my fire. I held out my hand using it so the blade would think it completed its mission once it slide through skin, bone and blood. It wasn't the first time I've been stabbed, so the pain screaming up my arm didn't cripple me. I pushed my fire out wider, for the space, so I could stand up Tree Trunk Cory and pull out the damn knife.

The pain grated while I pulled out the knife. My fire was changing colors. Something I had never seen before.

Thankfully, once the knife was out, all that was left was a small grey line on my palm. Ash. All metal wounds healed instantly once they were removed. Instead of a scab, my body produced ash to heal.

With a simple thought I took control of the knife and directed it towards the stained glass ceiling, shattering the glass. When the glass descended Cory finally faltered out of the hold one of the guards had on her. The glass distracted them perfectly. I extinguished my ring of fire, and pushed our way towards the doors. I couldn't teleport in or out of this forsaken place, which was a major problem right now.

Antrom lunged for Cory trying to snatch her ankle. Cory kicked and I slammed my fist into his jaw. Stunned, he dropped his arm, landing hard with a bright red fist-size mark on his jaw. It looked like a massive burn, and in truth, it was. My fire was too close to my skin. I hoped it served as a very important reminder for him.

I grabbed Cory's hand, burning her, on accident. Gah! I carefully pushed her towards the door making sure to only touch her clothes, just in case.

Escaping the hard way.

We pushed past the library doors heading towards the gate. Fifty yards out from the gate we saw a long line of centurions. The guardians of the white gates.

Cory stumbled as she pulled something from her pocket. I had an odd feeling that she was up to something again.

Ten yards from the guards, Cory stopped to pick up something from the ground. Antrom called out behind us, "Even if you leave, we'll find you," he said harshly.

The guards rushed forward. I felt pings all over my skin. My fire pushed harder against my skin and my control. Cory screamed as she dropped into a fetal position.

My fire won. I roared, incidentally letting my fire free. I felt the sizzle as it broke through my skin. My fire blinded me. All I could see was white spots. It felt as if I was dropped in a pit of feathers. I was light-headed. I tried to get some balance by flinging my arm out to steady me, but it didn't feel like my arms.

The white spots receded.

The guards stopped and then I felt pressure all over me again.

They were using their magic on me and thankfully it wasn't working. I tried to grab Cory but my arms missed her. Instead I felt my feathers brush over her.

What the hell?

I grabbed Cory around the waist with the claws on my feet. I moved my fire around her and then pushed it into her using the attachment she had made. She went limp. Shit.

I turned to keep all the guards in front of me. I needed to watch for their magic. I extended my wings and kept Cory below me where it was safe. Then I saw something cross my periphery. A blur of bright orange hair was running behind all the centurions attempting to get behind them. When she got within a close distance she paused, with hopeful and pleading eyes.

I hadn't formed any long-lasting friends within the fairy courts, I prided myself on it, but Theya was one of those people who inadvertently put a mark on you without even trying. Not love, not misery, but something good. And if my suspicions were right about her magic, she knew exactly what she was doing, and she knew we were getting out.

I squawked and let my fire fall from me as I flapped my wings, raising me off the ground a short way. The fire dropped like little red fire feathers, as I flapped harder pushing them towards the guards.

The guards dispersed, some patting themselves to stop the fire that was licking at their clothes. Some ran toward the water fountain nearby. No one noticed as Theya walked through the fire feathers, untouched. *Interesting.*

Antrom tried to send in some guards and they didn't get far before the fire burned them to ash. I backed up slowly, one step at a time, making the effort not to crush Cory. Theya crossed the gates before me. When I was past the gate I let go of Cory. Theya reached out, pulling her into her arms. I fought with my fire to return inside of me.

After great effort, I pulled back my fire, somewhat dazed from the morph that I had never known I could do. Cory was blinking at me, ash colored and wide-eyed. I pursed my lips at her absurd reaction. Reaching down, I grab Cory's waist and pull her into me. Not because I need her close, but because I plan to teleport her home. Theya grabbed on to my arm before I had a chance to tell her to hold on.

The next second all three of us have landed in Cory's living room.

* * *

"I am so sorry," Cory says, backing away from me. "I am so, so sorry." She says again and I can feel she deeply regretted what she did. Damn, I've got to figure out how that damn spell keeps opening up.

Ignoring her feelings, "Never trust a fairy. That's what I always say."

Cory watched me carefully, wiping her hands on her thighs. "I'll take it back. I have never not figured out a potion."

"What were you thinking?" I wanted to shake her.

"Antrom was going to punish my parents or who ever slept with a human. I knew he was going to force me to take his hand at some point. I couldn't find anything in my collection, so the only other option was in their library. I didn't know how I was going to stop him, and by the time I found that potion, I only had twenty minutes to get it done before he came back."

Disregarding her cleverly crafted excuse I ask, "Are you really my wife?"

Her shoulders slouched forward. "Technically the bond potion is just that, a bond. The fae use it in their hand-fasting ceremony, which is another form of marriage. We're not married, we're linked. I guess you could say, I belong to you."

"You belong to me?" I repeated carefully. "But do I belong to you?"

She looked away from me.

"Cory," I warned her. Cory looked around and I knew the moment she saw the door. I felt a spike of relief. I narrowed my eyes at her, "You're not leaving until you undo this."

She swallowed. Her emotions were swirling. She pulled the

necklace from her neck, breaking it. Holding it out to me she said, "I'll let you know when I find the potion."

I narrowed my eyes, not taking the coin back. "If you think you can run away from me, think again." She was solid once more, completely in control of every emotion. I couldn't feel anything but I could see she was biding her time. *Plotting.*

Cory turned, right before the door flung open to a very pissed off brunette. Cory threw the coin out the front door. I held out my hand stopping the coin from going far, it floated back via my magic. Her nose flared and her lips flattened, "I don't need another leash. There is nowhere to go that you couldn't find me, Shane. I'm bound to you."

Considering this was all new I didn't know that, but I also didn't like how she was acting as if she was ending things between us. Damn this was getting complicated.

"You're what?" Beth hissed.

I rolled my eyes before I looked at the other Carver, then back at Cory. I wasn't going to stay and talk this out with Beth. I couldn't care less about Beth and how she felt about our situation. In fact, she had a lot more to consider now that her sister was possibly a fairy outlaw.

I teleported to my car, which was hidden at the beginning of the ten-mile dirt road that led to the fairy gate.

CHAPTER NINE
BETH

I folded my arms looking at Cory. "I'm going to give you a chance to explain. But I'll be honest, I don't think there's much that will change my mind. But you should try, because I really, really want to teleport you to a science hut in Antarctica right now."

Cory's eyes followed something behind me for a moment, and then I heard the front door shut. I didn't care to look back around, I wasn't going to do anything to change topics.

I messed up last night by yelling first when I should have listened, but I was scared, pissed, and ready to take on the entire Magical Council after I found out that the same blood-sucker who broke into our house, took her from work.

That vampire burglar was going to get fire slapped next time I saw her. I looked forward to a hand print welt on her face.

When Cory looked back at me her eyes were guarded, or at least I thought they were. She shook her head and I saw them glisten. Tears? Not fair. She wiped away a small tear and whispered, "I went."

"I guessed," I was keeping my voice low.

She slapped her thigh, "I found a potion to stop that guy. It worked." She rolled her eyes, "Kind of."

I headed to the kitchen. She might need a drink. Actually, I needed a large glass of fizzy Coke and a seat. Cory followed me to the kitchen table. I pulled out a mug and raised my eyebrows.

"Lemon grass," she whispered.

I tapped her mug and it filled with lemon grass jasmine tea. I pulled out a red can of the delicious liquid and popped the top. "You used the bonding potion?" I had read about it once, but I had forgotten about it until I heard Shane say he was bound to my sister.

She nodded solemnly, "Yeah."

"Did you tell him what you were doing before you did it?" I waited for her to shake her head before I took a long sip from the cold drink, "And now, you're going to unbind yourself from him."

She took a sip of tea, "I am pretty sure he thinks he's bound to me, too."

"Is he?" I took another long sip.

"No." Her melancholy tone said more than the word. I knew all too well how it felt to like someone when they didn't like you back. "He's a Carver, he chooses who he's bound to."

My anger was satisfied. I really didn't want my sister bound to that jerk-face, but seeing her face, I felt sorry for her. She was staring at nothing, numbingly sipping her tea. I sat next to her in silence until she finished her tea. I offered to fill it up, but she declined and left for her room.

She probably just needs some time to work through it. I hoped she had a short-term heart break. Mine seemed to be a long term curse.

* * *

Cory didn't come out for dinner, not that I expected her to. I had just turned off the tv when I saw a human figure walk across the front window. I couldn't hear anything so whoever it was, was light footed. I pushed at my fire bringing it to my fingertips.

I thought I had warded my house against all super natural, but Shane was able to teleport in without a problem. I ran the words again in my head, wondering how he broke through the spell, but I couldn't think of anything. Now that there was possibly a prowler outside I needed to find a real ward to secure the house.

I heard something ticking by the front door. I shielded the inside of the house against a possible bomb, or whatever was ticking on the other side of the door. A moment later I heard the door snap unlocked. Crap!

I grabbed the door handle and let my fire run through it melting it closed. I herd someone say, "Ouch," on the other side. I didn't know how many people where around the house and I wasn't leaving Cory upstairs unprotected. And I wasn't going to fight anyone out in the open. I was already on the Magical Council's radar.

A thought entered my mind and I teleported to Cory's room quickly. Instead of landing in her room I was at her door. I tried to open it but the door was locked. My magic didn't open it and I was irritated and impressed at the same time.

I bang on the door. A moment later she opened the door, red eyed. I grabbed her hand and teleported us to one of our vacation spots. At the moment this was the safest place I could think of.

Cory looked around and nodded, "I don't think this is going to help."

I questioned her, "Help what?"

She walked slowly to her room, "To cheer me up."

Hey if that's what she thought, that's fine. I walked around our wood cabin and checked the doors and windows. Then I pulled out a glass and filled it with water. I drained half of it and tapped the top, filling it with fizzy Coke. I took a sip and poured the rest out. I wondered if their drink was magically copyrighted.

* * *

The next day I was gathering a few necessities at the small town's mom and pop store, when I saw a creepy chick, with short blonde hair and crazy orange eye shadow and matching lipstick, eyeing me from the door. She waved at me before she left me with a crawling sensation in my belly.

I checked out and walked behind the store to teleport to the cabin. I popped into the kitchen and saw the place had been ransacked. The table, chairs, drawers, and shelves were in a mangled mess. Pieces of furniture were spread all over the floor. Dropping the bags, I ran to Cory's room. The door was off the hinges. I grabbed the doorframe as my stomach free-fell straight to the souls of my feet.

She was gone. Her bed was gone. And there were various odd-shaped broken bottles scattered on the floor.

One Mississippi. (Inhale)

Two Mississippi. (Exhale)

Three Mississippi. (Inhale)

She's really gone.

Someone is going to die.

I let my fire fill me until it suffocates me. Who would have my sister? If I teleport to her, it could be an ambush, so I had to think carefully and teleport to who had kidnapped her. I picture the vampire bitch in my mind and teleport. She's the first on my list of people who might have her. She took her once already.

I land in a small, rain-soaked alleyway. It's drizzling and the air is humid, making me feel more uncomfortable. It smells like ocean and mildew mixed with a musky something that was tickling my nose. On both sides of the alleyway were hand-made cardboard and tin houses. Some houses had tin roofs, others had tarps. At the end of the alley I saw the toothy leach leaned over a young man, no older than twenty. He was limp and I supposed he was dead or about to be if I didn't do something.

One more reason to take her out. I held in my fire, patiently stalking my prey. Lifting my index finger, I crooked it and knocked it on the hollow streetlight twice.

With unnatural speed the black lady was facing me, white eyes, and fangs stained with the blood from her victim. She ran her tongue over her red stained lips. "They must have gotten her," she smiled as she talked.

I was momentarily conflicted. If I kill her now I would miss out on the information about the who took my sister and why. The desire to see her shrivel up to ash had its emotional satisfaction pounded in my head. My fire very much liked that idea. Or I could try and get the information out of her, although that could take hours maybe. I had never interrogated anyone before.

Decision made. I let my fire slowly slither up my throat and exhaled it out slowly. The fire slowly slid out of my mouth, like a snake, its small red fire scaly beads slithered around my neck and down my body heading straight for the vampire.

The vampire snickered, "You don't scare me, Carver." She watched the snake-like fire move towards her with amusement. Then as an after thought, she said, "I should thank you for challenging me. Now I get to kill you with no reprisal."

She crouched, hissing as her fangs elongate even more. The vampire blurred in my direction, I blinked waiting for a hit, but the fire on the ground exploded, shaking the ground and blowing the makeshift houses to splinters.

I looked around. Debris and ash chunks flip flopped in the air, falling with the rain. I brushed off my pants before teleporting to the next person on my list. The blonde chick with the ugly orange eye shadow. I don't know why she gave me the creeps but she just did. And if she had anything to do with my sister's disappearance, I planned on thinking of a very good punishment. My fire was out for vengeance.

I felt high on my own power as I teleported, keeping the creepy chick clear in my thoughts. I landed in an old campground. The ugly orange lipstick wearing chick sitting on a white, plastic chair picking at her fingernails.

I whistled.

She looked up and squinted as if she didn't know what she was looking at. Then she cursed and started running as if her life depended on it. My gut was right. Something was wrong with this chick because she acted as if she knew exactly who I was. And the fact that she was running from me alluded to a nefarious motive.

I pulled the fire to my palm and threw the ball in her direction, giving it a small lead. She screamed as the fireball missed her, she kept running toward the forest. I teleported closer to her and knocked her into a large, Sears Tower-sized tree. I grabbed her uncombed hair and kicked behind her knee letting her fall, "You have two seconds to tell me why you took my sister."

She scrambled out of my reach looking wide eye at me, "Shit, you're a fire Carver? You're her aren't you? Don't kill me, please. We have been looking for you." She licked her lips and looked around her as if anyone could help her.

I pressed my lips together keeping my rage in check, for the most part. I stopped before her and flicked my fingers letting my fire scales land perfectly in her mangy hair.

"No STOP!" She shook out her head patting it quickly. "I'll take you to her! Just let me go. I swear!"

Not bad for my first interrogation. I pulled on her hair to stand her up, "I have a special link to my sister. I know she's alive. I want her back now."

The girl's scared expression melted away as her eyes began to glow orange, accompanied with a wicked smile. "Richard. Say hi to the halfling's adopted sister." I turned quickly to see a tall man, with short, dirty blond hair and aqua blue eyes. He looked a hell of a lot like Shane.

"I'm impressed with your abilities, Beth. I can see why you are a perfect Carver for my son."

I ground my teeth. *The Carvers.* I thought I got away from them. I even did a special spell so that my parents couldn't find me, and if they so happened to pass by me they wouldn't recognize me.

"Why don't you let Fennel go and we can talk like adults," Richard said in a smooth voice as his eyes returned to normal, but I wasn't an idiot. He was dangerous and his calculating eyes were sparkling. He was smiling on the inside.

I dropped my hold on the ugly, orange-eyed Carver with a horribly embarrassing name. She stumbled, catching herself with her hands. I choose not to kick her back down because I am being the bigger person.

"Bitch," she coughed.

My foot perfectly connected with her hip. She slid several feet into another mammoth-sized tree. The old man tilted his head as if to ask if that was necessary.

The answer? *Yes.*

"Is this when you tell me you didn't know you took my sister? Is this when you placate me? Or is this where you give me a sentimental story about the Carver's War?" I blinked slowly, looking a combination of bored and ready to strike.

"Just like my son," he curled his hand into a fist. It was the only thing that alerted me to his feelings. "You don't understand how important it is to stop this war. You don't understand the genocide on our kind."

Okay so he was going to go with the sales pitch.

I clicked in my mouth, "I'll tell you what I told my parents. This is my life."

"Said the spoiled brat," said a boy with dark, messy hair, and a scar on the right side of his face. He was resting against a tree with a white ear bud in one ear while the other hung freely.

"Who are you? Nutmeg?" I asked.

His screwed up face didn't like my question, "You're so selfish that you can't see how much our kind is being exterminated one at a time. You're too high and mighty to even consider it. That's a spoiled brat. One who had a sweet life growing up and still has one. I, for one, wouldn't expect much from someone like you."

"Brad." Richard's warning fell on deaf ears.

Brad the Jerk pushed off the tree and I saw for the first time at least ten other people, surrounding us. "Must be nice to be so powerful that the Magic Council has ordered all supernatural to leave you alone. If you were like us, you would see what being a Carver is really like."

Yeah right. Like I got a free pass.

I didn't like this jerk. Another girl stepped up. She was wearing tight red pants and a white tank top. On her wrist was the beginning of a tornado tattoo that stopped at her shoulder. Around it were several outlined houses with a series of numbers inside of each one. There was only one that looked like a trailer house. Ah the irony was not lost on me. I squelched a smirk. She folded her arms and said, "The prophecy is wasted on someone like you, fairy lover."

"Oh, like you're any better Isla. How long have you kept your little wolf boy on a leash?" Another guy said, with dark olive skin, shoulder length black hair and a longer nose, with a set of blue eyes Mother Earth would be jealous of.

A gust of wind blew past me, towards the handsome Carver. His eyes glowed towards the trailer trash Carver seconds before he was flung back, hitting the gigantic tree behind me.

The earth shook and I held out my arms to steady myself.

"That is my last warning," Richard looked at trailer trash Isla and pretty boy. "You two better learn to get along or I'm going to let you both go and see how you fare on your own."

It shocked me to see the fear in their eyes. They were afraid of living on their own? Was this a cult of some sort?

Richard looked back at me, "You will have to excuse Isla and Amir. They aren't used to guests."

I couldn't keep in my arrogant huff, "They're Carvers." No excuse needed.

All of their eyes locked on Richard as if I just insulted him, "You don't know a thing about them little girl. I'd watch how you talk about your own kind." He had widened his stance taking up more space. His arms on his hips made him look bigger and it did absolutely nothing to intimidate me.

"You may run this lunatic's camp, but you don't scare me, and since you are stupid enough to take my sister from me you must have a few screws loose."

The group of Carvers seemed to encroach on Richard and I. I scanned their eyes. I dare them to try something. Mentally I was crossing my fingers, *Make a move kiddos*. Trailer trash Carver made the first move. I teleported behind her kicking her in the back of the knees causing her to land on her hands as she rolled over and shot out air in my direction. I teleported again next to her, dropping a small fireball in her hair. She screamed and the air around started swirling. It was no longer just coming from her, it was as if she was calling on all the air around her.

Interesting.

I dropped little fingernail sized fire scales over her bright red pants. She screamed that I was ruining her new pants. I felt like I was doing her a favor, they looked horrible on her.

I began to feel all the air around us swirl. I looked up and saw a funnel coming straight at me. The wind was so strong I felt myself being sucked towards the funnel. As I was being lifted into the air I noticed there was no one else around in the clearing. They must be watching from a distance. I was being smacked with debris that the tornado was pulling up along with myself. I grabbed a small pebble. Palmed it, letting my fire heat it. I threw it as hard as I could at trailer trash. Damn, she moved.

She flipped backwards in the gymnastics kind of way. Gusts were swirling crap all around me so I shouldn't have been surprised when a large tree smacked me from behind. Holding my head with one hand and grabbing for another rock, I warmed it with fire and this time added my magic. I told it to find the one in my mind. Then I threw it, barley escaping another tree.

The next second I was falling. It happened so fast I almost didn't catch myself. I hit the ground hard. I was blasted back once more with a gush of wind but it had an extra element to it. It zinged inside of me. I pushed off the floor, quickly looking around for the girl who needed a serious make over. I looked for movement but she was nowhere. Then I saw a lump in the middle of the clearing.

Not trusting her possum stance, I ran at the stupid girl and felt the ground rumble. I stop next to trailer trash and see Richard's beady glowing red eyes, "You killed your own. That's unforgivable."

I look down. The girl's hair was half shriveled and her clothes had small burn holes. I swallow. The side of her face had a silver dollar sized hole from the rock I threw. My mind wavered a bit. I had no intentions of killing her. I specifically told my parents I wouldn't join their crusade because I didn't kill innocent people. In fact, the first person I ever killed was the vampire, and she had it coming. So killing another person was not technically what I was after. I just wanted my sister. My fire on the other hand, was steady and unremorseful.

I wasn't going to excuse myself. I looked at the man who took my sister. "I'm taking my sister now, and if you ever think to take her from me again, we'll revisit what's unforgivable."

"Before you go Beth," he said my name like it was a disease, "I want you to know that we took Cory because we felt she was a distraction, Shane needed to find his true partner in life, which, and this surprised me, turns out to be you, the only other fourth generation fire Carver."

He was looking for some kind of response. I didn't give him any. But inside the idea of being with Shane makes me want to vomit.

"You see, I know your parents well. In fact, we made sure that you and Shane would meet one day. We made a special necklace that would draw you to my son. The odd part is, the necklace," he held up a small yellow charm. The one my parents gave me as a parting gift that I threw away a long time ago; Cory had fished it out and had been wearing it ever since, "found it's way onto your sister's neck, drawing her to him. And when he broke the necklace he broke the spell that drew the two together, collapsing any feelings he had for her. So much so that when I told him I would kill his little trifling crush if he didn't return to me, he said, 'Go ahead, might solve my little problem anyways.'"

That did sound just like the ass-hat and it would solve his bonding problem with Cory. My fire and I didn't like that. Not at all.

Richard was waiting patiently for my outburst. He was baiting me like the vampire, and just like the vampire, I was hooked. "You like to punish people who interfere with your goals? That sounds pretty childish to me. Or better yet, cowardly," I said.

Several things happened. The earth shook, and then a large piece of the tree closest to me splintered, as a large boulder headed for me.

I teleported out and straight to Cory, somewhat pleased I got a rise out of the old man. Cory was chained in a stone cellar. She was holding her legs close to her chest. Her head was tucked into her knees. "I I don't know where it is," she mumbled.

I kneeled down and let my magic run over her. I was right. She was alive but the room was cold, she was shivering and she was naked with odd black marks all over her skin. It looked like decayed skin. I slowly touched my hand to her shoulder and she moved quickly away from me, screaming to stop. I held my hands up, feeling even worse for leaving her in here. "It's me Cory. I'm not going to hurt you."

She looked around and I saw her eyes were pale, as if clouded. What the hell? I quickly grabbed her ankle and teleported to our house. I ran a scan of the house making sure no one was inside, and then I said another spell to ensure we were safe.

Cory was curled up on the rug, in the middle of our living room. I pushed my magic into her, demanding it heal her all the while using my magic to turn the coffee table into a blanket.

The spots on Cory had turned blood red and were beginning to fade to pink. The blanket floated above her. I grabbed it, laid it down, turning it into her favorite blue pajamas with yellow microscopes. When she no longer had any spots on her I continued to let my fire flow to check if anything else was wrong. There wasn't, but she had passed out.

They tortured her. And from the looks of it, it looked like she had been there for months, not an hour.

Then I remembered. I froze time once. Maybe they could too.

I stopped pushing in my magic so I could pull her into my arms. I teleported to her room, or at least I tried. I ended up at her door. I reached down carefully to twist the door handle. It was locked. I adjusted my hold and carried her down the stairs to my room at the end of the hall and laid her down.

From what I could guess she had frostbite all over her body. That's what those little black marks were. Except they weren't on her toes or fingers, which meant that someone touched her. All of them needed healing along with the cuts from the cuffs on her wrists. They blinded her, took her clothes, and put her in a freezing-cold room. I was far too lenient on them.

I herd a chirping sound coming from the kitchen. Cory's phone. I walked out of my room and shut the door slowly. I popped into the kitchen and saw her phone on the counter, next to a coin with a conquistador on it. I know that Cory would never leave her phone in the kitchen, and that coin was the one Shane gave her. He was in this house, and he knew exactly what his father did.

I sneer at the phone with Shane's name in white bold letters. With hatred in my voice, I answered the phone. "Meet me at the devil's playground," I say through my teeth.

"What happened?" He asked slowly, enunciating every word.

I looked down at the phone and ran my thumb over the red button. I dropped it on the counter.

I left my sister in my room, mentally promising her I was going to fix it. I hope my last spell would keep her safe for a few minutes, while I kill Shane, or at least critically maim him. I teleported to the devil's playground at Pikes Peak and waited with my fire at the ready.

An hour later I was seething when I saw him walk down the path. I rushed him. "You fucking bastard!" I punch the ground letting loose my fire. It blew the ground loose, ricocheting a cloud of rocks at him.

"What the fuck is wrong with you?" He blocks the rocks and a set of fireballs sailing at his head.

"You knew he had her!" I let the fire out of my mouth, grabbing all the million scales, and flung another fireball at him. He dodged the fire but not the follow up pyroclastic cloud I belched. The plume swarmed with hot ash, sucking the air from him, all the while dragging him several hundred miles over the cliff, down the base of the mountain.

Shane teleported back, with burned clothes and untouched skin and hair. My fire didn't even make a dent. I scowled. Shane took in a breath, his eyes glow arctic blue as he screams, "BETH! WHAT THE FUCK ARE YOU TALKING ABOUT?"

I felt the rage building in my stomach. He looked around him as if looking for cover. I watch him evaporate and pop up next to me. Shane grabbed my arm and moved quickly to put me in some sort of submission hold, "What the hell is wrong with you, Beth?"

I snarl, "You knew your father had Cory. And you knew what he would do." I spit at his face, I saw it land on his cheek, but then the skin moved. I saw red and yellow feathers shift and the acid hot spit had cleared. Not giving up trying to hurt him, I lift my knee into his ribs. "And they tortured her! You told them you didn't care if she died," my voice almost broke.

His grip tightened around my neck, "I would never say that!" I felt the fire sizzling at my skin. It wanted out. My hands were the first to lose control and I watched as they grew into raptor-sized claws. I swung out, slicing into his skin. Interestingly, I could see the same little fire feathers filling the spots of his exposed insides.

"Stop it! I don't want to fight you. You are not strong enough to fight me." Shane is starting to shake. His power must be swirling.

I shake out of his hold, reign in the fire trying to break out, and get my hand back. I reach down and grab a handful of sand. I let out my fire and blew on it, making several pieces into glass. I chuck them with all my force, "I'm a fourth generation Carver, you idiot."

He growls, hands shaking. I can see the back of his hand covered in little red cuts. But the fire underneath is already fixing the glass cuts. I rushed him again, slamming into his waist, making his head swing, crashing on the hard ground with a thud. I hear something behind me. I turn to see a tree engulfed in fire headed my way. I jump free and roll away. Shane rolls on his side and stands up slowly, "I'm the only fourth gen Carver." His eyes are ablaze and I feel the air heating up around me, then a long fire tail grabs me, tosses over the valley of the Devil's Playground, landing hard on the trail sign.

My heart is pounding. I look around and find Shane is slowly descending, using his arms that were now fire feathers or something like that.

Maybe I was wrong . . .

My fire is flickering inside me and I hate that my anger is decreasing as my amusement is rising. He is my match. The stupid prophecy made sense. I couldn't hurt him, not with my fire. It makes me feel good to know that he is the only one who would understand me, but he has to be punished. For what happened to Cory.

I lift my hands up to the sky. I call on my breath and suck in the cold and I hold my lungs to warm it up. I let it out and see the static in the air. The storm rumbled above me waiting for a target.

A gruff wrecking ball hits me from the behind and wraps around me.

Dar.

Stop this Beth! STOP THIS NOW! Dar orders. He is in my head and I can start to feel the foreign pressure on my blood. I scream and fight the pain that I know is going to happen. I have to obey. I can't breathe well. He is still holding me down, "You are so childish!" He says in my ear, and my whole body wants to press against him and his warmth, with him being so close. I fight the desire; I hate him.

No you don't. Dar says.

I let the storm go. Dar looses his hold. I drop, trying to push him away, "Get off."

Dar smirks, "I could . . . but," I can tell by the spark in his eyes he took my words to the gutter. Dar leans in so only I can hear him and whispers, "It wouldn't be worth it."

I wish I didn't feel a huge burning in my chest. I wish my insides weren't burning to touch him. Being numb would be a welcomed feeling instead of the shame. Dar has my heart and he doesn't want it and he doesn't hide his disgust for me.

"Get up," Dar says as he lets me go.

Looking around, we have an audience. Several wolves pace the perimeter. Then I lock eyes on Cory. Cory is shivering. She locked eyes with Shane as if she's bloody worried for him. And just like that my fire was back and I want to rip Shane to shreds. One feather at a time if necessary.

Dar grabs my arm and shakes me once, "Knock it off!" He must have felt my desire to go after Shane.

I did. He confirms.

"Privacy is not overrated," I say under my breath.

It's a privilege that you don't deserve.

"Get out of my head," I hiss.

Cory holds up a vile so that Shane can see it. I know what it does before I can even think of the words. The look on her face said it all. She was totally lost, as in, broken hearted and ready to give up. She opens the vile and I can see Shane standing a few feet in front of me, frozen like I am. She brings it to her lips and downs the drink. She looks at me and I know she is begging for me to understand something, and then she falls like a sack of rocks.

"CORY!" I hear Shane scream hysterically beside me. I turn to see him disappear from where he was sitting, then reappears next to Cory, ripping her from the arms of the werewolf that had tried to catch her fall.

I take a step and teleport to her, pushing at the stupid wolf who was getting between my sister and me. I pushed and pulled to grab my sister from the black-hearted asshole who pushed her to this. She always found a way, it was as if she couldn't fail a promise. Shane grabbed her from me so hard I thought he might have pulled her arm out of the socket and pissing me the fuck off.

He looks at me with glowing eyes, "What did she do?"

I can't even answer him because I don't know what the potion was, but I know that some potions are irreversible. A binding potion would be one of the harder ones to undo.

Several people are gathering around now and terror is gripping me. I reach down and try to push my magic into her but it won't go. It's as if there is something stopping my magic from entering her. Shane puts his hands on her and I can see his eyes squeeze. He opens his eye and he is figuring out the same thing as I did. She's blocked us. She's too smart for her own good. If she died, I was going to become the first Carver necromancer. I wasn't losing my sister today. Or ever.

I try shaking her. Cory has been out for too long, she's not breathing and she has no heart beat. I feel completely defeated, still trying to push my healing magic in her.

"I can't feel her," I say to myself.

"Me neither," he mumbles.

She did it. She broke the bonds she had with Shane and, incidentally, me as well. Shane is still pouring in his magic and speaking under his breath. Then he hits Cory on the chest and screams, "Wake up dammit! I didn't mean this…"

The people around me begin to fade from me. I can feel nothing and hear nothing. It's like a dark hole just swallowed me. Shane pulls her further into his lap and I see him grab her hand and kiss her open palm. "Prenez mon Coeur de Cory (Take my heart Cory)." He just gave his heart to my sister. She couldn't die now. I should feel relieved but instead I feel weak. I fall to my hands. I feel the very last drop of magic leave my body and I still push my magic into her.

My hands are bright red and burning. Without reason I begin to rock as tears are coming out of my eyes and I don't want anyone to see this. Shane is crouched over Cory and has wrapped them in a ball of fire. It would have burned me in the shoulder but I'm made of fire so he can't hurt me, either.

She's taken. Mated to a Carver. A jackass Carver who pushed her to her limits. She won't be able to fix that. My little sister is now a slave to Shane, the offspring of the man who tortured her. How could I let this happen? How could I have been so wrong? Now she's in the same boat. She's connected to someone who doesn't love her. I failed her.

I feel someone pulling me up and putting their arms under my back and legs. "Dar?" I hear a man say his name, as if it's a question.

"She's my mate. I am taking her home," his words are cold. If I had any energy, I would say something wildly insulting.

"They will find out," the man warns.

"Take those two back to the healer's house and get them help," Dar says with calm confidence. "Duretta. Let the council know that we have them."

"Dar," a young woman's voice says, "she's a Carver not a wolf. How can she be your mate?"

"How indeed," is all I hear him say. Then I feel the wind over my skin and I know Dar is running.

* * *

I wake up smelling way too much of Dar. I squeeze my eyes shut, hoping that I dreamt all of it. I couldn't have heard Dar call me his mate with disdain, and see my sister take a potion that might have killed her. Nope. That's not my reality, I decide. I am not going to open my eyes until my world is back to normal.

"I know you're awake," Dar says.

I want to roll my eyes. Considering he knows everything I am thinking and feeling, I guess the thought is good enough. It's stupid to hold in my feelings around him.

"Yea it's stupid to try and hide it," he says, in the same irritated tone he always uses with me.

"Where's my sister?" I ask while I roll out of a bed that's way too high off the ground. It has a hand carved backboard with several swirls that looked like wolf paws. The footboard is also hand carved but it looks more like claw marks. The windows are dark. I look for a clock of some kind to tell me what time it is.

"Four in the morning. Your sister is in our pack healer's house." He is holding a blue mug, sitting in a thick, dark brown leather chair with his feet on the nightstand. It looks so comfortable you could live in it.

Dar smirked.

I quickly turn around, causing my vision to blur. My head was filling up with fuzzies. I felt dizzy. Fighting the haze, I need to get as far away from Dar as I can.

"I can hear you!" He grumbles behind me as I stumble out of the bedroom I pray isn't his.

"I know. But I can't help it," I relent. My vision returns and the fuzziness fades.

"Try."

I look around the hallway and spot the bathroom. I can feel the film on my teeth. I feel gross. I haven't taken a shower since Saturday morning. It's been almost twenty-four hours.

"Actually it has been close to two days," he says as he opens a cabinet in the hallway and pulls out two towels.

I close my palm over my mouth. Eeeeww. I don't want to be around anyone with two-day-old breath.

Dar laughs quietly. "I had to open the windows," he snickers.

Oh gross. I walk past Dar to the bathroom grabbing the towels as I pass. I take in a deep breath and make sure I can feel my magic. It's there and ready.

Good.

"Don't you dare," I hear Dar say behind me.

"You don't run me, Dar. I need to get Cory and go home and find somewhere safe for us." My confidence is undeniable. He can't keep me here.

"You're not leaving," he orders in his tone.

I roll my eyes. But at the same time I can feel my fire flickering. I wait for the pain to ensure I follow his order. Dar inhales slowly. "You shouldn't leave," he amends, trying not to sound like an overbearing brute.

I am not a brute!

I chuff, "Overbearing brute." I step in the bathroom and try to close the door in his face. He stops the door with one hand. Dar shakes his head, "You can't leave. The Council has been here for a day to discuss the situation with the Carvers."

I don't answer to the Magic Council. The words wanted to come out but I didn't want to discuss it with him. Not with two-day-old breath.

Dar grimaces slightly then recovers. "Yep. Just like a Carver. You care only for yourself. After your tantrum the other day, all the Carvers will know you're here, or at least, they will know you were here. Which leaves the citizens and magical creatures in this area in danger. But of course, you don't care."

"I care about Cory."

"Everyone else be damned then?" His voice was condescending yet again.

I pushed at his rock hard chest and shut the door. I let the water warm and I stepped in, letting the warm water rush over me. I had to figure out how to take back my heart. It's obviously not something he wants, and to be honest it was time I did what was necessary. If Cory could fix a binding potion with limited power and resources, I could figure out a way around that spell.

I try picturing the hospital where I gave Dar my heart unintentionally. I reach out to the memory and take his hand... "BETH STOP IT!" Dar bangs on the door.

I step back against the shower wall and cover myself afraid he'll walk in, "You don't even want it!"

The door smashes open and I close my eyes attempting to stop myself from blushing from head to toe. He flings the shower curtain open and looks me in the eyes. His eyes are glowing bright amber. Then I watch his eyes look down. Damn it. I turn my head and feel the blush cascade down my cheeks to my toes. He leans into the shower putting one hand on the side of my face. In my periphery I can see him coming closer, "If you take your heart back now, you will kill me."

The words hang in the air and I wish them not to be true.

He continues talking in my ear ever so closely that I can feel each word he says, and I can't move back any further to give myself the desperately needed space. "Is that what you want? Do you want to kill me Beth? Not only did you force your bond on me, but now you are forcing my death. How perfect. I guess fate had it right all along." His words kill me.

I can't believe this accident between Dar and I keeps getting worse. He talks to me like I am not even a person. Like I am his curse. I need to do something. I need air, lots of it.

He growls as I feel hands pushing against my arms to keep me in place but I close my eyes and focus on being alone. I use my magic to push free of him and without thinking of where, I teleport.

When I open my eyes, I am still naked, surrounded by trees, gnarly, bare-naked grey trees. Everything looks dead. Wherever I am, it's winter before the snow. The ground looks unforgiving, haunted and decaying. To my right I see something dark. It's a large brown bear.

The bear looks me over and sniffs. I see something dangling from its neck. It looks like a silver charm. A bear wearing a necklace? I flash back to a conversation Dar and I had in the hospital. He had said the bear wore a necklace around its neck.

So this is the bear that attacked Dar.

Feeling more confident by the second, I pick up a twig and turn it into dark blue jeans. I pull them on noting that the bear is still watching me with vague interest. I pick up a rock and turn it into a grey-blue baseball t-shirt.

Then I pick up another rock and bounce it in my hand contemplating how best to get the beast's attentions. I have never done this before but right now I am not afraid of getting mauled. I am not afraid of anything – Dar, Carvers, death.

"Hey!" I yell out as I throw the rock in the bear's direction, careful not to kill it.

The bear yawns at me as if it knows exactly what I am doing. I point in its direction, "You and I have some unfinished business." The bear transforms quickly into an old lady with stringy, grey-white hair. Her fingers are skinny and long. They wiggle in a circle causing a blue fire to encircle us.

A bear shifter? I read that some powerful witches could shift. I didn't expect the bear that attacked Dar to be an old lady though.

I roll my eyes, "Your magic can't contain me, witch."

The witch rolls her eyes at me and says mockingly, "Carvers are so ignorant when it comes to practical magic." My jaw drops a little with her cocky attitude. "You're all unrefined potential. Always running into situations without a plan."

I shrug, "Yep that's us. But then again, we're left to human parents to raise us instead of getting real training."

"Top of the power pyramid and still whining?" She purses her lips. "Tell me what you want."

She was right. I didn't have a plan so I blurted out, "You stabbed a young wolf boy when he was young, nearly killed him." I was unsure if I was here to lecture her or hurt her.

The witch looked me over with a new appreciative smile, "Bethany." The way she says my name sounds like she knows me, "What took you so long?"

A little confused at her comment, I shrug. It would make sense for me to go after the witch that hurt Dar. If he died I definitely would have gone looking for her. "If Dar died I would have killed you," I say, sincerely. "But since he lived I didn't think about it."

The old witch seemed to contemplate what I said, "Hmm. So why are you here now?"

"I needed some air," I answer honestly. Knowing she wouldn't get it.

She smirks, "Mmmh." She nods and asks carefully, "So this is a chance meeting?" Her eyes narrow at me, "Or are you running from someone with glowing amber eyes?"

She was just guessing. I knew she didn't know anything.

Her bright, white teeth gleamed in her grin. "Ah. I see. Well, why don't you tell me what's going on. I am a witch after all. I have plenty of experience."

I can feel my fire tightening. She can't help with anything. "You're a witch. Your power is useless."

The witch stiffens and I can tell my comment bothers her, "I have more knowledge than you in every way. Your power does not define you." She says with cold disapproval. "Now, what happened with Dar?" She asks carefully.

"That's none of your business," I drop my chin, daring her to push me.

Her fingers touch her lips, then start tapping, thoughtfully. "You should be thanking me," she mumbles, while looking around me absently, "without me, you would be miserably ignorant of who your true mate is."

My jaw tightens, "You have no idea, witch. I am beyond miserable." I can see that my words have caused her jaw to drop some, "Ignorance would be preferred to this."

The witch chucks a blue felt bag at me. I grab it with my right hand and use my fire to burn it, except it isn't turning to ash like it should have. Curiously I look at the bag that is immune to my fire. I open it up to see several small bones inside. I drop it and back up. The witch rushes to me and moves me out of the way.

Crap! She's a seer. *The Seer?*

"No!" I try to push her away but she turns and smiles at me as if she is satisfied.

"Everything is as it should be," she says, wiping off her dress with a smile.

What? "Everything is ruined!" I try and grab her but she backs up quickly, way too quickly for an old woman. Then I hear her laughing. A big, long, relieved laugh. I want to scream, but instead I yell, "So Dar is supposed to hate me? He's supposed to be ashamed of me? Is that your brilliant plan?" I slap my thigh.

She was still smiling when she answered, "He does not hate you. If he hated you, he wouldn't still have your heart."

I point at her then in the direction I assume Dar lives, "That's because if I take it back he dies."

She snickers, "That's ridiculous. He doesn't die if you take back your heart." She watches me and smiles as if I'm a child. It's starting to get annoying. "Is that what you think will happen? Who told you that?"

"He did," I can feel my nose flare out.

She tilts her head like a sweet old lady. "No, sweet Bethany," Then she grabs my hand and pats it. "You will die if you take back your heart against his will. Once you make a promise with your blood language you bind yourself to it. If you break your promise you die. He has made no promise or claimed you as his mate so, he will live no matter what."

I pull my hand back, "Then why did he say that?" I ask myself out loud.

The old witch softens, "Because he doesn't hate you."

I scoff. She has no idea. She stands there looking hopeful, "You don't know him."

Her eyes glinted, "I do. I know you, too. I am the one who knew you two had to be together or the Carver's war was going to destroy this planet."

The planet? That sounds a bit brash.

Doubting her, I say, "The humans are pretty resourceful. If it weren't for them trying to eradicate the supernatural powerhouse, the potion master wouldn't have been forced to make the first Carver."

Everyone knew the humans had kidnapped and tortured the poor fairy until he made a creature that would overpower the supernatural. What the humans stupidly overlooked was that if Carvers were more powerful than the supernatural, we were too powerful for them as well. My mouth twisted a bit before adding, "Plus, if you're the seer then you're the one who told my parents about Shane being my match."

The witch looks me over and shakes her head like a mom would at a kid that didn't know better. "The Carvers misinterpreted my prophecy. And I had no reason to clarify it because their actions would set you and Shane on the right course, being that you would bond with your high school crush, making you stronger because Dar is a good anchor. He's smart, responsible and is easily the most powerful Alpha living today, and yet he keeps his dominance low so no one can tell."

I kind of already figured out the misinterpretation of match so I didn't dwell on that. "I don't think he hides it like you think. I can feel his power." Or maybe it was because I gave him my heart and had to obey him now.

"Want to know something? Carvers don't ever mate with other Carvers. So every first, second, third and forth generation Carver were born by two people who didn't have any affection for each other, they did it to breed a stronger bloodline."

My nose crinkled. The rebels that did that repulsed me. They hated the supernaturals on principle. It's supernatural racism. And it's disturbing to even think about it.

She continued, “As you’ve noticed, Carvers are not too keen on humans. Most Carvers hate them as much as the supernaturals, even though they are pretty defensive, unless you count their ingenuity. Except you,” the old lady smiled in pride, “because of Cory, you have a soft spot for them."

This was not what I wanted when I thought of getting some air. "Yes except she’s not all human." I should have teleported to her and not to… wherever I am. "I need to get back to her."

The witch shakes her head condescendingly, "She is not your responsibility anymore."

The hell she says! "She is MY sister!"

The witch picked up her blue bag, "She’s Shane's now, and you know it."

That pissed me off to no end. How did she know this? "Is this a fun game? Playing matchmaker? He only gave her his heart because he felt guilty for what she did to unbind them."

The old lady witch sucked in a haggard breath, looking to the sky before answering. "Cory would have fallen in love with Shane already if it wasn't for your meddling parents that put a love spell on that stupid necklace."

I laugh haughtily, "What are you trying to say? That I messed things up for Cory and Shane? Because of that damn necklace?"

"No." The old lady folded her arms. "Shane is a Carver, he would have felt the pull towards his mate, which is Cory. The reason he didn’t go after her was because his adopted family hurt him in every way they could. And his real father wasn’t any better. He doesn’t trust, and he doesn’t open up, and he is practically friendless. The necklace was made for you and Shane, so when Cory put it on the spell mutated. I think that’s why Cory started showing more of her fae power. The modicum of magic inside her began working non-stop against the spell. With her magic in over drive, it would also strengthen it, making her magical traits show themselves."

"What traits?" I heard myself ask, dumbfounded at how much this woman knew.

"Potions," The witch made it sound as if I should have known.

I should have.

She continued, "Carvers are special creatures." It was the first time I have ever heard someone say that word affectionately. To be honest, it was almost uncomfortable. Even I didn't talk too positively about my kind. "They have all four blood lines. Three of the four all have special bonds to the perfect match. Werewolves and fairies have mates and vampires have husband and brides. Witches have soul mates, and those are hard to find because we are more like humans, we don't feel a magical pull, we have the human pull which could be intrigue or attraction, and most of the time both at the same time. So when I say that you are Dar's mate you should believe it because deep down you know it's true."

I was beginning to doubt my doubts.

"You had a pull to Dar like no other boy you've ever seen, right? Carvers have the strongest pull to their mates because they have so many magical powers inside them. Dar wouldn't have figured it out immediately because he was young and was undergoing a very stressful time." The witch looked at her necklace with a dagger on it and frowned. I wondered if she felt sorry for attacking him. "But, his wolf would have known if you weren't his mate. His wolf wouldn't have allowed you to give him your heart."

Really?

She nodded at me as if she knew what I was asking but I know I didn't ask that out loud. "But Dar tries to control everything, because his life has been chaotic since he was a pup. You mated with him without his consent. That would be a big blow to his control issues." She smiled at me, reassuringly, "He knows that you can take back your heart. I know this because he came to me a long time ago to get the facts on Carvers and their mating formalities. So the fact that he still keeps you close is his only way of showing you how he feels. He is going to need you more so now, and in the near future, than ever before. I just hope that this time you don't abandon him."

With a strong annoyance I asked, "Are you blaming me for leaving after high school? I didn't know I was mated!" This is so unfair.

"No." She pointed her finger at me, "What I am saying is Dar is in trouble and he needs your help, but you can't help him until you are secure in knowing he is your mate. I am also saying that Cory is Shane's mate and that Shane's father is not going to allow them to be together, so you will also need to help Shane."

That goes without saying. He was tied to Cory so I had to help him on principle.

"You are my gambit Beth, I am putting all my hope in you."

Sobering to the added responsibility, I ask, "Is Cory going to be okay?"

The witch nodded warmly, "So are you." Then she looked behind me and narrowed her eyes as if she saw something in the air.

Hesitantly, I ask, "Am I really his mate?"

The witch peered back at me, "Yes." Then she looked behind

me again so I turned around and saw nothing. When I looked back, I saw her mouth move, but I couldn't hear what she was saying. Without warning she reached in her skirt and pulled out a black rock. She was looking it over as it began to clear to a white rock, "Your war is about to begin."

Not helpful. I shake my head at her.

"It's time to go back," she holds the stone in her hand for me to take. Before I reach for the rock she says, "The poison is still inside him. He is holding on to it." Her eyes tell me that this is really important. I would have asked why, but she dropped the clear rock into my hand, transporting me back to Dar's bathroom.

* * *

I look at my reflection in the bathroom mirror. I've had better days. I lock the door and rest my forehead against the wood door. I try and keep my mind blank instead of reviewing what the witch just told me. My way of letting my feelings putter out. I inhale. I exhale. Once more, I inhale and exhale thinking of only blackness. Not thoughts, no worries.

I'm a gambit. I don't even know what the hell that means. I squeeze my eyes and remind myself I need to… then I remember my cocoon. I feel the lightness around me instantly.

I open my eyes and my cocoon has a sweet, white leather chair. I jump feet first on the big lazy boy looking chair and snuggle in. Oh it's heaven. I can't see anything other than my chair but I can honestly say if this was my heaven, it would be worth being good for the rest of my life.

I started laughing and the fire came out in spurts. I covered my mouth, not ever having done that before. My fire was never predictable. Just like me. I felt a surge tingle inside of me. It was so sweet it made me want to sleep in this wonderful place.

I was relaxed. I smiled again at the tingles caressing my skin. Oh my gosh they felt so good. Like fizzy soda.

I closed my eyes and just sat there in the silence. This was exactly what I needed. I sat until I was practically humming with my fire at full strength. My fire was done sitting and wanted to get out and do anything. Since I was in agreement, I did just that.

Out of the white cocoon I was standing in the front room of Dar's house made mostly of caramel colored wood. Dar was at the bar in his kitchen, I assumed drinking something that looked a lot like scotch.

"What time is it?" I ask judgmentally. It couldn't have been past six in the morning and this guy was tossing em' back already?

"Time for you to meet with the council. They're in the den." He took another sip. His expressionless face didn't bother me. He seemed to have mastered that look. Leaving the glass on the bar, I followed him down a series of steps.

For a basement, it looked pretty clean. I looked around and saw the old witch-shifter standing in the corner. She was dressed in the same dress when I met her in the woods. She looked at me with indifference as if she didn't know me. Odd. Dar stopped once we were in the middle of the half circle of people.

"You may go, Dar," an older, Native American man with long hair, wrinkled skin, and small lips said. He had a round charm around his neck with four different colors. His knees were well above his hips as he sat in that rickety old chair. He was tall, broad and had a belly too. Naturally I didn't like him for dismissing the one person I trusted more than anyone else in the room of strangers.

Without another word, or even shooting me a mental warning to be good, Dar turned around and headed back up the stairs. I purse my lips in his direction, wondering how the hell I could have such a jerk for a mate. I am not the warmest person in the world, but I wouldn't have left anyone alone with the Magical Council. Not even Shane.

When the door shut above the stairs, the Native American pointed at the wicker seat in front of me. I shook my head. I wasn't going to sit down in front of all these people, I'm not dumb, "I don't plan to be here that long."

No one looked pleased by my presence, or my words. Unfazed, I jutted my chin towards the model looking man with a black t-shirt and red scarf. "Who are you?"

His eyes narrowed in amusement, "I'm Antrom." My fire flickered. He was the one who wanted to hurt Cory and her family. This was not starting off well, not that I expected it.

I rolled my eyes dramatically and looked at the person sitting next to him. This person was stocky, with dark brown hair, a red beard, and a plaid green shirt. I didn't have to guess, this guy was Irish. The woman next to him had red, bushy hair. She was pretty and even though I knew she didn't like me outright, I had to give her props on her navy colored dress.

The man pointed at himself with beefy fingers, "Finn." He crooked his head to the woman next to him, "My wife, Roisin. We rule together over the house of the witches." He leaned back and pointed at the old grey haired witch standing fastidiously behind them, "This is our advisor, Duretta. She's the seer."

The old lady was just staring at something or maybe she was getting a vision. Which to be honest, pissed me off. Mere minutes ago she talked to me like she was the Carver's defender and now. . . nothing.

Next to Roisin stood a man in a white button-up with grey

slacks, slick black shoes, and matching belt. He looked Slavic. He was clean shaven with a strong jaw line, dark eyes, and thick eyebrows. He half smiled, showing his vampire teeth. His way of letting me know he was a vampire, "I'm the Horde king, Deyan."

I hope my face didn't express my surprise. I heard stories about this guy. And even though he was dressed sharp, he looked every bit of the scary-ass man that I read about. Defensively, I would have to take him out first if I had any chance of getting out of here alive, if it came to that. Behind him was a Middle Eastern, tall man, with shoulder length black hair, and deep-set eyes. He had high cheekbones and an angular face. He was as tall as the Horde king.

"One of your enforcers?" I asked without sounding nervous, even though I was starting to feel it.

"Kresso is my head enforcer." His words sounded like they were friendly, but there was definitely something itching at him. His enforcer didn't look at me. He was looking behind me, studying something carefully. His eyes were moving back and forth as if he were reading something. Vampires must have good vision. The sidekick must not find me a big threat because he was ignoring me all together.

Interesting.

"And you're Dar's father," I say to the man who looked at me with the most disgust out of all the members. And that's saying a lot with a fairy in the room.

"Jeri."

The first one to speak after several moments of silence was Antrom. "We know the Carvers see you as their chosen. Our seer," he pointed in Duretta's direction, "was the one who first saw the vision. A Carver spy reported it back to your rebels when you were born."

Finn interjected, "We've heard this before Antrom. I doubt this is new." He looked at me pointedly, "Is it?"

"It's probably best if you just tell me what you want, or what you think you're going to charge me with." I took a moment to reflect to myself on how lucky I was to not only meet and piss off Shane's father, the leader of the Carver's rebellion, but now I am front and center at a Magical Council hearing, informally of course, because they were trying to keep this low key. If anything went wrong, they could twist the story. I wondered if they knew how stupid it was to put a person like me, a living fireball, in an enclosed area.

The Horde king turned his wrists at his side and I heard several joints popping from his arm joints. His expression, calm, but I felt anything but. "You killed my enforcer, Patra. Your sister has a contract out on her head because she's made forbidden potions and performed fae magic in front of humans. You were once under the informal protection of the Magic Council while we ascertained your power source and how to destroy someone like you. However, that time has passed. Your time is up."

I forced myself not to show weakness. Instead I used my only form of defense. I tapped my lips with my right index finger, looking dramatically confused.

"Is that straight forward enough, Beth?" The Horde king stood unnaturally still. Only his lips moved when he spoke. I wanted to do a full-body shiver.

I peered to my right, then left. I had a mouth full of comebacks. I opened my mouth to say something, but I shut it as the thought occurred to me.

I'm underground.

The entire Magical Council is right in front of me, and I stupidly thought they didn't have a strategic plan in place.

I exhaled, letting the dread surround me.

Carvers had strong power sources, but they weren't the only ones who could wield spells and magic. I had completely stumbled into their web. And their cocky attitudes were confirmation that they felt they had an ace up their sleeve. An ace, by the name of Dar, who had the power to control me.

I had another second before they realized I knew what was going on, so I pushed at my power and told time to stop. Amazingly it did.

I took a relieved breath and tried to teleport. Nothing. I didn't move.

Not good.

I walked up the stairs to confront Dar and to have a very fiery talk about giving me over to the Magic Council, but the door wouldn't budge. I pushed harder and then tried to use my magic. Nothing.

He locked me in? With the council?

Inhale. *One Mississippi . . .*

Exhale. *Two Mississippi . . .*

Inhale. *Three Mississippi . . .*

I made myself go back down the stairs, into the place that felt like it was already getting smaller.

It was just my imagination. I knew that and I wasn't going to let this situation get the better of me. No way.

It was plenty big. I didn't see a vent, but I told myself it was okay. There was plenty of air. I stood by Jeri and noticed the color under his chair was oak, not dirt like the floor was. Then another thought pinged my mind.

Fearing the worst, went to brush Jeri's shoulder and my hand swept right through him. Hologram. Crap!

He was watching me with sadistic amusement. They weren't even in here. They must be upstairs because there was no wood anywhere. I walked to each person to confirm my theory.

A few were smirking but no one said anything or laughed, they just sat there in their unlatching, raggedy looking chairs that could have been held together with a few nails, if that, and stared.

This was their move. They planned to catch me like a rodent in a cage. They were idiots. As soon as I figured out how to get around their dumb magic I was out of here.

I yawned at them. This was so beneath me. I rolled my back while I thought about a few things I could do to get out of this dumb cage. After a second I looked over to the wicker seat.

I sat down on the wicker chair and reclined in, getting comfortable. Then I felt something move underneath me. I sat up at the same time the movement slinked down my legs. Everything happened so fast

Something had punched through both shins and tied me to the legs of the chair. Then the same bone crunching feeling ricocheted up my arms as the wicker pushed through my forearms and wrapped my arms, tying me to the chair.

I screamed. And I kept screaming. And my fire ignited in my stomach rushing up my throat. My screams were coupled with fire similar to a flamethrower. My fire kept coming out and filling up the room. The chair tipped over and the pain vibrated through me like a massive electric current.

This was too much. I couldn't take this. Then I felt pressure and another snap as the wicker chair punched through my stomach. I instantly vomited blood. I think.

Die. Why wasn't I dead yet. There was a constant circulation of electrical current running through my body. I screamed fire. I vomited blood. Over and over.

My fire surrounded me and had taken hold of the house. I could have imagined it but my mind seemed to be in a world of everything and nothing. I knew without really knowing that the house was on fire and I also knew that I was the only one in the house. The fire knew and therefore, somehow, I knew.

My skin ripped. My screams changed to screeches. My vision blurred to white. I felt heavy. Really heavy. The pain stopped screaming inside of me. Instead it felt, bearable, like a fire ant bite.

I tried to move but I felt stuck, like inside a box. I pushed and I felt the earth below me move. I pushed harder and the box started to break around me. One last push and I was free.

The white haze started to fade. I looked around and my vision was different. I could see currents of colors. I was on the floor, on my belly. When I tried to get up I found my hands were claws, and my wings had claws, and my belly was large, and my legs were thick and strong, and I felt my… tail swish behind me.

Tail? Wings? What. The. Hell?

I'm a dragon?

I could see the entire basement was outlined in a pepto bismol pink. I could smell the fire still eating the house. It had not finished, and it wouldn't stop until the house was ash. The fire had planned to eat through the walls around me, the only problem I could tell was that the basement was already collapsed and the magic was still in place. I was trapped.

Inhale.

Exhale . . . ball of fire.

Inhale.

Think. I can do this. Cory said I limit myself to my own perceptions. My own rules limited myself. There's a way to do this. Think!

Time. I had frozen time. Was it still frozen? Dar could tell me. That bastard owed me.

Dar? I said in my head wondering if the blaggard would even answer me after ditching me to this fate. No answer. Typical.

DAR! I screamed mentally getting a picture of him in my head.

Beth? His voice was soft as if he was unsure.

Dar, is everyone still frozen? I asked letting my disgust for him coat every single word.

What the hell happened? His internal voice was small. *Beth? Where are you?* No way was I falling for that lame ass trick. He knew.

In the fucking basement where you left me asshole!

He was silent for a few moments and then I hear, *Did you blow up my house? Fuck Beth!*

I didn't feel an ounce of remorse for the bastard's house.

Wait, you're where? You would think he would at least pretend to be concerned. But no, not Dar, he was yelling in my fucking head!

And worst of all, this anger was starting to make me feel better.

Beth! Then I heard shuffling and his voice calling from above. "BETH!" I heard him move something above and then there was light where the door once stood. Dar bounded down the stairs and stopped. Eyes wide as he stepped back. "Beth?"

I snorted smoke. *Yes.*

His eyebrows spiked, "You're a dragon, Beth." He looked around, and I could see something light blue wrapped around his throat. And then I could see something white tied around his chest, where his heart beat.

"How did you get like this?"

I knew he could hear all my thoughts and from what he said before he could also see my thoughts, so I replayed everything from the time he left me. His eyes glowed as each new scene played out. I made sure he knew exactly what happened. When I finished he took a step forward.

I flinched. He saw and frowned. I wanted to believe he didn't knowingly leave me like a worm on a hook, but, I couldn't convince myself to trust him. I didn't flip that fast. There was nothing I could even think of that he could say that would make me change my mind.

In fact, I would prefer to throw him into the black sea with a thousand pound weight tied to his feet. He ditched me. I tried to move away from him, but it didn't work. The basement was too small. He kept moving towards me with one hand out as if he was urging me to trust him. I moved my wings, trying to stop him, but he ducked those. He dropped to the floor, eyes glowing and touched my face, "Turn back."

His words sounded soft, but it was a command, and my fire gave up the hold it had on my dragon form. My fire always felt worse when it was obeying him instead of doing what I wanted. I morphed back into my human form slowly, and with a lot of very uncomfortable moments when my bones shrank. When it was done, I was on the dirt floor naked.

Way too close, I moved away from him. He snatched my wrist in the process and crept closer. I felt him move my empty hands and pressed them on my stomach, "Dress." My magic responded to him and I was now dressed in a long, grey shirtdress that stopped mid-thigh. He pulled me up and his eyes were still glowing.

"I swear I don't remember anything after you teleported out of my bathroom," he swallowed. "Please believe me. I would never have left you." He leaned his head towards mine. Our foreheads touched and I could feel his skin on mine. I could also feel his guilt, as odd as that sounds. I hated myself, but leaned further into him, needing the warmth. I wanted to crawl in his lap but I was able to refrain being that ridiculous. He may not have ditched me, but he didn't want me.

"I'm sorry," then he pulled me closer into his lap, and pressed his lips on mine.

Stunned for a half second, I pushed him back. Dar shook his head and I was unsure if he regretted it or not.

He smirked and ran his finger across my lips. *Soft.*

I stood there, aware that I was scantily clothed and he was half dressed. He leaned in and my eyes closed when his lips touched mine. He was firm and fierce and I wanted to break under him. Stupid hormones.

His kiss intensified and I pressed my chest into him and wrapped my hands around his neck. Dar grabbed my waist and lifted me up against the stone wall. He pushed into me and rocked against my core. I could feel a steel bar between us.

Holy…

"Tell me to stop Beth," he said between kisses. One hand was holding me under my thigh and the other was inching its way over my left nipple.

Um…

"Tell me you don't want me," he hissed, then his tone softened as if he was battling something inside. The words sounded like an order, but my fire was not compelling me yet. "Tell me what you want," he whispered.

I would, but his tongue pushed inside my mouth and I accepted it with vigor.

He left my mouth and moved down, bring the tips of my breast into his mouth, through the thin shirt.

Oh damn…

"Tell me to stop," he commanded. His eyes were fading some.

"Stop?" I moaned. He felt amazing. But did he want this? I pushed myself against him because he was perfectly situated between my thighs, and his roughness was pressing beautifully against my throbbing need.

He bit my lower lip. I could feel him everywhere, "Not convincing, baby." Then I felt him run his hand up my dress, pushing the long t-shirt up and over my chest. His tongue slipped into my mouth as his thumb began to circle my nipple. He squeezed.

"Please…" I begged, and tried to push my clit against his jeans. I was so ready to come.

He pushed against my hands, stopping me from trying to touch him. "I can't baby," he said as if he was out of breath.

My need for him was overwhelming. I needed him, I needed to come. Slowly, he moved his hand between us and pushed a digit inside me. I bit my lip. Damn he felt good. He pushed up several times and I wanted to ride his long, thick finger. Then I felt myself stretching as he added another digit. I couldn't think. I need this. I begged him. I fucking begged. I was throbbing and I needed more. So much more.

He shushed me with a light kiss and brushed his thumb over my folds, slipping it in between, working masterfully, circling my combination.

It started from all around me, the tingling, the pleasure, the heat building inside of me. Oh yes, I wanted him so bad. I rode his hand and mounted my pleasure until it flowed out and through me like Niagara Falls.

He continued until I cried for him to stop.

Oh my…

I exhaled slowly, and my fire circled both of us. My legs were tightly wrapped around his waist and I had his shoulder in my mouth. I opened my eyes, worried about what I was going to see. I had bit him. Bad.

Dar was not looking at me. He was breathing heavy. He let go of me and I slowly stepped onto my shaky legs. And he walked away. No words. No nothing. When he reached the top of the stairs he said, "When I get you out of here, be prepared to be bit." *Hard*, he says in my mind.

I push my shirt down, not sure what I was feeling. I looked around at my new cage and wondered what exactly did we just do? And more importantly, could he actually get me out?

Unfreeze them Beth. His tone was back to being harsh and authoritative.

I obeyed and felt my stomach drop.

CHAPTER TEN
SHANE

I gave her my heart. I never thought I would ever give anyone my heart. I knew I didn't possess the ability to love like others, and so, I knew I would never want to give my heart to anyone who was willing to settle for my shitty kind of love.

But, Cory was dying and I couldn't allow her to die. Not that she is doing any better now. I've been watching her sleep for what feels like minutes, but it's been days now. The healer, Sidney, said Cory is in a coma. She said her potion was very potent and had begun to disassemble her from the inside. I wish she had bought that stupid potion from someone so I could beat the ever-living hell out of him. I'm so scared I'm literally steaming from my pores. My fire wants out, but I won't leave her for a second to let it vent. Giving her my heart is the only thing keeping her alive, it stopped the potion's attack.

When Cory had first arrived at Sidney's house, and her homemade werewolf hospital, she didn't waste a second. Sidney had me shoving my healing magic in her while she cleaned the potion out of her. It was horrible. I had to watch Cory's chest cut open, then watch her insides move around and bounce. Ugh. There was black slime everywhere. That nasty stuff was hard to get out because it would start decomposing anything that touched it. We went through rags, gloves, towels, and a lot of gauze.

I don't know how long it took, but when Sidney was sure the potion was all out, she sewed her back together. I kept pushing my healing magic into her but she was healing slowly, probably because I felt like I had done a thousand push-ups and I was physically weak, myself.

Sidney left a few minutes ago, rubbing the back of her neck where I saw the beginning of a scar. It looked like she had a huge cut that ran from the top of her spine heading down. It was at least a half-inch thick. Her short, dark, wavy, chocolate hair did nothing to cover it. If it weren't for my own magic I would have scars like that all over my body. I had already given her my appreciation for saving Cory. She worked hard and didn't once act like saving someone unlike her own kind was beneath her, and *that* is what earned her my respect. She's been checking on Cory every so often, but didn't say much other than, "She's getting there."

I reach out and grab Cory's hand. I press my lips to her skin. Needing to feel something from her. Her hand is limp in my hand, but I could feel the slight buzz around her. She is in there. I just don't know how to get her to wake up. I let her hand down by her side, but I refuse to let go. I'm not used to this need, and it's not something I can easily define, but I definitely can't stop the intense desire to merge with her. Her soul. Just…her.

Someone touched my shoulder. I peered up and saw a blue mug that said in white writing, "This Could Be Wine." I want to smile, but I didn't have the energy. I grab the mug and brought it to my nose. Dark, black, plain coffee, it was perfect.

"Thank you Sid," I whisper.

"It's decaf."

As odd as it sounds, I scowl at her, but I wasn't angry or annoyed. She laughs at me and it actually took some pressure off my shoulders. I may have… just met my first friend. I scratch the side of my head, wondering if that made any sense. I don't have friends, but hours with Sid, with her straightforward words and non-judgmental tones, made me like her from the start.

Yep. First friend.

"The faster you drink that cup the faster we can move Cory to a clean bed and you can sleep." Sid is standing over Cory, looking over the angry red marks all over her chest. Her wounds are healing. When Sid had placed her in here at the beginning the cut was still held together with sutures, now the skin had scarred the two pieces together.

I took another sip of the coffee that didn't taste decaf at all. I continue to hold Cory's hand, pushing in my magic.

I took another sip and ask, "Where are we taking her?"

Sid didn't answer right away. She was looking at her watch while holding her slim fingers on Cory's wrist, "Home."

Home? "What does that mean?" I set the mug down on the nightstand with white chipping paint.

Sid's smile didn't reach her eyes, "You claimed her, didn't you?" I nodded once. It was a little awkward acknowledging this. "Then your home is her home now." I nodded once more. *My home, is her home? Okay. I can do this*, I reassured myself. And I really can. I think.

* * *

I laid Cory on my bed. This was not the image I had formulated when I thought of Cory in my bed, but she and I will get to that later. At the rate she's healing, it will be much later, but I can wait.

She's still asleep. Sid assured me that I don't need to push any more magic into her. Her body is healing at a steady rate. But I have Sid's number in case Cory doesn't wake up in another 24 hours. Sid assured me that Cory would wake up, but I'm not taking any chances.

Before I teleported Cory from Sid's house-slash-pack-hospital she theorized that Cory's magic must have been pretty strong if she was able to make a potion like that. I hated to agree with her, but I did. Cory was less than half a fairy and yet she cooked up two potions, that I don't know if I would have been able to duplicate. A bonding or binding potion, whatever it was, it's not an easy potion. Which is why it only is created when two fairies are going to get married – not just because you didn't want someone to know what bloodline you're from.

I told Sid about Cory's bloodline, and that she was a descendant of a potions master. I didn't know what I expected Sid to say, probably because I never confided in anyone ever before, but her response was to smile with her eyes and choke on her concealed laugh. She said I was in for a constant adventure, living with a potions master.

I would have thanked her for everything but she side tracked me when she also gave me heads up on what to expect when Cory woke up. Either she is going to be weak because her magic has been doing double time to heal, or her magic would be thick and powerful after exercising so much. And that is what started me to worry. Because when she woke up, all this was going to be real. I was going to have someone who was forever connected to me for the rest of my immortal life. If that isn't something to knock a man down a few steps, then that man isn't living in reality.

Cory's scars are fading, and I hope she wakes up soon. If she knew how often I check her chest, she would probably blush.

I let the large grey shirt I magically put on her drop, covering her pale belly. She is laying on top of my bed, breathing shallowly. I'm sitting on a seat from my kitchen table I dragged in here. I am tired, but I'm not going to rest.

I have to think of some way to wake her up, so, with no other ideas, I start talking. "My father came to see me the other day. He told me that he had you and he would hurt you if I didn't come back with him." I ignored the twang of guilt in my chest, "I told him I didn't care what happened to you," I paused. The words were harder to get out than I thought. I didn't like to explain myself ever, but I wanted to explain it to her, even if she didn't hear me. "My father's a sadist. I thought that if I showed how much I didn't care, he would let you go and try something else," I swallowed, "I was wrong, and I'm sorry."

I let out a haggard breath, "I'm sorry I let him hurt you. I'm sorry you got wrapped up in this mess. When I first saw you, I thought that you were just a human, a silly girl who thought if you drank dirty martinis you would look more mature." I scratch the back of my neck. It was harsh, but true. "Until I found out you were sisters with Beth. Then, I was kind of jealous that Beth had someone like you who didn't judge what we are." I smile at a quick memory, "I like how you stick up for us, too."

Cory hadn't moved. It is easy to talk to her this way when she is like this, but I would prefer to talk to her when she was awake, even if that meant it would be harder to say the words out loud.

"When I was a kid, I would walk past this guy who always drank from a brown bag," I shake my head at how long it took me to figure out that he was drinking liquor every day. "I ignored him and he ignored me, until I saw him squirming on the ground. I remember being excited, thinking he was having a seizure. It was the first seizure I had seen. But he was not stiff like I saw on TV, he was whining and talking to people, telling them to get to safety."

I look up to the ceiling, wondering if I should even say this stuff out loud. It really isn't useful. "I tried to wake him up. He ended up grabbing me and almost choking me until my fire burnt his hands." I would never forget the look of fear that homeless guy had on his face when I burnt him. He scrambled back as if he knew what I was. "He started following me saying stuff like 'I know what you are.' My family already knew that I was different, so when this guy started following me it made my life so much worse," I frown.

"One day I confronted him. I asked him what I was. And you know what he said? He said, 'You're the one who killed them.' I asked, 'Killed who?' And he started crying. He said I killed his family. He said I was a murderer. I was not a good kid, not by a long shot, but I never hurt anyone. I made sure of it because I wasn't going to do to others what my adopted family had done to me. So I told him I wasn't the same guy. He said I was and that he would remember my face anywhere." I shake my head at my ignorance then, "I told him to show me. I told him I could see anything he pictured in his mind if I touched the side of his face. It wasn't easy to get him to let me touch him, but when he did, I saw everything."

I stand up from the chair and pace, "In his memory, the person who killed his family looked a lot like me. It was so horrific that I had cast a spell without realizing it. When the man had finished showing me his memories, his eyes blurred to white, then went normal again. When he looked at me I knew he was different. He acted like he didn't know me. When I tried to stop him and remind him about his family he said he didn't have one," I laugh without humor. "I had erased his traumatic memories. And as soon as you wake up I plan to do the same for you, right after you show me everything my father did to you, because I plan to do the same to him."

Two hard knocks sound at my front door, reminding me where I was and who I was talking to. No one knows where I live, so the one behind the door is about to die. I teleport to the other side of the door and had my fire in hand, ready to end… "Theya?" I open the door all the way. I look her up and down, not sure what to say. I didn't want to hurt her, but if she was here for Cory, then all my kindness would be lost.

She tilted her head to me, unafraid. "You're not going to kill me. And now that you're curious, I would appreciate it if you let me in. It's taken me days to find you."

I mentally amend the ward on my apartment so she can come in. She stepped through and walked straight to the kitchen. I shake my head and am about to push the door shut when she says, "Wait, the wolf wants to talk to you about Beth."

The what? I whip around and see, sure enough, the poser is walking down the hall toward my door, "What are you doing here?"

The poser stops at my door. I would have expected him to try and shove past. Pity, it would have gotten interesting fast. Ignoring my question, he says, "The Magical Council wants to speak with you. They are waiting in a warehouse a few blocks from here."

I hear Theya flit behind me towards my bedroom. I want to tell her to stay out of there, but I don't want this poser to know who is in my apartment, "You can tell them to go to hell." There is no reality where I leave Cory in my apartment to talk to those scumbags. If I see Antrom again I doubt we would be able to settle our differences amicably. I wanted him dead for what happened with Cory and I am sure he feels the same, but more on the principle that I am the wrong supernatural race.

The poser's expression didn't change, "I won't ask nicely again."

"You won't have to," Theya said beside me. It unnerves me to know she had been there without me sensing her. She had her arms folded across her chest but she looks totally at ease. As if she planned this. Which she may have. I may not know her specific magic gift, but she always seemed to know what was going to happen. "We will go on one condition."

I looked down at her in a "The hell we will" expression. She didn't look back at me; her eyes were solidly fixated on the poser. I hear my bedroom door shut. I dropped my hand from the door, turning all the way around as my stomach dropped to the floor, worried I missed something or someone in my house and they were going to hurt Cory.

My jaw and the rest of my energy drop when I see Cory walking towards us with a mug in her hand. She didn't spare a glace at me, she was only looking at the poser.

Theya continued, "You try our new vegetarian smoothie and we will go willingly."

What? I am at a loss for what is going on inside my apartment. I know I am awake. I had to be…right?

The poser's lip curled, "What's in it?"

Cory handed the cup out to him, "Wheat grass."

The poser's jaw relaxed for a second, "You eat grass?" He didn't make a move to grab the cup. He is perfectly still and his eyes almost glass over a bit.

Theya rolled her eyes, "We drink it. Now you have to or we don't go." She lightly brushed Cory's shoulder, as if to make this whole crazy conversation into a joke of some kind.

The poser's head tilts as he looks at the cup. I'll be damned, Theya's done it again. He seems to consider it. But then I swear I see something pass by his eyes and he fixes his head straight once more, "I don't need to make a deal. Shane's coming even if I have to drag him."

I open my mouth and Theya chirps up, "Or you could drink it and we can get this done faster." Not waiting for him to agree, Theya takes the mug out of Cory's hand and hands it to Dar.

The poser's eyes flash amber as he takes the mug and downed it like a shot. The glass falls with him when he lands on his knees moments later. He grabs his throat as if there is an invisible leash choking him. He begins thrashing on the ground. Unsure what's wrong, I grab Cory and back up.

Theya steps up, almost getting slashed from his half phased claws, and grabbed at something on his neck that I couldn't see. When she finished whatever it was, Dar fell forward gasping for air in between coughing up something that sounded like a fist sized loogie.

After he rights himself on the ground, I feel a current in the air. It is emitting from him and begins to get stronger as he stands up. Theya turned her back on the wolf and looked at Cory as if she didn't just feel the dangerous vibes flowing in the air. Ones that could be decoded as *you're all dead.*

"I'm going to need a place to stay. May I stay in your spare bedroom? I will take care of the house and bills until you decide what to do with the extra house."

Cory nodded but didn't take her eyes off the wolf, "Um. Yeah. I guess so."

Theya bowed her head and touched her fingers to her forehead, "Thank you."

She left just as the poser leveled his eyes on me. He holds them until he sways a bit. He grabs the door frame to hold himself steady. The poser looks around as if he has no idea where he is.

Interesting.

I watch as the recognition lights in his eyes when he sees Cory. I think I see him mouth her name before he shakes his head. Then his eyes glow as he grabs at his chest, "Beth." His eyebrows furrowed deeply, "She's trapped." He looked at me, not for help but for…I don't know. Clarification? "I don't know who trapped her and I can't get her out myself."

Cory takes a step towards him. I pulled her back and wrapped my arms around her middle letting my magic into her, making her skin just as deadly as mine. If he so much as touched either one of us, he would feel the effects for a long while. Now that I feel even calmer with her safety, I rest my chin on her head, "Cory's not leaving."

His nose flares lightly, "I must not have made myself clear." The vibes around him are unnerving, because again I shouldn't be able to feel them. And neither should Cory but she stiffend at the same time I did, so I know that this guy was a lot more than some wolf. He must be an alpha. A master alpha or whatever they call guys like him that are seriously packed with juice. "The Magical Council took Beth, threatened to kill Cory, tortured Beth because she's one of a pair that was fated to destroy the supernatural kind." His words were clipped but he was putting all his juice into them.

"Fated to end the tyranny of the Magical Council," I amended for him.

His eyes narrow, "And you know this how?"

"I'm her fated match." At my words Cory shifts as if something just pinched her. Worried, I look down in hopes that she's okay.

At his growl I lift my chin back up to see that he is close to shifting in front of me.

"You're fated to be with my sister?" Cory asks, as she struggles to get loose of me.

I hold her tight and mentally kick myself for not being clear. She growled at me before eventually giving up. "Match, not mate," I said slowly.

Dar seemed to relax a little but not much. So I added, "I've made my choice with Cory."

Cory struggled again in my arms, successfully jabbing me in the ribs, and this time I was offended. I just announced she was my chosen and she's trying to get away from me? What happened to the girls that swoon over you after you ask them to marry you?

"I have to help my sister," She grumbles, still trying to get loose.

I let her go on the other side of me so she is furthest from the Alpha poser, "I don't think there's a potion to untrap someone from a magical ward."

Her eye brows raise as her fists pop on her waist like magnets. "There is a potion for everything," she hisses. I take a step to her because I don't like the look in her eyes, but she stops me with a finger in the air and her eyes threatening me, "If you want this to work between us, now that you actually decided you want to be with me, then you will help my sister."

Like that huh?

"Fine," I mutter after another few moments of silence. Just Fine!

The poser's eyes watched us, but says nothing. He is

completely detached. I don't know if he is worried about Beth, or if he is naturally like that. I hold open the front door, amending my ward yet again, "Come in."

* * *

It turns out there is a possible solution to getting out of a ward.

Cory made me teleport her back to her room so she could "look" through her bookshelf. What I thought was going to be a quick in and out turned out to look like a troll terrorizing a library. But to be fair, the room wasn't organized when we arrived either.

I left her to look through her books. I shouldn't have been so shocked to find the kitchen lined with glass jars, I think they were beakers, I don't know, but I knew this was where she cooked up the potion that almost killed her. I didn't want to touch anything, but I also didn't want to leave it here.

If the ward was made for a specific person, Cory explained, then all we had to do was turn her into someone else. She used the poser's blood and made a potion that would turn Beth into him for five minutes. That should be long enough to get her out.

Sounded simple enough, but of course Cory wanted to go with the poser to make sure Beth got out. The poser and I both object until Cory threatens us with turning us into dung beetles.

"I told you the Magical Council is looking for you and you still want to go?" The poser asks. It is a legitimate question, considering it makes no sense to me either. She is turning into that girl that is walking to death's door.

Her response is that we wouldn't understand. I looked at the poser and we *shared* the same look of doubt.

I can't teleport to Beth because I'm not going to tempt the ward, just in case they made it where I would be stuck, too. And the only other person I know is Sid and I'm not going to even tempt getting her mixed up in this.

Dar took the potion and we all walked out of my apartment. On the car ride to his pack I asked, "Do you think the Magical Council put that spell on you, to get to me?"

"I have no doubts," he is radiating again.

"Then why did you have Beth unfreeze them?" I ask, because his strategy makes no sense to me.

"If they had Beth trapped, they were going to go after you next," he mumbled towards the window.

Still confused, I ask, "But you didn't know what you were doing. You were under a spell. One that I would have overlooked while killing you if you tried to take me in."

"I know," He says.

What? "I don't understand, you wanted to die?"

He looked at me condescendingly, "You can't kill me Shane." His tone and expression was firm and unwavering. He must have seen my reluctance to believe him so he added, "Beth gave me her heart when I was seventeen. I have been stabbed, burned, and drowned, and have yet to die. So I figured if you killed me the spell would die with me and when I woke up again I would be cleared."

Really?

"Beth's heart keeps me alive," he almost said that last part proudly, but his tone didn't inflect much.

"So Cory can't die?" I heard myself ask.

"Did you give her your heart the Carver way?" He watched me as if looking for my reaction, instead of the words.

"Yeah," I reply.

I heard Cory's small inhale. Probably not the best way to find out that I claimed her.

"You claimed me?" She whispered.

I reached behind me and felt for her knee. I rubbed it, "Do you object?" Not that it would matter. She isn't going anywhere.

"Do you really want me?" I could feel her insecurities in her words.

I can feel her! The wave of her emotions came at me full force. She is worried, and yet overcome with joy. "Don't doubt me. I don't do anything that I don't mean." And just because I knew she needed to hear it, I answered, "Yes I want you. And I will show you how much as soon as we get back home."

I could feel her blush. I look back to smile at her.

"Look out!" The poser yells. I turn back just in time to yank the wheel and avoid hitting the chick with glowing orange eyes. *Crap.*

The air around me combusts and the windows burst. A large gust of wind picks up the car and tosses it. I reach out, grabbing both the poser and Cory, teleporting to my Reservoir 11. As soon as we touch the ground we are all hit by another large gust of wind and Cory flies from my arms. I teleport to her, and look around for the poser. He has shifted to his wolf form and is running quickly with the potion in his mouth.

I would have let him take care of the rest himself, but I need to help Beth get free or Cory will be disappointed. With Cory in my arms I teleport to the wolf, grab his haunch and teleport to Sid.

Sid's house is in ashes. I look around and she is no where. The poser shakes me off and takes off. Cory grabs her head and I know someone is attacking her with magic. I teleport to Theya, who happens to be at a vendor at a park. She's sipping on a purple drink watching something when she lifts her head, as if she can sense me. She says something to the vendor and buys another purple drink. I walk to her with Cory in tow, hoping that Cory will do me a favor and let me fight this one without her.

Theya holds out the drink to Cory with a shy smile. Cory takes it and glowers at me, "I won't be able to think if you get hurt. Stay here with Theya. She won't let anything happen to you. Right?" I glanced at Theya.

"I'm not a seer Shane," she says.

"You've never been wrong yet," I return. She's never told me her power. In fact, she has tried to convince me she didn't have any power. Her sister, the one I spent time with at nights, would say the same thing, but I knew Theya had a special talent and I also knew she was never going to tell me about it.

I kiss Cory and teleport back to the poser's pack. Priorities first. Save Beth, fight the council, then take out my father and end this stupid fucking conflict.

I shake my head knowing it's not going to be that easy. The chick with the orange eyes is standing on a burnt porch with her arms folded. Dressed in black tights, fur boots, a jean mini skirt with rips in it, and a sports bra. *Trashy* Carver.

"You came back?" The chick says, surprised. She twisted her hand and I felt the air begin to move around me. It bothers me that she knows I was here before.

My father walks out of a half-burnt house, eyes glowing red. "Ah, excellent timing," he rubs off the blood on his hands on an already bloody towel. My fire and I trust the odds that that blood is not Sid's. But no matter, he hurt Cory.

I teleport the few feet, let my fire rise to my skin, and throw a wild haymaker connecting with the bastard's jaw. Hitting him in any other way would be unsatisfying. I feel his jaw give in to my punch, unhinging.

My father flies backward and hits the ash covered dirt so hard that he slides another few feet. His eyes find me. The look of death does nothing to me.

"You can't kill stone, Shane," he says, rubbing his jaw as he stands up.

He teleports a half arm-length from me and throws an overhand right. I lose my step and fall back. When I try to get up I feel as though I am in an invisible cage. I hit the air and it's hard, it won't let me out. I try and teleport but I am still in this damn box!

At once several rocks fly out of nowhere. I curl into a ball and protect my face as the rocks strike my arms. The Trashy Carver starts to laugh, "Get caught in a snare Shane? You can thank the witches for that. They put them all over this wolf park."

"Shane," my father grates out, "do you know what a witch's snare is? No? Had you stayed with me and trained, we wouldn't be in this mess, and you would know how to get out of the witch's snare." More rocks hit me all over my body. I think I have several broken ribs, as well as a large gash somewhere on my head; I can feel the wetness and a throbbing pain. He leans down and whispers, "I will always be stronger than you. I don't care that you are made of fire. I can't die."

My fire wants a go at him and I let it out, breaking my skin and turning me into the firebird that lurks beneath my skin and shares my soul. Now I see the pink lines around me in a box shape. The rocks stop coming at me and now I can feel water sizzling around me.

"Why isn't it working?" My father yells.

"My water's evaporating before it reaches him," shouts a guy with dark, black hair and a black tank top, arms covered with tattoos. His eyes are glowing light blue.

My fire pushes out towards them until they teleport further back. I can see my father saying something to the other Carver. All of them walk into another house and I don't see them, but I can hear screams from men, women, and children.

My fire and I push against the lines with all our might but nothing is happening. I scratch, claw, and screech until the ground begins to shake. I look around and watch as two posers walk out from a house that has collapsed. After two steps, one of the posers morphs into Beth. My indifference to her has evaporated like water. I need her help, and I know she will be more than willing to give it, considering that my father is here. He is the one who hurt Cory and he is also attacking the pack of her… whatever Dar is to her.

The poser morphs into a hellishly large black wolf, with patches of dark brown on his paws and belly. I can see he has a white rope around his chest, as if it is guarded, protected. Beth has the same white rope in her chest. It is odd to be able to see the magic, and yet see her normally at the same time.

Beth looks at me for a second before she teleports just outside the box. She holds up the vile. There is still some left. I pulled my fire in and feel my skin once more. I hear a wolf howl and I turned to see the poser pulling the water Carver out of a house. The wolf is soaking wet, and the Carver is trying to create a ball of water around the dog, but the dog isn't letting go of the Carver's neck.

The Carver lets go of his water and tries getting free of the wolf that had just pulled out a large chunk from his collar. The blood sprayed the wolf's fur. The black wolf grabs the man's neck once more, and I swear the dog's mouth is so large the man's neck fits in it like a bone. The wolf chomps down and pulls, separating the head from the body.

The body sizzled and gushed water, spraying out at least fifty feet. Beth threw the vile at me and ran to the wolf. The Trashy Carver came out of one of the houses and charged at the wolf and Beth.

I grab the vile, letting every last drop down my throat. I hope the potion is strong enough to effect me. I can feel the change happening immediately. Interestingly, I feel a lot deadlier.

I push up off the ground and walk out of the box. I teleport to where my father is using his magic to hit the poser with a rock the size of a small car. I am able to grab the poser right before the rock hit. I dropped him off near Beth and returned to my father.

Once more, I noticed his hands had more blood on them. Remembering the old homeless man from when I was younger, I have a vague idea what he was doing in there, and it was too much to even let those thoughts linger.

This time when I teleported with my arm cocked back, I slammed into a large boulder. It didn't crack it. It didn't even phase it. I touched it with my palm and pushed my fire into it. If I couldn't beat him to death, maybe I could cook him to death. When the rock had turned to a bright red, it still didn't budge.

I continued punching, regardless of the affect. The rock moved only when the poser joined me punching the rock. The rock reformed into my father, quickly grabbing the poser around the waste, and teleported.

I spare no time in following them, keeping my father's picture clear in mind. When I pop into a forest of gigantic trees I see the poser leave a dent in one of the Titan sized trees, just as my father teleported behind him. My father sends the poser into the ground with a right hook. I teleport to my father's side, slamming my shin into his unprotected body, hopefully knocking his liver into a state of no return.

Richard's eyes glow when he sees me. He turns, pulling back his fist. I knew it was going to hurt because he was made of stone. All third generation Carvers have a connection to earth and stone. But before he was able to connect with my already shielded face, he stumbled. His eyes bugged for a moment as if he had lost control of his legs. He would have fallen on his own but the poser, in wolf form, latched onto his neck, effectively breaking a large hole in the side of my father's neck.

The wolf continues to snarl and rip apart my father's body. I stand, numb, not feeling anything for what bloody mangled mess my father ends up as. He can't hurt anyone now, and there is no way of healing past that.

That's the interesting thing about Carvers. They have the potential to be immortal but if someone chops off your head, pulls out your heart, or wounds you so far, you can die. We were not infallible; we are just like the other super naturals that can succumb to death.

When the wolf finished, he phased back to human. His eyes are still amber but I hold out my arm, unafraid, offering to return him to his pack lands. He wipes off the blood as best he can, but he is covered in bits of flesh.

The poser took off the second we popped into his pack lands. He was headed to Beth, who has Trashy Carver in a triangle choke hold. The girl's face is bloody, her eyes are glowing orange, and it is pretty clear that the tornados circling were her power.

I run to the last house my father had came out of, and let my fire rise to my eyes, effectively turning them into the Phoenix's eyes. There are no pink lines, or any color lines keeping anyone inside.

I found the basement door magically locked, so the people are obviously down there. I burn the door to ash in moments. When I am half way down the stairs, I am tripped and several big men start punching my face. I fill with fire, letting it out of my hands, "I'm not here to hurt you, but if you don't get off me, I'm going to burn each and every one of you to ash." They got up, amber eyes glowing from most of them.

The floor is sopping wet and I am covered in mud. One older man with buzzed, light hair clearly doesn't trust me. Another man is next to him who could pass as his son, ridden with tattoos on his knuckles, arms and collar looks like he is about to snap, except, his eyes aren't glowing. He looks at me with the same scowl as the man that looked like his father.

The others are all crowded behind the two macho heads. I pointed at the stairs, "They're gone." The father and son stayed in between the rest of the survivors and myself. As they leave, single file up the stairs, I look around to see what had happened down here.

Behind me I saw a lump. It was covered in mud. It looked dead. Looked back to the two men wondering if they were going to take the dead body up top.

The older man had been watching me, curiosity mixed with hatred, "She's a bloodsucker. We don't share our blood with them." I wasn't sure if he hated me or the dead person more.

The Menace, next to him, flinched when he talked about blood.

I turned back around, not sure I wanted to actually… wait. Blood suckers turn to ash when they die. I kneel down next to the body and push the face back that was malformed and practically skinned. Sid.

No! "Sid?" I felt for a pulse in the sagged water saturated skin. Not sure exactly if vampires had pulses. Nothing felt alive under my skin. I can feel my fire rattling in my chest. I don't want her to die. She had helped me when I needed her the most – she healed Cory.

The Menace had somehow walked over to me without a sound. He knelt down and let his finger turn into a claw. "If you want to save her, you have to give her your blood, Carver. Are you willing to do that?"

"Do it," I told him.

He sliced a huge gash down my arm. Blood erupted, and so did some of my fire. I told my fire not to harm her. The boy slowly backed up as my fire floated in the air around Sid and I.

I let the blood drop down to her lips. It wasn't seconds before her eyes opened, shining winter-white. In a frenzy, she grabbed my arm and pulled it to her mouth. I expected it to hurt worse than it did. I expected I was going to want to throw up, knowing what I was doing, but the feeling didn't come. Instead I was mesmerized, watching her new skin solidify over her face and body.

Sid threw me back as her eyes darkened back to their natural color, "You idiot! You can't feed me fresh blood!" She was pissed, the ungrateful chick.

Unrepentant, "You were dying."

She wipes the blood from her face. She closes her eyes and starts shaking. "Get out," she growls. Her fangs elongating.

My fire floats over to her. She opens her eyes as the little red beads fall on her like rain. Her skin soaks them up without any harm done. I have no idea what my fire is doing. I stand up next to the Menace. We watch as she begins spasming on the ground.

I try calling to my fire, but it isn't listening so I rush to her side. Her eyes switch from winter-white, to amber, then to my Carver-blue. I grab her wrists to stop her from moving and to pull my fire directly from her.

Finally, the red beads came out her mouth and she fell limp. The fire took its place in my skin and I wait. This time, when I touch her neck, I feel a pulse.

She slapped my hand lightly, "I'm fine Shane. Stop pawing me." She opened her eyes that were not glowing and sat up. Then she smiled from ear to ear, "That's pretty intense."

"What is?" The Menace behind me asked. I can hear the curiosity in his tone. He isn't disgusted, he is seriously curious.

She looks at him for a half a second before looking back at me. She pushes herself up and offers to help me up, oddly. I stand up with her help, "So does that mean you'll live and that you're not mad at me anymore?"

"I've heard that vampires that drink fresh blood can't drink anything else. They are instantly addicted," she responds.

"So you're addicted to my blood now?"

She shakes her head, "No, I don't think so. But I feel different. Like I could run for years."

"Vampires *can* run for years," Couldn't they?

"Not me. I'm half vampire, half werewolf so I get tired after about 100 miles or so."

That explains the amber eyes and white eyes. "But now you have a pulse, does that mean something?"

She bites her lower lip, looking every bit as worried as I feel, "I don't know."

"Mikhail!" The old macho dad calls from upstairs, "If the bloodsucker's alive, tell her she needs to get up here. There are several bodies and more wounded in Gunner's house."

I turned around to Mikhail, the Menace. He is looking somewhat conflicted. Ending his conflict, he presses his lips together and tilts his head to the side, curtly. "You're the only healer we have, Sidney."

Before I can say something, Sid walks past me, yelling up the stairs, "Coming McGrave." I think she murmured the word asshole under her breath. She jerks her chin at the boy when she passed, "I won't forget what he did."

He looked unaffected.

I follow her out and the old man looks at us both and sneers. "Tell the vampire that the bodies are over there," he points to the house my father had been in.

Sid snorts and walks in the direction of the house. I want to follow, but the poser grabs my shoulder, "They're still here."

I turn around, pissed, fueling my fire. Waiting for another dumbass Carver to come at me. I see a line of people floating in the air. Antrom is the first I recognize because he always wears that damn red scarf. He is watching me carefully, guarded. Reminds me of playing poker when your opponent is thinking of calling, but is unsure if they have a good enough hand to win.

Next to him is a large, Thor-sized man with a grizzly beard. He stands next to a ginger with a long-sleeved pioneer blue dress on. Beside them is Duretta, the witch from the restaurant. Beside her is a Russian looking vampire, and a Middle Eastern vampire. Finally, at the end, is a Native American man with a large belly, and his eyes are on the poser next to me. In fact, they might even have similar qualities.

They continued to float there until one of the vampires started talking to the Native American, whose eyes started glowing amber. Then they all left.

Beth popped next to me, glaring daggers at the spot where the group of super naturals had just been, "I know he's your father Dar, but I really hate him."

The poser stepped on the other side of me, "Join the club."

"That was the Magical Council, right?" I asked the poser. He nods as he holds his hand out to Beth.

Beth hesitates before she takes the poser's hand. Then she levels her eyes on me. "They'll be back, for you, for me, and anyone else who's on our side," Beth says.

"Our side?" I repeat with lifted brows.

"My father won't stop looking for a way to kill you and Beth, and the rest of the Carvers," the poser spoke to me, but didn't take his eyes off Beth.

Beth looked around, "I'm sorry for all the fire damage I caused." The words didn't match her tone, but I could understand the conflict. I had let my fire out when I was caught, and I had burned down plenty of houses and trees, too.

If Cory was here she would want to help her sister. I let out a deflated breath, "I'll help. I caused a good chunk of the damage, too."

The poser's surprise doesn't bother me. I am surprising myself. I really don't consider the problems of others to be mine. I had detached from everyone in my life so that I didn't feel obligated to always help. Except this time it isn't that I feel like I am being pushed to do something I don't want to do, I am going to do something that I know will make someone I care about happy.

The poser holds out his free hand to me, "I'd appreciate that Shane." Then he stops and rolls his eyes at Beth, as if he heard her say something I didn't. "I know," he said to her before his jaw tightened. "Speak out loud. Stop being rude."

Oooh. With all her sass she can't push over that wolf. I like him even more now.

Beth looked at me, "I don't think they will come after us again so soon, but I think it's best if we stick together."

I did agree Cory would be safer with two Carvers protecting her. But, I wasn't sure if Beth was suggesting all three or four of us living in my apartment, or her house. Both options aren't acceptable, "Not too close together."

The poser shakes his head and bumps Beth with his shoulder, "That's none of your business, Beth." Then he looked at me, "You're welcome to stay here in the pack area. My guys will start rebuilding tomorrow, if you want a house I will make sure you get one."

I am unsure if he is offering something he has no power to offer, "Are you able to make that offer?"

His eyes flash amber for a second, "My father was the alpha of this pack before he left and found his way into the Magical Council. The pack does not recognize anyone as alpha because my father never officially left, also because he didn't appoint anyone in his stead, and no one has challenged him for this pack." His comments about being over-looked are not lost on me, "No werewolf wants this pack because we have a few mixed-bloods, and most werewolves are purists."

"Mixed bloods like Sid?" I ask.

"I found her years ago. She was trying to make it in the human world as a doctor. The day I found her was the day that she had it out with one of her administrators who found out what she was. She was on the run, and looking for a safe place. Her parents were already killed by the Magical Council for an indiscretion they made up. I took her in because our pack never had a healer. Since she's been here, she's saved several lives, including your mate, from what I hear."

"She did. And I repaid her in kind."

Both Beth and him wait for me to explain. I was about to walk off because I never explain myself, but again, Cory is in my mind. She wouldn't have explained but I felt like she would want me to tell them. "The water Carver did something and I found her on the ground almost dead. I gave her some of my blood and now she's back up and healing people in the next house."

"You gave her your blood?" Beth asked, almost disgusted.

"She's never had fresh blood," the poser added.

I shrug dismissively, not willing to discuss it any further, "I'll be back tomorrow with Cory, but I do have a job, and if I haven't been fired, then I will have to work tomorrow night."

"Cory can't go back to work. She was kidnapped from there so I don't think she will be safe there," Beth adds.

"I have a feeling she's not going to like that," I add.

The poser huffed in amusement. He and Beth were talking in their heads again. It is mildly irritating, and yet I am kind of jealous. I want to do that with Cory. But then, that thought died when I remembered she would be able to hear all my thoughts. It was best that she couldn't.

"I'll let you drop that news," I say.

"It's only fair that you remain here, too," the poser says softly to Beth. Then he shakes his head and his contemptuous tone returns. "You don't get to tell your sister to do one thing and then you get to do the same thing you told her she couldn't do. That's being a hypocrite, not that being a hypocrite is new to you."

"You don't run me, Dar," she pushes his shoulder and it looks like they were about to get into some kind of lovers spat, so I teleport to Cory.

* * *

I find Cory in her room with a purple smoothie on the nightstand, and a book in her lap. She looks up and immediately closes the book, "Is it over?"

Refusing to lie to her, I shake my head, "No, but we made a dent in everyone's plans."

"I don't understand?"

"The Carvers and the Magic Council are going to have to regroup before they come after us again."

Cory places the book on her nightstand and scoots closer to me. "So what now? How do we prepare for them again?"

I take a drink of her smoothie. It is divine, so I finish it before I answer, "Antrom will continue to look for a way to get you back, but now you have my heart, so Antrom and anyone else who thinks of taking you again will answer to me. As for the rest, Beth and I will always be in danger from both the Carvers and Magical Council because we have resisted them both. The Carvers don't have two lackeys like they planned, and we didn't die like the Council hoped."

"Oh," she sat back and folded her arms.

I reach over and tap her nose, "I've arranged for us to stay with your sister and her guy," *or mate or whatever he is*, "so that you will always be safe." Unable to stop myself, I leaned in and kissed her sweet, soft lips, "Are you okay with that?" As soon as the question was out of my mouth I realized what I just did. Never had I asked if a choice I made for myself or others was okay.

This little fairy really is affecting me, in a good way. And I need to show her exactly how much she affects me. When I pushed the kiss harder, she backed up, grimacing.

"What?" I asked probably a little harsh. I am not really use to anyone pushing me away.

Her cheeks blew up to small balls for several heart beats before she let her breath out oddly, "You should probably shower first." She showed me her dirty palm. Mud from the basement or maybe the cage I was in for a while. I grabbed her wrist and pulled her to the shower.

"I don't need a shower," she tried to argue.

I pull off my shirt, catching her off guard. She stood still and just looked. I turned on the water with my magic and let her watch as I finished undressing. I don't remember anyone ever looking at me like I was a specimen, but with the critical look in Cory's eyes, that's what it feels like.

Slowly I grab the ends of her shirt and pull it off. I need to do this slowly. I need to reassure her.

Maybe I can try talking again, "My father's dead."

Her face scrunched up, "Oh." She looks miserable and feels guilty and relieved, "Um, I'm sorry for your–"

"No that's not what I meant." *Okay. I suck at talking.* I move Cory under the water and start lathering up the soap. "You never answered if you were okay with living with your sister's new pack?"

She held up her arm when I scrubbed her sides making sure to give attention to her beautiful, handful-sized breasts. "I didn't answer because I didn't have an answer," She lifted her other arm for me next.

Moving down, I knelt on tile. "So where do you want to live?" I slowly ran up one leg and then the other.

"I… uh, I don't…" I grabbed her thigh and slowly cleaned her soft pink skin.

"You don't know?" I ask, keeping the conversation alive to keep her distracted mentally.

"Um," she is breathing heavy and I love it. "I can't think."

I stood up and waited to see if she would look up to me. She didn't. She chewed on the inside of her lip. I pushed a few drops of water from her cheek and said, "Try." Then I leaned down and ran my lips over hers for a second. I stopped just to draw this out. "You want to stay with me, right?" I stood back to watch her expression.

With a slight blush she nodded, "Ye –Yes."

I hummed in my chest, gaining her full attention, "Forever Cory? I need you to tell me you want to be with me forever," I pulled her to me, not touching lips, but everything else did.

"I do," she whispered.

Not good enough. "You do what?" I pulled back entirely.

"I do want you. Forever." I smiled at my victory and rewarded her, ravaging her mouth, like the desperate man I was. I let her go to catch her breath and I saw that look I have been wanting to see on her face since I first saw her. Utter desire.

She watched me and waited as if she were waiting for me to lead the way. When I didn't say anything, she swallowed and said, "I'm going to wait for you out there." She pointed, to the door.

I pulled her in for another kiss and I could feel her urgency. After I let her up for air a second time, I breathed, "Give me three minutes."

Cory's green eyes sparkled a knowing look and she left, still dripping wet.

I finished washing all the mud, blood and grime from me. In my bedroom she still is wrapped tightly in her towel. She is drinking from my dark brown mug, a favorite of mine. I take it from her and take a sip. It tastes familiar. I looked down and see her lip is bleeding. I bite my own lip and drank the rest, feeling the same wiggle inside of me. But this time, I knew what it was and I was warmed to know she wanted to be bound to me in the fairy-way.

"It binds me to you forever. Not you to me, like I let you think before."

"My magic binds me to you, and you to me," I was confident in this.

She shrugs, "It's still good to make sure."

Yes it is. I pull her towel away, bringing a fresh blush to her cheeks. It is now that I realize something, "Am I your first, Cory?" The blush deepens and I don't think I can be any happier. "And your last," I say to myself.

I start at her neck while I rubbed her down with my free hand. Her skin is soft, and warm and everything I am going to enjoy forever. I wanted to make sure that she loved every second of this because it was her first and no one ever forgets their first.

I made her moan, I watched her scream and I loved watching her fall apart in front of me. I have never been weak after sex, but I had pretty much fallen onto Cory's back when I finished. I roll off and grab her, pulling her to me as the last feelings dissipate.

I breathe deeply with Cory. Matching her as her chest rose and fell. I have no idea what just happened but I am confident it is the bond between us. Being bonded has its benefits, this being the top of the list, thus far. I look forward to seeing what else the bond does, considering I have never read anywhere about what it is like as a bonded Carver.

CHAPTER ELEVEN
BETH

I check my phone. No messages. With a huff I lock it again. Cory's at work and Shane is in the viewing room connected to her lab. He's not willing to let her out of his sight. I guess they worked out a schedule where he went to work with her and she went to work with him. He somehow didn't lose his job, instead he now owns Amber Line. I doubt the owner just gave it to him, so I am pretty sure his magic has something to do with it. But all in all, Cory sounds happy.

Dar, on the other hand, isn't happy and neither am I. He hasn't stopped working with his pack to rebuild the houses that were burned down. It's been two months and they have practically redesigned everything about this mountain town.

It looks more like a campground now. Instead of houses sporadically being built here or there, they are now outlining the grounds. There is one big community center that the pack decided they would use as an all-encompassing place. I have yet to go inside. It's easier to ignore all the looks from his pack mates. Some girls look at me in pity. Oddly enough, I never thought I would see that. Other girls look at me as if I took something that was theirs.

In a few I see seething hatred as if I was the one that hurt or killed someone in their family.

The men all look at me with disgust. That, I expected. I don't care what they think, and I never will.

Currently I am in "time-out." Dar said it is tedious to keep monitoring me while he is trying to focus on work. He didn't blame me outright, but I felt like he had alluded to it a few times.

I refuse to think and feel while I am sitting in a black, fire-licked chair. I'm not going to think about how hot and cold Dar is. When I was stuck in that cage I was sure he wanted me, even before he admitted it. Now, he is acting like before. Like I am something he's ashamed of.

Ugh. I am thinking of him again. I would leave, but he ordered me to stay. As if I were a dog. Gah! I hate this. I could be at work. Or I could be at my real home. Being here in the time-out chair, sucked.

"She can't stay here," a man with light buzzed hair is pointing at me. I stop cleaning my nails and lean over on my knees. *This should be interesting.* Dar was on his way over with a juice in one hand, and a plastic wrapped sandwich in the other. He did this twice a day but the times always varied so either he was busy or he forgot about me entirely.

Dar walked past the man, not giving him any eye contact, "You don't make the rules MacGrave."

The man's sausage forefinger moved from me to Dar, "She doesn't belong here and neither do you."

Dar handed me the sandwich and put the drink on the floor next to me, not giving me a small grace period to grab it myself. He turned back and started walking, not giving me or MacGrave a second of his time.

But at least I accepted the fact that I was being ignored. This guy's face reddened before he shouted, "Everyone loyal to your father is going to try and kill this bitch of yours. She's a freak and you know it."

Dar's jaw clenched. My fire teased my skin, hoping to get out. I had learned over the past month that there was a fine line to his orders. For example, if he fights right now, it will release me from his order to sit here and be safe. The fight would change the rules because sitting would be come unsafe, giving me the freedom to get up and out.

"She's my mate. She stays. Pack law." His upper lip curled at the older man. "The council didn't make an official ruling and you know it. My mate and the other Carver are not condemned; they haven't broken any rules. The council's corrupt; they tried to kill them because they're scared. And so are you, because you experienced first hand what a low grade Carver can do to you, let alone someone like her," he jutted his chin in my direction, "a fire Carver."

The man looked back at me, defeated and disgusted. He gazed over my neck and said, "She's not marked. Which makes me question if she really is your mate."

Dar's jaw clenched. In between his teeth he said, "She's a Carver, they don't have to be marked. Their magic solidifies the bond."

The older man squinted, "It's unnatural to have an unmarked mate and you know it. You can't feel bonded to someone you haven't claimed, and that thing is unclaimed. And that thing," he pointed at me again, "is not pack and never will be."

I watch closely, waiting to see him agree with that statement.

If he so much as hinted that he agrees, I am fucking leaving. Forever!

Dar's eyes glow as he looks at me. He knows what I am thinking but I'm not hiding anything from him. Let him hear me because I mean it. I return the look, letting my magic flow through me. I know my eyes are glowing when the old man curled back.

Dar didn't agree or disagree to what the old man said. He simply turned back and continued walking. I looked up to the sky to focus on anything other than the rage I felt. I have felt low before, but he was taking me into the depths of a place I never wanted to be. A place where I was worse than an unwanted pet, but the owner was too much of a piece of shit to find it a better home.

I needed to get out of here. In my mind I told Dar, *I need some air.*

Dar didn't answer. Typical.

The older man followed Dar back to the pack, but he spit in my direction first. The fire inside me was getting hotter by the second and if I didn't –

Get your air, Beth. But come back when I call you.

I stood up and narrowed my eyes at Dar's back. I would have screamed it but my voice might have cracked so I yelled in my mind. *I'm not a dog!*

Dar hadn't turned around and it bothered me. I know he ignored me and I anticipated it but right now it bothered me so much I wanted to burn everything.

Dar finally turned around and lifted his eyebrows. *Don't be dramatic Beth. I'm doing what I can with what I have. But you seem to forget that you are not the center of the universe. I know you're the number one target for the Carvers and Magical Council, but so is Shane and I don't see him in my face making my life a nightmare. Instead he's working with me and the pack getting this town back to normal. But you haven't noticed because it's all about you. Has it escaped you that if you die, I die? This is why I treat you the way I do. You react without thinking about the consequences. That's not safe, Beth. And instead of caring about the person you're bonded to, you start fights with my pack members when you should try to be the bigger person and understand that they're scared of you. You're bonded to me remember, so you have to accept I am a part of this pack. And since you are my mate, this is your pack too, but do you care? No. You want to get some air.*

I walk away without responding. I don't teleport because, damn it, his words sunk in so deep my mind feels shredded. My fire that was strong and blazing a second ago has fizzled. I can feel it, but it feels like a million bricks in my stomach. It's so heavy I can barley walk.

I stumble for a while and end up in front of the house that trapped me. His house. I look around and notice that his house is secluded, backed into the forest a way. The whole pack land is at the base of three mountains. There are only a few on the outskirts. Then there are several dirt roads that lead into the forest.

I kick a few burnt chunks of metal. I try not to remember what happened in here, but the memories are too fresh and I see them and practically feel them vividly. My fire swirls up my stomach, alleviating my despair but not my anxiety. I let the magic flow to my eyes. My stomach boils as I behold the pink strip surrounding the crumbled basement. It didn't occur to me until now that if I was ever caught again I would need help to get out, and I would be damned if I had to ask Dar again. I pulled out my phone and sent a text to Cory.

Me: Need you to make me something just incase I get stuck in another trap.

Cory text back a few second later. Cory: Will do. Shane checks for the pink line(?) before we go anywhere.

Me: I bet. How long will it take?

Cory: Three days maybe. Shane and I are going out of town for two days.

Oh yeah, I forgot. Shane is always taking her to new places on his weekends. I don't let it get to me to see the vast difference in mine versus Cory's relationships.

I looked down at the ashes and charred wood. I don't know what Dar has planned when he rebuilds his house. He hasn't even started on it, which is why we have been sleeping outside in sleeping bags. I miss being on a bed. At this rate I doubt we will have a house when winter comes in a few months.

I squat down and get a good look at the mess. Not that he would ever ask for my opinion, but, there is a better place for a house a little way over. Plus, it would have a creek in the back yard.

"I would like to see you rebuilt over there," I point to the space. My stomach wiggles a bit and I watch curiously as the ash starts swirling and then it falls abruptly. Interestingly, the small chunks are now bigger chunks. I fold my arms and stare. Could my magic really put the house back together? I could fix things sure, but ash is millions of little pieces.

Hoping that Dar isn't listening, I say the words out loud, instead of my head where I know he listens closely, "Reconstruire la-bas." My stomach drops and I feel my words become reality.

It was like watching someone doing a million small, grey Rubik's Cubes. Dust was floating off the ground and surrounded each Rubiks Cube that was growing larger and larger. Everything is happening at once. Then I see the dirt begin to move where I want the house to rebuild. I see pipes and concrete, and stone all rolling to their rightful spots.

I look around to make sure no one is watching this. And thankfully everyone is on the other side of the village. I looked back and smile at how amazed I am that this is actually working.

The foundation seems to bubble from the ground up. The wood slides in like a crazy game of Tetris and the frame work solidifies into place. I even see the vines from his plants slither to their new spots. Tomatoes and herbs line the side of his house.

The tree that had fallen from the fire is forming and slowly moving next to the other trees to claim it's spot. It was amazing because that tree was thick. I kept looking around because I worried that someone was going to see, or that Dar would stop me at any moment.

When it was finished I checked to see if there was a pink line outlining the basement. It wasn't there. I step up to the new porch and run my hand over the doorway. It is wood and it smells fresh. Inside, I see the kitchen, table, and bar to the right. In the middle is a big, open living room with several big, lazy boy seats. I walk to the almost empty bookshelf. There is one brown leather notebook, and then a picture of a boy with long black hair and copper skin. He had some looks like Dar, but more like his father. It dawned on me that this was his brother. The one who had died when we were in high school.

I put down the picture and wonder what happened. I don't get a chance to wonder long because the front door creeks open. I look up to see Dar's awed face as he looks around. His eyes find me and I want to mentally stab myself for being such a daisy. His look of appreciation and awe has my belly twirling like ballerinas.

He laughs softly in his chest, "Ballerinas?" I try not to show how his mood affects me. I am sure this happiness is a fluke. Dar's eyes sparkle in laughter, "Come on. We are all eating together in the hall and I know you didn't eat the sandwich." He holds out his hand to me and I hesitate, wondering what has come over him. Then I see something pass behind his eyes and I can feel the change in his mood.

His eyes narrow at me. "But if you'd rather stay, no one would care."

I let my magic up to my eyes.

Knock it off. He orders.

I let my magic go, pissed he can stop me from even thinking to myself. I stomp to the door. Before I open it I remember something and wrap myself in my white room before Dar can stop me.

I knew he was going to be pissed but at this point, who cares. Not me. He was probably going to order me never to go here again so I needed to make sure this time I formulated a perfect plan.

I am leaving. That is going to happen and he is not going to stop me. I just have to figure out a way to get out without him stopping me. And I was also going to have to stop being tricked by his niceness. I swear it was like bi-polar or possessed or . . . then I remember what the witch said. *He still has the poison in him.*

Poison? It looked more like something was inside him, not just a liquid poison. Or maybe that's it, the thing inside him was poisoning him from the inside. What if the poison made him that way? Actually, the better question is, how do I get it out of him?

I sit on the white lazy boy for a while, turning several options over in my head. All options will take too long and I will only have seconds when I leave this white heaven. I can't ask the healer to help get it out, that thing inside him would stop me. I have to think!

Then I remember Cory's birthday and how my fire attacked the caffeine potion she made. Maybe I could do the same with the poison. What if I use my fire to kill it? I can do that, and I'm sure it will hurt like hell, but if I was ever going to get away from Dar, I was going to have to talk to the real Dar. The one who smiled at me from time to time. The one I hope I can reason with.

With one last long breath, I leave the white heaven and am grabbed immediately by Dar's powerful hands.

"You may never go there again," his words solidified and I feel my magic accept his order. I fight to free my arms but he has pushed me against the door and leans into my face, his eyes searching me. He begins to say something but I quickly say, "Posion, entrent en moi maintenant." I almost fear my words didn't work because I didn't feel my stomach drop for another two heart beats.

Dar's tight hold stays as he opens his mouth but nothing comes out. He opens again and still nothing. He narrows his eyes and I can see the wolf in him warning me he's coming.

Then his eyes fade back and all I see is black moving back and forth like dull slimy tar. Dar's grip has loosened finally. I wiggle out of his arms and watch as he remains fixed forward but his body is tilting back and forth.

Then his black slimy eyes turn my way and in a tone I have never heard before, he asks, "What did you do?" I watch as his beautiful skin fades away and I see thick white scars appear on his skin. They are gnarled, jagged scars crisscrossing as if he had been whipped and sliced to ribbons, and somehow he healed. I stand up and look over every single scar.

They were awful. One scar looked like his head had even been severed. Every joint looks like it has been cut and the man I once knew, the perfect gorgeous man, looked emaciated, frail and sewn together by his scars. His cheeks swallowed and his lips were cracked.

The poison began moving past his eyes once more, but with his skin so translucent I could see the slime moving under his skin.

The black recedes from his eyes and I see the brown eyes I know belong to Dar. He looks stoned as he slowly looks down and observes his arms, "What did you do Beth?" He flips his arms the other way and he swallows in between shallow breaths, "Why can I see these?"

The film takes over his eyes again and it makes my stomach tense, "You shouldn't have done that." His mouth curls up at the side and I can see something coming out of his mouth. It's greyish black and it is not only coming out of his mouth, but his pores. It floats in the air like vapor slowly wafting in my direction. I tense the closer it gets until it reaches me. I watch disgusted as the cloud surrounds my exposed skin and is sucked down like water would in a desert.

Several sharp pains run up my arms and into my head immediately. But it's not just a sharp pain, it's full of all Dar's old emotional scars. All the bad memories flash in my mind as if I am experiencing them, too. I can see and feel someone sawing into my neck. I can hear the poison telling me that I deserve it. That everyone hates me because I'm mated to a Carver.

My vision is black and all I can see is what the poison is showing me. Then it moves from my eyes and I feel my skin being cut from my body. It's unbearable and I just scream and scream.

When that memory fades I open my eyes and see Dar's face start to blur. My eyesight is fading again. I don't want to see anymore of these memories. I don't even know why anyone would hurt him like this!

I see his outline fall to his knees and then curl over, pounding the wood floor.

"Beth..." My name sounds weak on his lips. I can see a puddle of blood on the ground but I don't know if it's his or mine. The blood is slowly heading my way and I slowly sit on the ground to accept it. I can't watch the poison come into my skin, so I look away and focus on some odd-shaped black lump shaking violently in the center of the entryway.

The blood has reached my fingertips. AH! It slices into my skin. It feels like glass in my veins again. I try to focus on my fire to help burn his poison. It is not like a potion from Cory. It is hatred, anger, bitterness, and grief. It is enough to make me want to kill everyone and everything.

I take in a breath and let out my fire, letting it wrap around me. The fire is melting the poisonous glass in my veins, but more hate and rage and wrath keeps pouring in by cutting into my skin. I have never felt like this. I have never been this bitter. I have never hated like this. Dar had shaped the poison to his emotions. He fed the poison. Everything in the way he thought was poison. The way he would move, was one more way to hurt someone, to separate himself from others. To stew in his own filthy thoughts. A large glass ripped through my lower back and I screamed.

The fire inside me rages on. It took a while, but the baseball-sized shard of poison finally melted. I can't feel the floor anymore. The heat is intense. I scream again, and I feel something break. My skin. Another rip down my back and I am sure the poison is killing me. My own fire is trying everything to keep me alive. I claw at the air. I can't tell where my skin ends and the fire begins. I can't see anything but white.

My scream morphs. I feel heavy. And then I see my wings. I

don't feel the pain anymore. I take in several clean breaths and search myself for any lingering poison. I slowly move my head because I am kind of cramped being in my dragon form.

Under one of my wings is a black and brown wolf curled up. He has black with brown patches on his feet. He looks at me with his ears flat against his head. I try to reign in my fire but it doesn't budge.

Can you hear me Dar? I ask mentally.

Yes. His voice was scratchy and deep. Not his normal voice. I bowed down my nose. *Come here.*

He eyed me, hesitantly.

You are going to give me the rest of the poison and my heart.

The wolf put his head down but backed up from under my wing. When he was by the door he morphed back to a human. He stood naked for a moment before holding out his hand and I hear him tell me telepathically, *Take your heart. But leave the poison. The poison is my punishment, not yours.*

I nudge his hand with my nose and use the rest of my magic to take the poison. It is in small pieces, but I take it all. It must be just as painful to him as it is for me because his whole body is shaking and his jaw is hard as steel.

He drops his hand from my nose and rubs his eyes. *I told you not to take the poison.* He looks up and waits for me to say something.

I didn't know the answer myself. I guess he didn't mean it because I didn't feel compelled to leave the poison inside him. I'm not going to think of why right now.

Now I need the last piece of what belongs to me, so I can finally be free of him. I let my memory fall back to when he was young. I picture him in the hospital. He chest and neck are almost all wrapped in gauze. I remember grabbing his hand-

I love you Beth. He says the words as if they are sacred. I feel my fire recede a little. I shake my head and force my fire to listen to me and not my emotions. I'm not going to let my feelings get the best of me. I push on my fire, but it recedes even more until I am naked and human again.

I stand up, unashamed and shake my head, not letting him stop what needs to be done. He is the one who keeps saying I bonded to him without asking. Well I am going to give him what he wants. And I know he doesn't want my heart, so I am allowed to take it back without the fear of dying.

Dar's eyes are downcast but I hear him in my head. *I was already broken before you met me. I couldn't heal myself from the hatred. I didn't know how. And whatever it was that was inside of me didn't let me rest for a long time before I was swirling out of control, even back then.*

I went looking for a way out that day I attacked the bear. I hoped it would kill me. But I was lying alone in the forest, I was even more angry that I let that thing get the better of me. So I yelled for help, unable to turn into my wolf because I was so weak.

I woke up in the hospital knowing I was going to have to work harder against the thing inside of me, until you came to me in the hospital. I couldn't see you but my wolf knew you the second he sensed you. I prayed every day hoping that you would know what to do. I'm sorry. I never meant to hurt you Beth. I swear. But I was so broken. And the only thing keeping me together was my pain, and the only thing giving me hope was your beautiful heart.

"No! Don't mess with me Dar! Don't mess with my head!" I have a feeling that I'm crying but the tears, thankfully, are evaporating.

Dar steps to me, and in one quick swipe he wraps his hand

around the back of my neck and pulls me to him. Our foreheads touch and his eyes are still closed. "I lied Beth," he said haggardly, "if you take your heart you die, not me."

I know.

My fire is circling both of us, but the intensity is changing. It is fading, slowly. Dar is still holding me close enough to feel his breath brush over me. I can feel the anxiety in him and it's the first time I can feel anything from him other than his anger. What surprises me the most is his scent is still so incredibly addicting. I still want him. I guess that is something to be expected when you give your heart to someone.

He leans in the last few inches and kisses my lips. I am hesitant at first. If he was broken when I met him, then who is the real Dar? I put my hand against his chest to push him away, but I never find the strength. I love the way his body feels against mine. A new fire is awakening.

I feel his mouth open and his tongue run across my lips. He is putting his whole heart into this moment. This is my moment to decide. I could finish this. I could. I could leave him with his disoriented brokenness. But if I stay and accept him, I am going to have to accept the person he really is underneath all that poison. The person I don't know.

His chest vibrates and I can feel an ache coming from him. A pleading in the form of his kisses. His emotion is exposed to me and I feel that the words he said about me are true. He needs me and he is willing to take me however he can get me, even if he looses me now, he will follow me forever. He didn't say the words, but the flood of emotions coming from him verify it's true.

It isn't a hard choice. I open for him. I let my chest fall against him to feel his skin. I need to feel him. His kiss is ragged and desperate. I bite his lip and grab him, letting my nails dig into his neck.

Dar kneels, bringing me with him. I can feel his nails scratching down my thighs, and then a moment later I can feel him cupping my sex. There is nothing separating his skin from mine this time. He runs his mouth down my neck and I can feel tingles all over. He nips my skin and the tingles shoot right to where his hand is.

"Don't hold back this time," I beg, because I need all of him this time.

"Shhh," he continues to explore my skin with his mouth. When he is just above my breast he bites his lip. "I promise not to hold back," he says with a tone I swear is more wolf than man.

I feel triumphant. He wants me. I arch my back into him wanting him to take what I am offering.

I heard him growl. He covers my nipple and his tongue is doing something I have always dreamed about. I moan because that's all I can do to encourage him to keep going.

He stops long enough to walk me into the bedroom.

"Hurry..." I whisper.

"Shhh," he says again, a little firmly.

He pushes me on the bed. I am fully aware that his eyes are starting to lighten and I am even more excited now that he's letting loose for me. He moves over me, roughly moving his hands up my hips and gripping them hard. Taking in an incredible view of Dar, I hear him say, "I'm barely holding on." I had dreamed about this a thousand times and this is so much better than I imagined. He was so much more intense.

So m u c h… (exhale).

His eyes are a little wild and I feel him thrust into me forcefully. He grabs the back of my hair and flips me over on my stomach, and takes me with a hand around my hip and his mouth my by jaw, he says, "MINE." His rhythm is hypnotic and I feel my body melt into his. Tingles tease me all over until I start to feel my need to build again. I am going to finish again if he keeps this pace. Before I am about to climax he sinks his teeth into my neck and ups his tempo, and I came a second time.

The bite is intoxicating. It was liquid gold – the feeling running and lingering in my womb. Dar bites down again, where my neck and shoulder meet and this time he growled, finishing with long serrated beats. I was in a haze of ecstasy combined with euphoria sprinkled with muscle spasms from my long-lasting release.

Dar flips me over, landing hard on the bed. It is perfect.

That… was intense. I think to myself.

"That's how wolves claim their mate," He whispers, with a smug smile.

* * *

"Beth, we need to go to the hall," his tone is light. Much lighter than before. I nod to him. I try not to think about it but I can't stop my mind from wondering what is going to happen now? Now that all his poison is gone, what exactly is he going to be like?

Dar starts laughing.

I cast my eyes to the bedroom where he's finishing getting dressed. "I hate that you can hear everything," I say.

"I know. I try to give you as much privacy as I can, but you're always just in my head."

"No you don't," I run my fingers through my wet hair, and then shake it. Dar walks out of the room and lifts me up to kiss the top of my head.

I look over his clothes, it pained me to have to cover it up. Once the poison was gone his skin looked beautiful once more. All his scars were gone and his fullness was back. He was enchanting as always. With a black nylon shirt and dark blue jeans, he looks so good I want to go another round. Damn he is sexy. I feel the core of me squeeze with a hopeful anticipation.

"Don't tempt me," his tone is light and playful, but the look in his eyes says he would go another round with pleasure.

I try to think of anything else to keep my mind off taking his clothes off. Then a picture jumps in my mind. A boy with shiny black hair. He was skinny and he had a smile almost the size of his face.

I watch Dar flinch.

Not sure what to do, I tried to think of something else. I thought about anything, letting new pictures enter into my mind as if I am flipping through a picture rolodex. Dar is looking at me with curiosity, while guiding me to the door. *What are you trying to hide from me, my little dragon?*

I shrug and change my pants and red shirt into a light peach sundress. Dar's eyes have a look in them, and I then I feel him reach under my skirt and rip my panties off. "You should know that any dress you wear will be handled just like this." I am pushed into the door, effectively closing it once again. And then I feel him inside me for the second time.

* * *

After another shower, I look in the mirror touching the several marks he left there.

"You've been marked well. And I have to admit, that you wear my mark nicely." He has his palm against my neck, taking in his handy work.

I slap his hand away with a roll of my eyes, but I'm not upset. I like this side of him. It's the side that always made me feel weak to him. A good weakness I think. "Are you afraid anyone won't notice?" I ask, mockingly.

He laughs and shakes his head. "They will be able to smell you before they see you. You smell like me. And with my mark they will know how I feel about you." He grabs my waist and pulls me in. "You are mine and no one will mistake that," he is firm and possessive. I love it.

On any other girl I would probably say she was trashy, but on me, knowing what it means to Dar, they are less trashy.

They are not trashy! Dar hissed

I laugh even though he is kissing me because I can't help it. I let my mind wander a moment and then seize on the picture in my mind. I teleported us to a place I always wanted to visit for years. I open my eyes and see beautifully shaped buildings and smell several odd kinds of spices in the air.

"Beth," I can hear the confusion and excitement in his tone. "Where are we?"

I smile at the market swarming in front of us, "Cambodia." I grab his hand and we walk down the many aisles of people selling all kinds of hand made crafts, food and OH MYGOSH! I jump back, "Is that a spider, on a stick?" EEEWWW Gross.

Dar started laughing, hard. A deep chest laugh that almost made me laugh.

He grabs me around my waist and presses his lips to the top of my head, "I love you."

I could tell he wanted to go, but he was letting me experience this, which was so different from the old Dar.

We didn't buy anything, not for the lack of not wanting anything, but we didn't have the currency or the language skills to pull it off. We walked for a few hours, then I gave in and agreed to return to his pack.

Our pack. He corrected.

I close my eyes, trying to picture the place but something else filtered in. The boy with the black, silky hair. He looks so happy and for some reason I could feel how much Dar missed him. It must have been one of the memories I took from Dar. With his arms wrapped around me I teleport us.

I clear my head and I open my eyes pulling out of his arms. We are definitely not back at the pack land. As soon as I feel the cold ocean air I know I failed. We are on sand, near a large, metal building. I can hear the ocean but I can't see it. I would say the building looked as big as a hotel with several doors, but it is ugly and dark and I know I would never stay in a place like that, and that thought is the one that worried me most. Why would I teleport to a place I didn't want to be?

Beth?

"Honestly I have no idea where we are, Dar." I answer his unasked question. I scan the place. I feel something, so I know there is magic around but I can't pinpoint it and I don't see anyone else so I didn't know who was here. It doesn't feel right. I really don't want to be here with Dar. It isn't safe.

We need to get out of here Beth.

Just then a woman walked out of a small shed. She has a tight bun, no make up, and she eyes me carefully. Her lips purse as she assesses me. My defensive nature held true and I lift my chin at her.

She recoiled, "New recruits are not allowed without an escort." I know she is trying to sound domineering, but her sallow face made her less threatening and more revolting.

I look at Dar to show that I am giving it some thought. In my mind I say, *There's something not right here.*

Dar grabs my arm, "Let's go get our escort."

The lady nods and watches us walk in the opposite direction. Dar walks beside me for a few seconds before he grabs my arm and turns us around. Dar sniffed the air and I feel him still next to me. I heard an ear-wrenching howl rip through the air.

Cort?

"What?" I ask quietly, wondering if I heard him correctly. I look back to make sure the sickly-looking woman didn't notice we stopped. She punches in a series of numbers at the front metal door of the dark building. The one that creeps me the hell out.

My brother. Dar leaves me heading in the direction of the creepy-ass building. He moves so quickly I have to teleport to keep up. He had squeezed in the metal door just as it was closing. We snuck in and I swear I've never been so worried for another person in my life. Okay I was worried when I saved Cory from the Carvers, but right now really bothers me.

Dar left me again as if he had a one-track mind. And to be honest, if it was Cory so would I. I did my best to keep up as he sniffed, assessing each intersection, hallway, and door.

I follow a step behind, because his damn long legs are just too fast. The halls are suspiciously empty. Dar phases into a wolf on the second floor and begins sniffing quickly from door to door. I am tense, not really knowing where we are going or what kind of place this is. I let my fire come to the front, just in case something happens. It should have been my first reaction, but all I could think about was Dar and hoping he didn't get hurt. Talk about a change in mindset.

Dar stops and I almost run into him. He phases back and I quickly make him some pants after taking off my top. I use my bra to turn it into a tightly fitted tank top with built in bra so that I'm not walking around free busting it. He kicks in the door and follows in with a growl and smashes into something or someone.

I don't think I was prepared for the smell that permeated the room. It was rancid and I worried it would eat through my clothing. When I got my gag reflex under control I could see a wolf on his side. He was cut open from his chest to his lower stomach. I froze for a moment at what I was looking at.

A fat, bald man was screaming as Dar's wolf was tearing into his ribs. The man's fist had done nothing to stop him. Blood was everywhere.

I don't know if this is Cort, but the wolf looks dead. Although I thought he was supposed to have been dead for years, he looks freshly dead. But we aren't leaving here without him and I will be damned if I let Dar's brother's body stay in this hell-hole of a room.

I know he needs to get the cuffs off before I can teleport. I try to push my magic in him to help with his wounds, but it won't go, again reinforcing that he's dead. I try once more before I refocus my efforts on the chains and I can feel the body take the magic. No way!

It takes longer than it should have, because I am trying to get the damn cuffs off and push in my magic at the same time, which is not easy. Imagine you are climbing stairs as fast as possible, that's what it's like to push your magic into someone.

The silver ate away at his ankles so much so that I think I saw bone in some areas.

"Beth. Take him to the healer's," Dar yells out to me when I drop the last chain. I put one hand on the wolf and held out the other to him. He's naked with blood on his face and chest. He shakes me off, "No. I'm going to kill them all." His eyes begin to lighten and I know he's turning back into his wolf.

I close my eyes and transport his brother to the healer's new extra-large house. We land hard on the wood floors. Sidney screams as she drops her glass of wine. I yell, "Help me dammit!"

She recovers quickly when she sees the wolf. She springs to my side and sniffs. Sniffs!

"It's Dar's brother." I say hoping she understands how serious it is that he lives.

Then she tilts her head as if she's looking at a ghost, "Cort?" She said his name with reverence and admiration, "I thought you were dead." She was whispering. Covering her mouth.

I bump her with my shoulder, attempting to knock some sense into her. "Can you heal him?" I ask, with coldness in my voice. I need to get back to Dar before he gets hurt, and I don't have time to worry about her emotional state. I need to make sure the healer can do her job.

The healer didn't answer me. She is mumbling under her breath and rummaging over him, while pinning his skin together. She holds my hand against the stomach and tells me to keep pushing in my magic.

Then she runs out of the room and grabs a bottle, "Cory

made this for me." I don't know if she was telling me, or herself. She drips one drop carefully on the wound and I can feel the added magic along with mine. Sidney runs away again and comes back a moment later with a shot.

"What's that for?"

"To keep him unconscious. That potion only gives him a boost, it's not a cure all. He needs to heal." She pats my hand, "His lungs are formed again. You can let go."

He has a lot of scars all over his body. I worry that he has poison in him, too, so I tell my magic to look for it. A moment later I know that there is no poison, those scars are his that haven't healed. I didn't even know that was possible. I have never seen a more ragged looking wolf. He is skinny and his hair is nasty and clumpy. And to be honest, he still looks dead.

"Are you sure?" I ask again, because if I let go and Dar's brother dies, I won't be forgiven.

The healer nods as she continues to look him over. I watch as tears run down her eyes. Her red mascara is smearing, making her tears look bloody, "Who did this?"

"I don't know," I know I am getting loud, but I need to return to Dar.

She let out her breath when she pulled a long, thin, silver colored needle from the dog's spine. "He'll live," she said, and I think she was starting to phase because her teeth elongated. She was able to tap it down because I noticed her nails remained white and she didn't grow any fur.

With nothing left to say, I teleport back to the building. I arrive back where I left Dar. The room is empty and an even bigger mess than before. I refuse to let my fear get into my head. He's going to live no matter what.

Where the hell is he?

The fire alarm began ringing. I cover my ears to alleviate the nose.

Dar? Where are you! I scream, hoping that he can hear my thoughts.

No answer.

I begin to let the fire inside me grow. I take a deep breath and let it out so it circles me. I leave the room, teleporting to Dar.

I am in a large room. There is a circle of people staring at me. I let out another breath, making the fire around me larger. They all step back, exposing Dar's wolf being held down with several silver chains. He is not moving. I step forward and the group steps back again, all except one.

The man that stood out from the others reminded me of Richard, with the same annoying, arrogant smirk. He stands there with his hands at his sides, "Another one? How fortunate."

Then someone throws something at my feet. The vapors are hostile and attack my nose and senses. I let my fire burn them as they try to enter my body. I cough and shake it off before I narrow my eyes.

The man with the arrogant smile stops smiling. He cuts his eyes behind me and I hear a loud crash. I turn in time to see a large blue light pointed at me. I look back at the man as if he had tried to drown me in feathers.

The arrogant man snaps his fingers behind me and the light turns off. This would have been amusing but my mate is still on the floor unconscious. Whipping around, I see him study me for a moment before asking, "What are you?"

I'm assuming he is talking to himself more than me, which made me happy because he probably means it, he doesn't know what I am. This is a boon for me.

I look at Dar and I hear the man make a clicking sound in his mouth. As if he could stop me from getting to my mate.

"You don't want to do that little witch."

I lazily look at the man and realize he has to be a human. No witch on this planet can control fire like me. Or at least I had never heard of one, "You can't stop me."

His smug look was back and it was really annoying, "Oh I think I can. You touch that and your body will be charged with so many volts your brain will fry. Werewolves can reassemble, but witches can't." He tipped his fingers into a triangle, "I would know, I already tried that."

Okay. I'll bite, "Who are you?"

His eyes sparkled, "Someone who knows all about the supernatural."

"Good for you," I said in a bored tone, but mentally I wondered if the council knew about this guy. I mean it seemed like this might be something they should know about, but then again why would the council do anything they were supposed to. I almost laughed at my ignorance.

"Now how about we make this seamless…" His words trailed off and I jumped to the left, anticipating whatever was behind me. I missed the first three darts but I felt four more tag me in the back.

The arrogant man said something, but I had already started to teleport to Dar. I couldn't see, but I could feel Dar. I told my fire to soften the chains. With the last of my ability to stay awake, I teleported us to his house.

We land on the floor of his house and my body goes limp just as my mind fades to black and a familiar voice says, "This, I can work with."

* * *

My body feels like I am being weighed down by a house of bricks. I can't move. I call on my fire to help. Slowly my fire loosens the weight and I can open my eyes.

Another few minutes later and I am looking at Sidney, sipping from a blue mug with white writing. Something about it being wine.

"Thank you Sidney," I don't know what she did, but I know that she's here to help or she already helped, but either way I wanted to thank her.

She nodded politely before looking behind her.

I follow her gaze at a crowd of women huddled around the front door. I look at Sidney again, questioning why we have an audience. Sidney huffs before she tips her mug all the way up and finishes the last of it.

My eyes are heavy and I was about to close them when I hear one lady ask in a whisper, "How is Cort doing?" I peer up and look for who's asking and why she's in my house asking about Cort. Sidney left the mug on the kitchen bar and sat down next to me.

Now that I was looking, I noticed I was on a cot in my living room and there were two clear bottles on my side. I don't know what they are, but I can clearly see Cory's writing on the labels. I look over at Dar and he, too, is on a cot, and he has an IV in his arm. That can't be good.

Sidney checked my pulse as she answered, "He's alive, only because werewolves are hard to kill."

Was she talking about Cort or Dar? She must have seen the question in my eyes right?

I was about to ask, but another women asked, "Is it true that he has scars?"

I cut my eyes to them. The healer chastised the young woman with a glare too, "He's not your business, Clair."

Dar is unconscious and all these bird heads want to talk about is Cort and if he has some scars? Unacceptable. I clear my throat. When they looked in my direction, it takes a lot of effort not to vaporize them right then and there. Their contempt was clear in the curl of their lips. It is as if I am beneath them to even talk in their direction.

"Get out," I didn't yell it, I said it. And I meant it.

"Cort is the heir to our Alpha," Clair makes sure to sound condescending, as if she is giving me a history lesson. "We are bound to our Alpha and his heir. We are obligated to help." Clair pointed at Sidney, "But she won't let us in to help!"

Sidney ignores them and hands me a bottle of water. I take a few sips before responding, "Dar's father hasn't been alpha of this pack since he joined with the council."

Their jaws drop at my words and I smirk at their ignorance. One redhead steps forward, "Speaking against our alpha is a punishable offense." She looks devilishly delighted, "I plan on letting our *Alpha* know and the council will see to it that you are properly punished."

And then the blonde girl, Clair, points at Sidney and says, "We plan to tell the Alpha what she's done too. She broke her promise to our Alpha and will be punished, too."

Thank goodness Dar was unconscious for all this. It was like talking to a spoiled brat who had no concept of the world around her. These *female dogs* were going to turn me in for telling the truth and Sidney for something equally as stupid (whatever it was she did). This is why I didn't mingle with Dar's pack. Because they made me crazy. I just wanted to shake them all until all their stupidity dropped out.

"Well he's not here in this house, I can assure you, so get out, or I will make you." I take another swig of water and use the bottle to point to the door. They didn't like that so much. All their eyes glowed amber.

"You can't harm us. I see the marks on your neck. You're bound to the pack like we are. You can't kill a pack member," Clair says, with her hands on her hips.

Sidney patted my arm, futility attempting to calm me down. She doesn't know me well enough. I would need a liter of fizzy Coke to calm down emotionally ,but thankfully my fire didn't give these birds a second of it's time.

The healer stands up and check's Dar's IV. She pulls it out and wraps the tubes around the liquid bag. She picks up the bottles and stuffs them into her pack and walks out, not addressing the women or myself. The women, thankfully, follow her, saying something about telling the Alpha that she drank blood.

I lift Dar to his bed and lie down next to him. I run my fingers against his skin, memorizing every bump and curve. Then for the next several hours I let my mind wander and plot about the humans in that creepy building. That place is a large torture chamber to the supernatural. Either way, that building needs to come down. And everyone in it is going to go down with it, after a few questions.

Two hours passed and I still can't get my eyes to close, so I take a shower and dress in a simple pair of jeans and a t-shirt. I look through the refrigerator and notice there is nothing in it.

I shake my head and remember that it was probably just yesterday that Dar and I made up. It just felt like all the events streamlined together. I close the door and frown. There was nothing in the house.

Pouting, I walk outside to get some perspective and fresh air. Again, I didn't hear anyone walk up, but when I heard someone clear their throat softly, I turned ready for another bird and her ignorant comments.

I saw the chick freeze, as if she lost her nerve to talk to me. I raise an eyebrow at her. What ever she says better not piss me off right now. I am on a caffeine deficiency. After a few seconds she bowed slightly and said, "Beth?"

My eyes squinted at the short woman with reddish-brown hair. I pride myself on knowing if a person is dangerous or not the moment I meet them. And this chick was submissive. She is kind of soft in the middle, with a pale, round face and pretty green eyes and pouty lips.

"Yeah, I'm Beth," I rest my hands on my hips and wait.

"You're mates with Dar, right? The healer said to give this to you." She is not looking at me as she holds up a wine glass with straw colored liquid in it.

Uh. What? It kind of bothers me to see someone being this submissive. I mean for heaven's sake she could at least look at me.

"I don't drink."

The girl pulls the drink back and casts her eyes down, "I'm sorry, I didn't know." Then she frowns, "I mean she probably didn't know." She blushed hard, "I mean, I sometimes help Sidney out when she's busy. You know about the other girls hounding her, right? She said you were there." She looks away as if thinking, and then changes topics yet again, "You're the beta's mate."

I bit the inside of my mouth to keep from laughing. Curious little thing. I like her. "What's your name?" I ask softly. Also changing the topic because I had no idea that Dar was a beta.

"Mina," she says softly as she peeked up at me.

"Mina, look at me," she looks scared and shakes her head, looking at her feet.

"Look at me, now," I say, letting her know it is not a request, it is an order. She looks at me slowly, but I know she doesn't want to.

When her green eyes look back at me, I hold them. And hold them until I know she's about to break away, and then I say, "Thank you, Mina."

Mina made a weird crinkle with her lips. She swallowed, "I have never met a magical creature."

I smile at her. By all definitions she's a magical creature, because even werewolves are considered supernatural. "Do I scare you?" I ask, curiously.

"Yes," she answers honestly, switching from one foot to the other.

I frown, "Don't be."

She continues to look down, "I can't help it. Your blood is so strong," she says in a whisper. It's comments like that that make me think of Cory.

I let my hands drop and walk back to the side of the house, where we can both sit on the steps. "My blood makes you uncomfortable?" I can tell this is going to be an interesting conversation, "Explain."

Mina follows me to the steps and sits down. "Your eyes… they glow. Like a wolf's. But they are green instead of brown." Her tone has changed from light and anxious, to a deeper confidence. Cory does this too when she's talking about a topic she knows well.

"Yeah I know," I say, nonchalantly.

She turns the glass in her hand, watching it like it was a specimen. "You must have wolf in you," she says with a confidence. I can tell that she wants me to say I do, so I nod. I am sure I have wolf in me. Four generations of Carvers there is bound to be a wolf in there somewhere.

As stubborn as you are...I can guarantee it, Dar says in my mind, and I instantly feel my fire waking up in me. I want to end this conversation to go see him. But I have to be nice, she is pack, and that is important to Dar. I am trying to be good.

Mina is waiting for something so I shrug, "Carvers are mixed bloods. So we have almost all magical bloods in us."

Mina considers this and looks as if she agrees with me. How did she not know this? "That would make sense because you and the other *one* don't smell the same. The magic in your blood is different. And then his woman has a different scent, too."

I am going to assume she is talking about Shane and Cory. Sometimes talking to people like this you have to figure out their references that usually only they know about. It's somewhat vexing, "The woman is mostly human. Have you smelled humans before?"

"Yes. I know what humans smell like," she says softly, "my mother is human." She continued to twirl the wine glass in her hand, not spinning it too quickly because the wine looked like it never really moved.

Oh.

She continues, "But the woman who was sick is not fully human. I can smell the magic blood in her. I would say that she is only part human and mostly magical. But if you say she's mostly human, then she is, and her magical blood is just really strong."

She was nothing like Cory. Cory would never agree with me just because I said so. I guess there is only one Cory in the world. But this girl obviously trusted me enough to believe me, and that in itself was…nice if not a bit foolish.

"What do you mean you can smell the magic in her blood?" I ask Mina, because I can just tell she wants to talk about this.

She looked down, "Um, just something I know how to do."

I can't help pointing out, "Can't all werewolves do that? You can smell if another supernatural is around right?"

"Yeah," she kicks a rock at her foot and it plummets down the stairs. "Werewolves can smell other magical creatures, but they don't smell it in their blood." She stopped swirling the glass and took a sip of the wine, "And…I'm not a werewolf," she finally looks up, waiting for my reaction.

Really? "Okay," I shrug, "I give up. You're human and what else?"

She drinks the rest of the wine and whispers, "I'm similar to Sidney in a way. She's a vampire and werewolf mixed-blood. I'm a human, vampire and witch mixed-blood."

Mixed-bloods.

Her ears prick up when she sees the expression on my face, which is full of curiosity. "I had no idea the other bloodlines could mix," I said it out loud and wanted to slap myself after I said that.

Mina looked lost for words because she was holding in a smile. For whatever reason she didn't want to fully express how she was feeling. Which was fine because it's not like I wanted to hug this out or anything.

"Not that there's anything wrong with mixed-bloods. I'm the last person who could say anything about that. So that's how you can smell the magic, because you are a vampire and witch? That's cool."

Mina's chin rose a little, "You really don't care that I'm mixed with a vampire, do you?"

I could tell this was a heavy question for her. She really wanted me to accept her the way she was. If anyone, I knew what that felt like. But before I could answer she said, "I heard that you killed one of the Horde King's head enforcers."

Ah, now I get it. "It wasn't because she was a vampire." I felt a twang of guilt, "Well, okay, yeah I didn't like any supernatural pure-borns. I don't like how they think they're better than me. But," I pointed at her, making sure she understands the line, "that vampire broke into my house threatening my sister and I, and then she laughed when she told me that my sister was gone, so she kind of had it coming."

Mina bit her lip before asking, "If you and the other guy don't hate mixed-bloods, why do the rest of the Carvers hate everyone?"

I can feel the weight of the question. I wonder what Shane did that eluded that he and I feel the same way, but then again he is bonded to a half-breed.

Mina hadn't moved. I answer as best as I can, "The reason why I don't hate everyone is because I had a good relationship with my adopted parents and Cory, my adopted sister, who turned out to be half-fairy. Or maybe it's a quarter. Anyway, when my parents tried to sell me the story that everyone is beneath me and they deserve our vengeance, I told them to stuff it. That kind of mentality just rubs me the wrong way." I shrug, "And I don't know why Shane is okay with mixed-bloods. And I can't agree that all Carvers hate everyone. I'm sure there are more out there that haven't been exposed to the supernatural world and the Carver's war." *At least I hoped so.*

This seemed to pacify her. She nodded and I could tell her eyes looked a bit glossy. She mumbled a thank you and left. I waited until she rounded the corner before I walked in and found my handsome man making steak and eggs.

I seriously love this man.

He turned to me and smiled, "You love me?"

I covered my mouth with the full implication of what I did. He watched me for another moment before leaving the stove and pulling me into his arms. I brushed his lips on mine, "I told you I loved you the other day and I meant it. I was just waiting for you to say it back."

I blush. This was so mushy. Then Dar started laughing while he pulled me to the kitchen and lifted me on the counter so I could watch him finish making our breakfast.

EPILOGUE
BETH

Cort woke up from his drug-induced coma a week ago. Sidney finally announced he was mended and began shooting him with "wake up shots." Every one, especially the girls, waited outside to greet him back to the pack. Dar and I were among the group to see him when he woke up. Not that it mattered, because the moment he woke up he screamed for everyone to get out.

He literally threw anything he could grab to run Sidney from her own house. I wasn't very understanding towards Cort; I felt that he didn't just overreact, he was outside his damn mind!

I don't know if Dar was afraid he would demand to take over the pack, or if he would hate Dar for not looking for him after all that time, but either way Cort was still a very touchy subject. One I just stayed away from.

The pack pretty much started disregarding Dar all together and I know that hit hard. He had to calm me down, saying it's the way things have to go. The pack has to get used to the change. Patience was never one of my virtues. I hated every time they slighted him and every time I had to keep my fire in check or he would order me to control it.

Sidney and Mina still look up to Dar, but no one considers him in any position of authority. And if that wasn't bad enough, their father has yet to show up and say a damned thing. By the end of the week I had waited long enough. I teleported to his brother, still inside Sidney's house.

"Get out Carver," he sneered.

I folded my arms. A big *fuck you* was on the tip of my tongue, but instead I raised my finger in the air and said, "I saved your fucking life, so shut the fuck up."

Cort was standing in the doorway of the smallest room. He wasn't leaning or looking cocky, he looked like he was ready to strike. He was in a defensive position and for the first time I really looked at him. Damn. I was wrong about him.

Cort growled a warning, but now that I knew what I was looking at I let the fire go that was blazing on my skin. I looked around the kitchen and noticed all the wine bottles were broken. I walked over the glass and hopped up on the counter, making him come out of the room to keep a keen eye on me. "I have nothing to say to you."

Now, how to word my proposal…,"What if I told you I have a house outside the pack territory, that's two stories, paid up, sitting empty?"

Cort didn't respond so I continued, "I will give you full reign of the house for as long as you want. And then, when you're ready you can decide what you want to do about…" I pointed out the windows, "all of this."

Cort's chin raised, "I don't need your help Carver."

I smiled. Oh he was going to take my offer, I could see it in his eyes. I jumped off the bar and picked up a broken glass and turned it into chalk. On the door I wrote my address and then flipped the chalk back on the floor turning it back to glass.

The magic bothered him. I knew that, but…I'm working on being a better person. I'm not perfect.

* * *

Cort waited exactly twenty minutes before he left. Not that I blame him, after Clair snuck into the house and tried to sweet talk him into coming outside with her. But I don't know that she deserved to be thrown out the front door like a bag of trash.

Dar didn't say anything when Cort walked out. Instead, he held up a pair of keys to the truck he parked in front of the healer's house. Cort grabbed the keys while he continued past the people who were all trying to talk to him or stop him from leaving.

Cort didn't waste anytime to peel out and head to my house.

By day two my curiosity was killing me. I had to know if Cort was settling in to the house. I also wanted to know if he had demolished the place. Four hours of wearing down my Mate, and a promise to wear his favorite pink and black lingerie, we had a deal.

I teleport with Dar to my old house. The second we land in the entryway Cort came flying out of his bedroom with a gritty look.

What is wrong with him? I wonder.

I look at Dar, he shrugs. I see something orange sitting on the couch. I lean back to get a better look around Dar. Some chick with chin length, bright orange hair, sitting on the couch with her hands in her lap. She is looking at me with calculating eyes. I walk to her, slowly taking in my own guess of who she might be. She isn't the orange-eyed Carver. That was my first thought. Thankfully this chick seemed more, what's the word, reserved.

Dar is on my heels. When I stop in front of her, I fold my arms, "Hi. Who are you?" I ask in clipped words.

Cort walks past Dar and stands to the far side of the living room. The chick's eyes shifted, as if she was following Cort in her periphery. Her demeanor is stiff and she definitely doesn't like being cornered.

"I'm Theya," she says, in almost a whisper.

Dar sniffs and says, "What are you doing here, fairy?"

Fairy? How can you tell? I ask Dar mentally.

Freckles, pale skin and smell.

The fairy was reserved but she didn't look shaken up, which means Cort didn't throw her out a door. That's growth right?

Her smooth, sweet voice cut into my thoughts, "I kinda hitched a ride with Shane and his girl."

"Hitched a ride?" I ask, possibly letting a little fire into my voice. When the hell did this happen?

Theya straightened up and looked at me, "The girl is part fairy and Antrom extended an invitation for her to come and see the Fairy lands."

"I am well aware of her time there. But she failed to tell me about you, so you can see how I don't believe you." And my hands are on my hips. Right. On. Schedule.

Cort snorts.

She's not lying.

Oh yeah, werewolves can smell lies. So then I refocus my questions, "You hitched a ride back with them? Why?"

Theya tensed, "It's personal," she says quietly, but firmly as if she is drawing a line in the sand.

"Try again fairy," Dar says, and I saw her shiver just as his vibes run over me as well. Interesting, did everyone feel his dominant vibes?

The fairy shakes her head, "It's personal." Then she looks at me in the same calculating way as she did earlier. Now she looks at Dar for a few seconds and lastly, Cort. It takes a few heartbeats before she nods her head. She says, "Okay." As if she has made a decision. The fairy walks around the couch and heads to the front door. The fairy pulls open the door, but I am right behind her. I slam the door shut in her face. I am not done with her. I need to know who she is and what she is doing here, and if she had planned to hurt Cory.

"Wait. If Cory brought you here, then I should at least give you the benefit of the doubt."

The fairy grabs the doorknob again and says in a cold, clipped tone, "It's clear that you don't want me here." The fairy pulled at the door, it didn't budge.

"How do you know Shane?" Dar asks with a weird look in his eyes, as if he were assessing her still.

Theya doesn't look at me, she shakes her head again, staring at the door. "There is nothing you could say that would motivate me to tell you anything."

Cort growls at her and I watched as she responds to him. Her shoulders stiffened and her breathing slowed. She turns to him and stares as if she is trying to win some dominance war that she is going to lose, because werewolves don't back down. She doesn't look away for several moments. Impatient, I am not about to stop Cort mid-fight with a fairy. "How about I take a few licks at that face of yours and see if that loosens your tongue?"

The fairy flinched. Maybe I hit a nerve. Maybe they don't like physical touch and I was about to give her a crash course in Carver fighting.

The fairy takes a few moments to answer, but she is still looking at Cort. "He used to sleep with my sister. I met him a few times between the front door and her room," she says bluntly.

Dar coughs and my jaw drops, "And after a few hello's he brings you back to my house and drops you off?" I asked because that sounds ridiculous that he would help out a sister of a chick he used to sleep with.

She finally turns to me and says, "He didn't really care one way or another about me when he teleported me here."

Dar tilts his head, assessing her.

Theya eyed Dar and then she turned back to Cort quickly, and her eyes narrowed. "If you have nothing else, then I will take my leave," she said quickly, attempting to get the door open.

"Headed home?" Cort calls out to her in a tone that sounds like he is trying to bait her. Odd that this is probably the most civil I have ever seen him. He is getting off on this little fairy fight. Gross.

I see her turn and I know the 'fuck off' look she's giving him. "No," she hisses lowly. She tries to pull the door open again and I keep my hand on the door, making it impossible to move while I am there.

"I don't think so, fairy. You stay until we talk to Shane and

Cory," Dar put his body between the fairy and the door, and I teleport out.

I teleport to Shane's door, a house that is as far as he could get from the pack. In fact, it is on the other side of the third mountain. I knock, as hard as I can, hoping to break it open, but I know it won't work because he has more wards on his house than I have on mine. I start yelling until the door opens with a sight of Cory I never want to see again.

She is in a long sweater that is two sizes too big. It looks like a dress and I pray she had panties on underneath it. Her hair is a mess, she has hickeys all over he neck. Her cheeks are blushing, like bright red.

Shane pulls her away from the door and quietly says, "Meet me upstairs."

I cough. "I don't think so," I said, while putting my hand on both of them and teleporting them back to the old house.

As soon as we land at my old house I let go of them and regret my impulsive nature. Cory is not dressed for visitors. Dar coughs and Shane glares at me, making her sweater into a long sweater dress.

"Shane. Do you know her?" I pointed at the fairy.

He rolled his eyes when he looks at me, "Beth you really need to relax. Is Dar not doing his husbandly duties?" His words are heavily drenched in sarcasm, "Do wolves even consider themselves husbands?" Shane said absently to himself.

I hear Dar growl, which is bad because we don't need to fight right now. I get in his face again, "Why is she here?"

Shane looks behind me and I can see something in his eyes, even though I don't know what it means. After a few seconds he says, "I knew her sister. Theya also helped Dar remove his magical collar, although I assume he doesn't remember any of that, do you?"

Dar is looking at the chick as if he was willing himself to remember.

Shane continues, "Fairies can't leave their lands without permission from the courts. And you can imagine how often they give permission. And even if they do get permission, they have to return shortly thereafter. As you know, they frown upon mixing their blood with others." He looks over at the fairy with an odd 'I told you so' look. "Theya hated it there. And she just happened to be there when I was taking Cory away."

The fairy looks at me and oddly enough, she doesn't look so tense anymore.

I watch Shane for another second before asking, "Do you trust her?"

Without hesitation he answered, "Yes."

Do you think she will be safe here with Cort? I ask Dar quickly.

He hasn't killed her yet and he hasn't objected to her living here like by the way he treated Clair, I know he wouldn't have any issue with voicing that opinion.

I tilt my head, annoyed that he made is sound like Cort is going to toy with the fairy as a predator would it's prey.

Shane nodded once at Dar and then grabbed Cory, "Next time wait for an invitation Beth, which should be about…never."

Dar was shaking his head when he held out his hand to me. He looked over to his brother to say something, but Cort huffed something on his way to the room on the bottom floor. Our guest room. Theya moved out of the way and walked back in the kitchen. The way she moved made me think that she was far too familiar with my house.

I didn't like it.

Dar squeezed my hand a second time. Let's go.

I teleported us out with the hope that my house remains in tact and Cort didn't kill the fairy, because there was something in the way he looked at her that made me think she was probably in danger. The crazy part was, when she looked back at him, she wasn't afraid. An explosive mix if there ever was one.

THE CARVER'S PROBLEM (BOOK 2) EXCERPT CORT

The smell of coffee wafts into my nose. I've been lying in this ridiculously uncomfortable bed of fluff most of the night, unable to sleep. I kick my feet off the bed and pull on a pair of black cutoff sweats.

The pixy just bought a new electronic coffee pot yesterday. In the kitchen, I pull a blue mug from the middle shelf and drink the contents of the pot. The very little I'm not able to drink, I pour out.

The orange-haired pixy hasn't gotten it through her thick skull that she's unwelcome. So everyday I try and find something to remind her that I don't want her here.

If she hasn't figured it out by tomorrow, I'm going for her shoes.

Her door opens and I can smell her lavender scent from where I'm standing. I set the mug down on the countertop and wait for her explosion. She's going to be pissed and I am itching for a fight.

She rounds the kitchen and ignores me until she sees the coffee pot. Then she eyes me with frustration. I can feel the hair on my neck begin to prickle with anticipation.

The pixy taps the counter a few times, then begins to make a new pot. When it begins to drip, she folds her arms and keeps her back to the pot, as if she's guarding it from me.

My wolf almost howls in amusement at her pitiful attempt to

keep her coffee safe. The feeling is a little uncomfortable because this is the first time in probably ten years that he isn't snarling at someone. That's why I haven't thrown her out the door yet. But I still don't want her here, no matter if my wolf seems to be unaffected by her presence. It's maddening to smell lavender all the time. And that's what fairies smell like to me – lavender.

I watched the pixy tense at the same moment I smelled charred wood. Fire Carver. That's what all fire Carvers smell like.

I turned my head and followed her gaze to the living room. Shane held his phone in the air, looking straight at the fairy next to me, "Why aren't you answering my text?"

I look back at her and her eyebrows raise slightly, "My phone is upstairs." Then she blew air out her cheeks and shook her head, "What do you want?"

Shane slid the phone into his front pocket, "I need you to watch Cory tonight. She's not feeling well and I still don't like leaving her alone."

Now my eyebrows raise slightly. He sounds like a werewolf protecting his mate, but he's a Carver and they don't feel those kind of things.

The pixy fixed herself a cup, giving the Carver her back. Stirring in some sugar, she says, "If Cory agrees, I will *hang out* with her until you get home tonight, but I'm never going to *watch her*."

He pulls his phone back out and starts texting. I keep my eyes on the Carver. My wolf is poised to attack if he so much as moves in my direction. I hate Carvers. Every last one of them could burn on a pitchfork and I would have no issue watching each of their fleshes bubble and fall off their body. I know Shane and Beth aren't like the Carvers who kept me a slave for ten years, so I haven't tried to kill them, but it's not easy to keep my wolf at bay.

For ten years my wolf was shackled inside me as my body was under a love spell. Isla Carver tricked me ten years ago and every second with her was hell. A living, tortuous, hell. The things she made me do, and the things I did to others, makes me want to shred my insides to ribbons. And if I wasn't bad enough to do all those disgusting things we did together, she used her Carver magic so that she could use me to sniff out the supernatural.

As a wolf I could always smell the different species- human, wolf, fairy and witch. But after the spell, I can smell Carvers and their designation along with mixed bloods, half bloods, and all pure bloods from just one sniff.

I shivered and I think the pixy picked up on it because she stiffened a little. It hasn't been that long since I woke up from that spell, and if she were smart she would have left by now, because my wolf may not mind her right now, but that doesn't mean that he is going to be able to stop me if she ever triggered a flashback.

I watched Shane's eyes lighten, "She said she would love to hang out." He lifted his eyes, "When should I drop her off?"

My wolf punched at the seams of my skin. Shane is trying to invade our space. Hell no is that going to happen. I opened my mouth as Theya took a step in my direction, totally cutting off my thought process and focusing on the fact that her body was so close to mine. I could practically breath on her vibrant orange hair.

"No. I will get my things. You can take me to her."

As she took a step back I could smell eucalyptus swirling around her. I tilted my head, wondering if that was her lotion, and then I wondered why I only just now smelled it. When I found her eyes they were watching me carefully. Another moment passed and she nodded and then walked away.

I watched her leave, wondering what that meant. Did she

just stop me from pouncing on Shane? And if so, how did she know? I've learned to school all my facial expressions so that no one, not even Isla knew what I was thinking.

Shane waited until she was upstairs to say, "I asked your brother to let Theya stay in his pack."

My wolf growled. He was interfering with something that wasn't his business.

Shane must have sensed my thoughts because his eyes glowed ice blue, "She needs to be somewhere safe, because they will come looking for her."

They?

The smell of cinnamon hit my nose just as the pixy rounded the corner. Her finger pointed at Shane, "I already told you no, I am not leaving here." And then she pointed at me while still talking to Shane, "And you are not going to lay my safety on anyone else's shoulders. Are we clear?"

Shane's eyes were back to normal, "We will talk about this later." Then he walked to Theya and I could feel my claws descending as I saw him get closer to her.

When they both disappeared my wolf growled again. Without another thought I headed up to her bedroom in search of her new heels. My wolf had plans for those hideous looking things.

* * *

I left her shoes where she would see them the second she walked in the door. But she didn't come back that afternoon or later that night. In fact, I had completely forgotten about the shoes when I heard the front door and smelled lavender in the early morning.

I dismissed her coming in until I heard, "You've got to be

kidding me." That pricked my ears up and I sat up, looking at my bedroom door.

I thumbed the bed for a few more minutes before I pushed myself off the bed and pulled on a pair of white, knee-length basketball shorts. Opening my door, I was assaulted by an overwhelming presence of cinnamon. I could taste it; the smell was so thick.

I quickly made it to the front door and stepped outside to cleaner air. I took in a few deep breaths before I looked at my '51 Chevy truck. I could go for a drive and find a desolate spot to let my wolf run, because letting him run where there were too many people wasn't safe. He would attack anyone within smelling distance. Or, I could just go for a run now and not waste the time going for a drive.

I looked down at my bare feet, deciding if it was worth it to go back inside for shoes. Deciding against it, I turned left at the end of the driveway and ran.

I ran past the houses and the near by park. I ran past the sketchy parts of town and into the undeveloped end of the city. I ran until my wolf no longer felt stiff with anxiety. I was thirsty but there wasn't a place nearby for water, and I didn't want to continue down this dirt path that lead to my brother's pack. I don't know how I ended up this close or why I even went this way.

Shaking off the odd feeling in my chest, I began the trip back to the house, stopping once by the first park to get a drink of water.

At the house I walked in, knowing my feet were leaving wet outlines and my shorts were wet with my sweat. I headed to my room and stopped short.

I smelled something amazing. Something I have not

smelled since I was a boy. Unique meat. Raw meat.

Karaboo?

"What am I smelling?" I asked out loud as I walk in the kitchen, but I am pretty sure it's Karaboo.

The fairy didn't answer me, in fact I noticed her shoulders tense up. She's holding her phone to her ear and I can hear Beth on the other side telling her to leave the meat until the sides turn a light shade of brown.

I walked in and stopped right behind her to look over her shoulder at the pan as the meat was being seared. I look down at the pixy who is stiff, and her smell changed from lavender to eucalyptus. I ignore the questions racing in my mind, asking why the hell am I getting so close. I reach around her and pull the tongs from her hand. I have successfully enclosed her in and there is no way out, so I am not surprised when she pushes back against my chest. In fact, it doesn't even register as a threat. She tries to push me again and then groans. I can feel the vibration of it. She turns around and lifts the phone to her ear, never taking her eyes off me.

That is when my wolf pricked up. He wasn't sure what to expect, and I was also unsure what she was going to do. Her eyes didn't look angry, not the angry I was used to seeing in Isla's eyes. The look that I was going to be punished, severely.

Nope, instead, right now, her eyes are drawing me in and every single inch of me is aware of her. I can feel her on my skin and against my thighs. A hint of peppermint swirled around her. Her breaths were shallow and I leaned down to get a better smell.

Then I heard Beth yell through her phone: *Theya? You still there?... Why are you – Is Cort there? What did he do? Theya!*

I grabbed the phone and crushed it in my free hand. I

threw the phone in the living room and was starting to feel my claws descending.

I can't explain why I just did that, but I couldn't have stopped myself if I wanted to.

The pixy wiggles out from in between me and the stove range to pick up the pieces of her phone. I can see her eyes are shimmering with tears unshed. I watch, unable to look away because something inside me is making me watch this and it's drilling it into my memory.

She finally takes the pieces to the trash and I am free to look down at the pan with two large steaks in it. If I remember correctly, fairies don't eat meat. They were all leafy green eaters or something like that.

I narrow my eyes at her back. She is breathing slowly and I wonder if she is crying, not that it should matter, but it's making that hole she just drilled in my chest feel… awkward.

The pixy sits at the table behind me, and it should bother me that she's in the perfect offensive position, but I push past that and focus on the steaks.

After the steaks are done, I grab two plates and put one steak on for her and then on the other for me. I put her plate in front of her and I take a seat on the opposite side, facing her.

She stands up and grabbed two forks and knives, giving me a pair without looking at me and then sits down.

For some reason my interest in the food has ebbed. I am curious if the pixy is actually going to eat it. And if she is, I want to see what her reaction is. In fact, I don't think want is a strong enough word, I *have* to see how she likes what I cooked.

I wait as she cuts a piece of steak and slides it into her

mouth. Then she stares at the wall and chews. After she swallows, she nods absently. After her first bite I saw her squirm in her chair and I realize that I have not stopped staring at her.

I almost ask her if she likes it, but I can't get the words out of my mouth She narrows her eyes at me for a half a second and then picks up her plate and walks out with a swirl of cinnamon left in her wake. I hear her footsteps stomping up the stairs and I am left to eat the rest of my food alone.

* * *

I place my plate in the sink and notice my mug from earlier isn't there. I open the cabinet and see the blue mug is right where it's suppose to be.

The doorbell rings and shakes me from looking curiously at the blue mug. I don't know why it's bothering me to look at it, but it is. The door bell rings again and the pixy hasn't come out of her room. The door bell starts to ring a third time and I swing the door open with a growl.

The man at my front door looks at me, then looks down to the cigarette in his hand. He flicks the cigarette into the grass before looking towards me. His hair is dirty blond and buzzed short. He has a tattoo on his neck sticking out of his light-grey t-shirt and both his arms are full sleeves of ink.

I breathed in slowly, and for the first time in a long time I found my voice, "I know what you are."

"Don't you mean who I am?" He was standing taller, not backing down from my glare.

He couldn't intimidate me even though he has the same wild look in his eyes as I have. His wolf must be just as close as mine is to the surface. He looks ready to throw down and I am all for it. "Nope, I meant, I know what you are," and then I looked at the cigarette butt on the lawn, "and *that* won't cover your bloodlines from me."

The man narrowed his blue eyes at me and then pursed his lips as if he was debating what to say. Then he looked behind me as if looking for something, "I'm here for the girl."

No.

My wolf and I aren't letting the pixy anywhere near this guy. Not because we are protecting her. We aren't. But this guy is bad news.

The guy's phone chimed and he pulled it out of his jeans pocket. On the other side I could hear my brother, Dar.

Where are you?

"Standing in front of your brother."

And?

The guy was hiding something. Not just what he was, but he was up to something. Not like I needed another reason to not like him.

"I don't smell blood so I am pretty sure the fairy is alive."

At my snort the man glanced at me with an evil smirk.

Hand the phone to my brother and get back as soon as you can, you're leaving for Alaska tomorrow morning.

The man snarled, "I'm what?"

I got a tip from a buddy of mine, he thinks he found your brother.

The man stilled, "Did you tell my father?"

No, I don't plan to tell him anything until… everything is sorted."

The man took in a deep breath, "What aren't you telling me?"

There was a long pause and then I heard my brother say, *My buddy says he was seen with a Carver.*

The man's eyes began to turn. He looked away and dropped the phone heading back to the black SUV in the driveway.

I watched him drive away before I picked up the phone.

"Dar," Was all I said because I didn't trust myself to say anything else. What I had just heard had me reliving my worse nightmares and I felt for the person that was under the thumb of a Carver.

"This is your new phone. I will text you the number after we hang up. I need to be able to get a hold of you."

I didn't agree, but I didn't say anything.

Dar didn't say anything for several moments. I remained quiet because even though I hadn't been around my brother for a long time, he still had a hard time with the hard topics. And whatever he was going to say, was going to probably piss me off. "Jeri wants to meet with you. I have held him off, giving you time to settle in, but he is getting very persistent."

"I'm not pack. He's not my alpha," A dark rage was building inside me. I found out what that bastard did to my mother and I hated him for it. My claws were out and I could feel the changing start.

Theya's door opened and shut loudly and I turned my half-changed wolf face at her. She was heading down the stairs, acting oblivious to me, holding a white plastic basket of clothes. She turned the corner, still ignoring me as she walked daintily to the laundry room.

I couldn't help but notice she had changed. I could see her pink bra straps through the white tank top and I couldn't see any underwear lines under a pair of very short shorts that made her legs look incredibly appetizing. I could almost imagine how soft her skin would be if I trailed my tongue over it.

I shook my head. *No. Stop it.*

"I'll tell him you are still adjusting," Dar's voice shook me from a variety of colorful images.

"There is nothing to adjust, this is who I am and I am *not* pack, yours or his. I am practically rogue."

Silence.

"If you were rogue, that fairy would be dead right now, but she's not and you are not rogue."

"I'm not pack."

"You are pack, you're my brother."

"I can't be controlled by you or anyone else."

"What are you trying to say?"

"I wasn't trying to say anything Dar. I said you can't control me."

"You think I am trying to be your alpha?"

"You are acting like it."

"No I'm not, you asshole. I'm acting like your brother."

I didn't know what to say to that, so I didn't say anything.

"Keep the phone near you. I'll call only when it's important."

"Fine."

"Fine." And then line went dead.

The pixy just exited the laundry room and I saw her walk with her head down towards the stairs. I watched her carefully, taking in every single curve. I think I saw her blush right before she bounded upstairs, giving me a very good memory of watching her pert ass swaying up the stairs.

The wolf in me growled and this time I knew it wasn't to scare her away.

26317913R00183

Made in the USA
San Bernardino, CA
24 November 2015